He hadn't realized
how much he missed her

Clea had married him because she was a good sport and she'd wanted to do him a favor. They'd made a deal—a marriage so he could get his inheritance and start his own business and so she could get her tuition and finish school; and then, with no strings attached, they'd get a divorce—and they stuck to it.

Austin had his business, and one look at Clea told him she was thriving, too. Everything had worked out just as they had planned.

He never let himself look back, but tonight, lying in her bed, he couldn't help it. He found himself remembering what it had been like being married to Clea, found himself wondering what it would be like to be married to her again.

D0808488

ABOUT THE AUTHOR

For Anne McAllister, ideas for stories are everywhere. She has found inspiration from a variety of sources—a childhood memory, a phone book, even a fortune cookie. In all her stories she writes about relationships— how they grow and how they challenge the people who share them. In this book, Anne picks up the story of Austin, Miles Cavanaugh's mischievous brother, whom we first met in *Body and Soul*. Anne makes her home in the Midwest with her husband and their four children.

Books by Anne McAllister

HARLEQUIN AMERICAN ROMANCE
89–STARSTRUCK
108–QUICKSILVER SEASON*
132–A CHANCE OF RAINBOWS*
186–BODY AND SOUL*
202–DREAM CHASERS

*THE QUICKSILVER SERIES

HARLEQUIN ROMANCE
2721–DARE TO TRUST

HARLEQUIN PRESENTS
844–LIGHTNING STORM

Don't miss any of our special offers. Write to us at the following address for information on our newest releases.

Harlequin Reader Service
901 Fuhrmann Blvd., P.O. Box 1397, Buffalo, NY 14240
Canadian address: P.O. Box 603,
Fort Erie, Ont. L2A 5X3

Marry Sunshine
Anne McAllister

Harlequin Books

TORONTO • NEW YORK • LONDON
AMSTERDAM • PARIS • SYDNEY • HAMBURG
STOCKHOLM • ATHENS • TOKYO • MILAN

To my parents,
who gave me a childhood full of beaches

And to Karin, Rosemary, Todd and Kevin,
who each gave me a piece of this book

Published February 1988

First printing December 1987

ISBN 0-373-16234-0

Chapter One

"I'm married?" Austin Cavanaugh opened one slightly bloodshot eye and stared at the man standing over him. Granted, Baxter knew more about most of his business than he did, but Austin doubted even Baxter would know that first. He raised himself on one elbow and fixed his lawyer with a baleful one-eyed stare. "To who?"

"Whom," Baxter corrected automatically. He cleared his throat and tried not to look officious, difficult for a man wearing a monocle. But at last, consulting the letter in his hand, he read aloud, "A Clea Maxine Bannister."

Austin fell back against the pillows and started to laugh. "Clea?" He opened both eyes now and grinned at his attorney's disapproving expression. "Hey, Baxter, that was years ago." He folded his arms behind his head and laughed again. "By God, I think you're developing a sense of humor after all."

"I'm afraid this is no joke." Baxter's voice was as starched as his shirtfront.

Austin made a face at him. "Of course it is. For cripe's sake, Bax, that was ancient history. Clea and I were married for ten months aeons ago. We've been divorced seven years."

"You *think* you've been divorced seven years," Baxter corrected him loftily.

Austin frowned. Hauling himself to a sitting position, he pulled the blanket up to cover his hips, then raked a hand through sleep-rumpled blond hair, and fixed Baxter with a narrow-eyed stare. "What the hell are you talking about?"

"This," Baxter said, holding the letter just out of Austin's reach, determined to have his moment of glory now that he'd got his employer's attention. "Shall I read it to you?"

Austin rolled his eyes, knowing Baxter was determined to read it no matter what. "Go ahead."

Baxter cleared his throat. "As I was saying, this arrived yesterday in the mail, and I flew right out because I felt it merited your immediate attention."

He gave Austin an assessing look as if he were trying to determine whether or not his employer was paying attention now.

"I'm all ears," Austin assured him. Half the time he felt as if he were a schoolboy and Baxter a disapproving teacher.

"It's from the clerk of District Court in Alameda County, California. That's in Oakland," Baxter added for Austin's enlightenment.

"I know where it is, Bax."

The lawyer's eyes narrowed for a moment. Then he gave a brisk nod, bent his head and proceeded to read, "Dear Mr. Cavanaugh: We regret to inform you that, due to failure to file the final papers, the divorce proceedings instituted on your behalf, which were conducted in our courts seven years ago, are invalid. Unless you have obtained a divorce elsewhere, you are still legally married to Clea Maxine Bannister. Ms. Bannister has been similarly notified. If you still wish to consider divorce proceedings, you will have to refile. Hoping you are not unduly inconvenienced, we remain, cordially yours, blah, blah, blah." Baxter folded the paper and presented Austin with one of his smug lawyer smiles. "I checked. They're right. You're married."

"Read it again," Austin demanded.

Baxter, now stern, obliged.

"God Almighty!" Austin fell back on the bed, chuckling for all he was worth.

Baxter's scowling disapproval deepened. "This is hardly cause for merriment, sir. I suggest we institute proceedings immediately. It will undoubtedly be a much thornier case this time, though. Your Miss Bannister will be able to ask for an enormous settlement now, whereas eight years ago," he said with a sniff, "you didn't have a feather to fly with."

Austin grinned. "It was Clea who got me the feathers, Bax."

Baxter blinked. "Got you the...? I don't understand."

Austin reached for the phone. "Let me call room service for some breakfast. Then I'll explain it to you." He was already dialing. "Want something?"

"No, that's quite all right. I—"

"When'd you get here?"

"This morning."

"You flew the red-eye from L.A. to Boston to tell me this and you haven't eaten a damned thing but airline food, right?"

"That's correct, but—"

"So you need something to eat, too. Ah, good," he said into the phone. "I want to order breakfast, please. I'll have two eggs, over easy, toast, hash browns, sausage, and coffee." He glanced at the other man. "How do you like your eggs, Bax?"

"I, er, boiled. Four minutes, please."

"And another just like it with four-minute eggs," Austin said into the phone. "Thanks, I'll be expecting it." Then he bounded out of the bed, grabbing his clothes. "I need a shower, Bax. You want to listen to the story while I shower or can you put your curiosity on hold until I get done?"

"I—I'll wait, sir."

Austin turned around halfway to the bathroom and glared at him. "How can you call a naked man 'sir,' Baxter?"

"Er, well, I..." Baxter's hard-won composure was getting badly ruffled.

"Never mind," Austin said. "You're a good lawyer in spite of it."

Baxter smiled, mollified. "Thank you, sir."

Austin groaned and went to take his shower.

Breakfast had arrived when he came out, dressed now in a pair of sand-colored canvas pants and a dark red polo shirt, barefooted and toweling his hair dry as he came. Baxter had rolled the cart over by the small table that looked out the window overlooking the Boston Public Garden and was busily uncovering the dishes and lining up the silverware.

"You should've been a butler, Bax." Austin ran a comb through his hair, then came over and dropped into the chair opposite.

"Sir?"

"Never mind." Austin began buttering his toast. "Dig in."

They had almost finished their meal, Baxter waiting in polite silence for the tale of Austin's marriage to Clea, before Austin began to speak. He'd been too hungry to start sooner, and besides, he couldn't think of a place to begin.

His life with Clea seemed almost like a fairy tale to him now. A part of his childhood—untarnished and beautiful, but gone. To think of her again as his wife—as a part of his present—blew his mind.

"When I was a kid," he began finally, "Clea Bannister was my best friend. She was the daughter of the woman who cleaned for us. And she was every bit as much of a rabble-rouser as I was." He smiled to see the very proper Baxter flinch. "She was a year younger than me, but she thought she could do anything I could do. In fact, she thought she ould do it a damned sight better. Sometimes," he admitted with uncharacteristic humility, "she could.

"Anyway, we'd known each other for years. And we were close all the time we were in high school, though she went to some local public school and I got the military bit." He grimaced now, remembering. "I stood that, but when the old man decided I ought to continue with it in college, I disagreed."

"But I thought you spent a year at Annapolis," Baxter protested.

"I did. It took me a year to get them to throw me out."

"Throw you out?" Baxter spluttered around his toast crumbs.

"You didn't think the old man would let me quit, did you?" Austin said flatly. "Huh-uh. Deviousness is the only way. Anyway," he went on, "my second year I spent at Berkeley, and Clea was there. She was doing art history or some damned thing, and I was doing business and architecture, so we didn't see each other a lot. Except if I needed a date and didn't want an entanglement, I'd call her. She was my friend, you know."

Baxter looked doubtful.

But Austin ignored him. "She was always game for anything. The only girl I knew who would get up at three in the morning and drive up to the Sierras to go hiking for a day, or who'd dress up and attend one of my dad's damned parties without expecting me to come through with a hundred-dollar dinner beforehand."

He cut a piece of sausage with his fork and nibbled on it, thinking back, remembering, a smile lighting his face. "She was something else."

Then his thoughts took him further and he frowned. "Then I graduated, and I thought I wanted to go to work with my dad."

"Just so," Baxter commented politely.

"But you know what a bastard my father is."

Baxter cleared his throat and looked away, embarrassed at Austin's bluntness.

"The architecture degree didn't mean a thing to him. The business classes weren't worth the paper the transcript was written on. Only he could deem what was worthy knowledge, and he didn't think I had any."

Baxter sucked in his breath, gave Austin a polite smile and cut off a piece of his toast, buttering it with care.

"He was still pissed off at me about the Annapolis bit. He wanted me to do what he wanted me to do, not what I wanted. But, grudgingly, he let me in. Of course, I had to start at the bottom of his worst company. I'd call it being a glorified gofer, but it wasn't even glorified. It was scut work. And I wanted to make something of myself. I wanted to build, create, design. I had ideas, vision, talent." His voice got stronger, more intense. He leaned toward Baxter. Baxter leaned back.

"And there was no way on earth he was going to give me a chance. My brother Miles always said I shouldn't let it get to me, that it was just the way he was, that he pigeonholed people and expected you to fit in whatever hole he decided on." Austin shrugged. "Well, I never fit the hole he wanted for me."

He sank back in his chair and lay his fork down on his plate, the weariness he always felt when confronted with his father's attitude overtaking him for a moment. Then he straightened and went on, "I tried it his way for about six months. I was getting nowhere, and damn it, I think he was glad. He kept saying, 'You got to learn what it's like from the ground up.' Well, damn it, I knew real fast what it was like on the ground, and he wasn't ever letting me up. I wanted to strike out on my own. So I did." His chin jutted out just as his father's did.

"Ah." Baxter dabbed his mouth with his napkin.

"I needed money, though, and I didn't have a red cent. He wasn't paying me a living wage either. I was due to get a trust from my mother when I was twenty-five, but there was no way I could touch it earlier unless I was married. So—" he shrugged "—I married Clea."

Baxter's eyes bugged.

"It was right there in legalese," Austin assured him, assuming that Baxter's amazement had something to do with the trust fund. "Twenty-five if I was single, twenty-one if I was married. I was twenty-two and there was no way on earth I was going to be able to last under the old man's thumb for another three years. It wasn't a big trust, but it was enough. I paid Clea's tuition her last year—that was what she got out of it, the opportunity to only have to work two jobs instead of three to stay in school—and I started my construction work. You know the rest."

The rest was a matter of public record, really. Austin Cavanaugh had gone into business for himself, first in construction, then in hot tubs, then in patio furniture and redwood decking, then in custom reproduction furniture and in— Well, he'd even lost track anymore.

He found that he liked construction, he liked design. But he liked a lot of other things, too. He liked challenges. And building up his own business had been a challenge. When he'd got it going well, he had even competed with his father for a time. Then the old man, instead of taking him back into his own firm, which is what Austin had expected, had bought him out.

The pattern had persisted, occurring time and time again. It made Austin rich, it made him powerful, it made him wary. Only with this latest business had he found something that finally his father couldn't take, something that he could call his own.

Baxter's mouth was opening and shutting like a fish's. Finally he stammered, "You got married for how long?" He pushed his plate away and lay his napkin down alongside it.

"Ten months. Clea's last year of school. It was the deal we made. Then she went her way and I went mine, and we got the divorce."

"Or thought you did," Baxter corrected automatically. "Amazing," he murmured to himself, his eyes never leaving Austin, as though his employer might do something even more outrageous at any second.

Austin sighed and stretched out his legs, crossing them at the ankle, contemplating his bare toes. "Or thought we did," he concurred.

The circumstances were still boggling. He shook his head. "That son-of-a-bitch lawyer. Rawlings, his name was. Got him out of the phone book. No wonder he was so cheap. He was incompetent."

"Begging your pardon, sir, but why did you get a, er, cheap attorney?"

"Because, as you so aptly put it, we didn't have a feather to fly with then."

"But the money from the trust—"

"Was all tied up in the business or paying tuition. We scraped by, that was all. And I could hardly ask Clea to hang on while I made more money, could I? I mean, we had a deal, you know. Besides, I thought, one lawyer is just as crooked as another." He grinned. "No offense intended. So what difference did it make? We had our lives to get on with, for heaven's sake."

"Yes, of course, but—"

Austin looked up. "But what?"

Baxter spread his hands, palms up, as if he would never understand his employer as long as he lived.

"But what now, you mean?" Austin asked.

"Among other things," he said disapprovingly.

"What other things?"

Baxter hesitated. "But whatever possessed her?" he finally demanded, unable to contain the question any longer.

Austin shrugged. "She was my friend."

"Yes, but friends don't just marry because—" The lawyer waved his arms in disbelief.

"Clea did." He gave Baxter a defiant glare.

The other man subsided, taking refuge behind his napkin again. "Er. . . quite."

He didn't seem convinced, though, Austin thought, disgruntled. Though he personally couldn't see why it mattered. What had mattered at the time was that Clea had—God bless her—married him. And what mattered now was that apparently she still was.

So, what now, indeed? Austin folded his arms behind his head and leaned back against them, staring out over the garden. It was a glorious view, one that he'd had little time to appreciate. He'd been here almost a week and he'd been working almost the whole time. But what he'd seen of it, he'd liked. He'd like to see more.

He wondered if Clea had ever been to Boston. She'd have loved it, he was sure. Clea loved everything old, glorious or not. If it was glorious, so much the better. But even if it was ancient, rotting, dirty and virtually useless, Clea could see potential in it. She would know how to make it beautiful again. In a city like Boston, where so much restoration was always taking place, she would be in heaven.

Ah, Clea. He smiled again, remembering how her eyes would flash with enthusiasm, how her whole face would light up, making him laugh and call her "Sunshine."

"I wonder if you see the seriousness of this," Baxter prodded when it was clear that Austin had drifted off on a cloud of his own. "I do think we should get right to work on filing again."

"Huh?" Austin frowned, steepling his hands in front of his mouth.

"Miss Bannister could take you to the cleaners," Baxter said, his lapse into the vernacular indicating how grave he felt the matter was.

Austin shook his head. "Clea? Nah. Money never mattered to Clea—beyond her tuition at least." He smiled again, his eyes lifting heavenward, though it wasn't the crack in the ceiling he was contemplating. It was the memory of Clea, sitting cross-legged on the lumpy old couch in their married student housing apartment, saying to him, "Tell your father what he can do with his millions. Who cares as long as we're happy."

"God, Clea," he mused, shaking his head. "I wonder what she's doing now. I wonder if she's still in San Francisco."

"I couldn't say, sir," Baxter said stiffly.

Austin ignored his disapproval, reaching into his rear pocket to pull out a small weekly calendar, an idea beginning to form in his head.

"Really, sir, I do think we should start making inquiries to find Miss Bannister so we can—"

"Forget the inquiries." Austin was running his fingers down the lines of his calendar. "Good. I don't have to do the competition sculpture for another three weeks." He stuck the calendar back in his pocket, then surged to his feet. "Come on, Baxter, time's a-wasting."

Baxter jumped up. "Sir? What about the divorce, sir? Shall I file again?"

Austin was already across the room, reaching for the phone with one hand and his suitcase with the other. "I'll let you know when I get back."

"Back, sir?" Baxter stared after him, confused.

"From San Francisco."

WITH LUCK, Ken would be late. Clea flew up the steep front steps of her most prized possession in the entire world, the Italianate-stick row house she'd just purchased, jiggled the rusty useless lock, pushed open the door, and heaved four books of wallpaper samples onto the tiny table in the entry-way. Then, jumping over the rotten floorboards just inside the front parlor, she snatched the cover off the bird's cage, whipped open the drapes, coughing when the dust billowed into her face, and raced up the stairs.

Drat Mr. Carruthers anyway. Pompous pea brains like him shouldn't have beautiful old houses anyway. She'd told him she had to leave early today, had told him that all his dithering had to be done before five o'clock because for once she had to get home by six so she could meet Ken, who was coming to pick her up for dinner. But oh no, he had to wait until four forty-five to show up and tell her that Mrs. Carruthers had said that the borders Clea had ordered for the front parlor of the Victorian she was restoring for them just wouldn't do.

Wouldn't do! They were authentic, for heaven's sake. If he hadn't wanted an accurate restoration, why had he hired her?

She knew the answer to that, though. He'd bought the house to impress the president of the insurance company where he worked who was a San Francisco history buff, and to placate his society-conscious wife who wanted the latest in everything. He didn't care in the least about the house himself, he just expected Clea to satisfy them both.

And she was having the devil's own time doing it. If she didn't love her job so much, and if she hadn't needed the money to restore her own newly purchased house, she wouldn't do it. It was certainly playing havoc with her personal life.

She kicked off her sneakers in the hallway and raced into her bedroom, snatched her plum-colored gypsy dress out of the closet, grabbed clean underwear out of the drawer and hotfooted it to the bathroom.

Lord, it was six-fifteen. He was going to be here at six-thirty, and he wasn't going to be late. Kenneth P. Hollister was never late. The P., she thought, ought to stand for Punctual or Prompt, even if his mother insisted it stood for Parsons, which, she had informed Clea, was her maiden name.

Her own middle initial, M., Clea thought, ought to stand for Mess. She pulled her grimy sweatshirt over her head, reached down and turned on the water taps, grimacing as rusty brown water sputtered and gurgled for a full minute before turning remotely colorless. That meant she needed new water pipes. She sighed. More money. She should have had her head examined, buying this place. But it was so perfect. Exactly what she'd been looking for.

Her jeans dropped around her ankles and she kicked them off, then plunged under the water and stifled a shriek. The new *hot* water pipe would have to come first.

Well, at least there was no temptation to linger. Forty seconds was as long a shower as she'd been able to stand in the week and a half she'd lived there. Shivering, she groped for a towel, wound it around her head, then grabbed another off the hook and briskly dried off.

Outside she heard a motorcycle tear down the hill, farther off she heard the sound of the bell clanging as the cable car came to the corner. If she stuck her head out the window and craned her neck she could see it. And if she looked out the front, she could see Coit Tower. A bit of local atmosphere, she'd explained to Ken when she'd told him she was buying it. Not a bay view exactly, but preferable to the cracker box in the Mission district where she had been living and better for her restoration and renovation business—when she eventually got it restored.

Unfortunately, at the moment she didn't have time to enjoy it or restore it. Six twenty-three and counting.

Dropping the towel to the floor, she donned her underwear, then skimmed a slip over her head.

The door bell rang.

"Drat." She looked helplessly at the plum dress and its cascade of tiny buttons, then at the stairs.

The doorbell sounded again.

"Why aren't you ever late?" she muttered to an absent Ken. "Or on time even? Why do you have to be early?"

She poked her head out the bathroom window. There was no way, even craning her neck, to see him on the covered porch below, but she knew he was there. The bell was ringing once more.

"Come on in," she called down. "I'm getting dressed." She'd wanted to meet him at the door, dressed and ready. She hadn't done much more than let him get a glimpse of her monstrous purchase yet. He hadn't thought it was the wisest move she'd ever made, and seeing it for any length of time would only confirm his impression.

But it couldn't be helped. He was here, and she still had to dry her hair and put on her dress.

She rubbed her hair with the towel, trying not to think what Ken's impression of the parlor would be. Early in their relationship she had learned that he didn't have the vision to see silk purses where he thought only sows' ears could be. But he had plenty of other sterling qualities, not the least of which was that he saw the best in her. So perhaps he would do the same for her house, focusing on the glorious oak woodwork that would be even more noticeable when she had refinished it or on the hand-carved newel posts or the stained leaded glass windows.

God willing he wouldn't pay much attention to the ratty draperies, the bare bulb hanging where the chandelier was supposed to, or the floor.

Oh, my God, the floor!

Still in her slip, she shot out of the bathroom, down the hall and took the steps two at a time. "Watch out for the boards in the—"

But before she could finish, there came a splintering crash, and as she hovered helplessly half up the stairs and half down them, a man began to extricate himself from the now gaping hole in her floor.

"Oh, God, Ken! Are you—" She started down the stairs, and had reached the bottom before she realized that it wasn't Ken at all, but—

"Austin?" She grabbed the hand-carved newel post for support.

The man was grinning Austin's grin, and he had Austin's heavy wheat-colored thatch of hair. But it wasn't, of course. It couldn't be. Not her ex-husband. She hadn't even seen him in six years.

He didn't know where she lived. He'd never even sent her a Christmas card. And he had absolutely no business here. It was the last place Austin Cavanaugh would be.

Which was probably why he was here.

"Watch out for the floor? Is that what you were going to say?"

It was, indeed, Austin.

He gave a mighty heave and hauled himself out of the hole, then got to his feet, and began brushing the dirt from his pants. They were white jeans, and they were suddenly the worse for wear.

He grinned and shook his head. "I should've known better than to wear them around you," he told her. "You haven't changed a bit."

Austin had. He'd got even more gorgeous than she remembered. He'd filled out. His shoulders were broader, his chest more obviously muscled even through the bright blue T-shirt he wore. His hair wasn't quite as long as he'd worn it when they were married, but it was still shaggy and wanted cutting. She wondered if he sat still any better now for whoever tried to cut it than he had for her. He'd driven her nuts, wriggling around on the stool while she tried to trim the ends and make him presentable so he could go bid on a job and not look like the kid he was. And all the while he would be telling her his plans, turning around to see her re-action, making her miss and almost remove his ear. Then he would grin at her and those lively blue eyes would posi-tively dance with laughter. The way they were dancing now.

Her mind jerked back to the present. "What on earth are you doing here?" The very sight of him was making her feel as if she were the one who had gone through the floor.

"You didn't get the letter?"

"What letter?" Had he written for once after all these years? "I don't get any mail at all half the time," she ex-plained. "I just moved here a week and a half ago, and this place has been vacant so long I don't think the mailman knows I'm here yet."

"Oh." Austin was still brushing himself off, but he was looking at her, his eyes pleased and warm and friendly, and totally and completely unnerving. Just the way they had al-ways been.

"So," Clea said briskly, "tell me why you're here."

"I came to see you, Sunshine." The old nickname seemed to fall unbidden from his lips. His blue eyes stopped danc-ing and skated slowly down her, taking in the damp hair which was sticking out all over her head, the woman's body that was still firm and well-toned from climbing all over old wrecks of houses and wrestling furniture up and down stairs. He traced every curve the slip so faithfully outlined, and Clea was horrified to find herself burning just like sun-shine under his gaze.

It was all she could do not to wrap her arms protectively across her breasts and beat a hasty retreat upstairs. But she wouldn't, even if she'd wanted to, because she'd never backed down with Austin. She'd have been a goner years ago if she had.

"Well," she said irritably, "you've seen me. Literally. Now what?"

A lazy grin lit his features. "Is that an invitation?"

"No, my dear, it is not." *Not on your life,* she thought. "And, as much as I would like to stop and chat with you, Austin, I really have things to do. As you can see, I'm not even dressed and I have a date tonight."

"A date?" One blond brow lifted. He wandered over to the bird cage and bent over, peering in, taking his time. "Does this thing sing?"

"No, it doesn't sing. It's a parakeet, not a canary."

"What's its name?"

"Austin, I'm busy."

"It does have a name, doesn't it?"

"Its name is Thurber."

"Thurber?" Austin was grinning. "As in James?"

"Yes." Ken had just thought she was being odd and a bit whimsical when she named her bird after the American writer. But Austin would remember her obsession with him from college, would remember how she had insisted on naming their illegal rabbit, Mitty Bunny, and how she'd said that if she ever had a daughter she was going to call her Saralinda after the Princess in "The Thirteen Clocks."

She gave him an impatient, irritated look and found that he was looking at her indulgently, tenderly, which had the effect of irritating her further. Then he bent down again and poked his finger into the cage. "It's nice meeting you, Thurber."

Thurber made a cheeping sound and hopped from one perch to the other.

"I think he likes me," Austin said, looking over his shoulder at Clea.

"No doubt," Clea said dryly. Birds, rabbits, girls—Austin could win over anyone who didn't steel her heart. She did. "My date, Austin," she reminded him now.

"Right." His grin vanished. "Is it serious?"

"Serious?"

He straightened up. "Your date." He was looking at her intently.

Clea ran her hand through her hair. It was damp still, but drying fast, going stick-straight and limp. Drat. She had to get it blown dry, and she had two minutes to do it in before Ken would be there. "Yes," she said to Austin. "I think you could say it's serious. I'm getting married."

"Tonight?" He sounded horrified.

"No, not tonight." She started up the stairs. "But to the man I'm going out with tonight." She turned and looked down at him, wondering again what had brought him back into her life at the very moment Ken was destined to ring the doorbell. "Listen, Austin, if you really do have something to talk about, why don't you drop around tomorrow. I could see you then, but I honestly don't have time tonight. This is the man I'm going to marry."

"I don't think so, Clea—"

"Austin..." she warned.

"Really, Clea, I—" He had followed her to the stairs and was beginning to climb them.

Clea's fingers clenched. She did not need him trailing her into her bedroom, for heaven's sake. "All right, damn it! What?"

"That's what I want to talk to you about."

"What's what you want to talk to me about?" The clock was chiming the half hour. "Austin, for Lord's—"

"We're still married."

Clea's foot slipped off the step. She caught herself by grabbing the bannister, then glared down at him with narrowed eyes. "Not funny, Austin."

"But true." He was digging into his pants' pocket and pulling out a letter. "Here." He bounded up the steps and thrust the much-folded paper into her hand. "Read it yourself."

With nerveless fingers, Clea opened it, scanning the contents, disbelieving, then reading it again word for word. Scowling, she held the paper up to the light.

"What're you doing?"

"Looking for water marks."

"It's been notarized, for God's sake."

He was right; it had. She folded it up slowly and stared at it as if it were something incredibly slimy and very much alive. "It's ridiculous," she said firmly. "How can they just say that after all this time?"

"I gather they didn't know before." He grinned at her. "You know how slow the court system is these days."

She frowned fiercely. "I suppose you think this is a big joke."

"Don't you?"

"No, damn it, I don't. I think it's totally absurd. I think— Oh, God, there's the bell. I'm not even dressed." She slapped the letter back into Austin's palm.

"I'll get it," he said brightly.

"No!"

"But—"

"I said, *No*!" She flew into the bathroom and yanked the dress off the hanger, jerking it over her head and fumbling with the buttons. "I'll be right with you, Ken," she yelled out the window.

There was no time to dry her hair now. But limp straight hair was the least of her worries. She ran a comb through it, grimaced at her reflection in the mottled mirror, finished buttoning the dress and hopped out the door, stuffing first one foot into a sandal, then the other.

She was halfway down the steps when the door opened and Ken walked into the entryway.

"It was open," he apologized, smiling up at her. "And I didn't think you'd mind."

"N-no. I'm glad you feel free enough to— Watch out for the floor!" Looking up at her, he had almost walked right into Austin's hole.

Ken jerked back, staring down at the jagged opening in the floorboards. "My God, Clea, did you—"

"No, I didn't." She shot a hasty glance around for Austin. He seemed to have disappeared. Had he left? She was sure that was too much to hope.

It was. Two seconds later he strolled in from the kitchen. "I did," Austin said conversationally. "So I thought I'd check out the rest of the place while I was at it," he said, then, he nodded a polite hello to Ken.

Ken simply stared at him.

"Er, Austin, this is Ken Hollister, my fiancé," she said bluntly, putting her hand on Ken's arm and aligning herself definitely with him. "Ken, this is Austin Cavanaugh."

Ken offered his hand. "Cavanaugh. And you are...?"

"Her husband," Austin said.

"I CAN EXPLAIN." It seemed to Clea as if she had been saying that all evening. It was not turning out to be a dinner to remember—at least not in the context she would have wished. They had been planning to toast their recent engagement. Now it seemed they were going to be dissecting her nonexistent divorce.

"Run it by me one more time." Ken was sipping his after-dinner coffee and regarding her as if she had just grown another head. All evening long he had been looking at her strangely. She supposed she shouldn't blame him. He had, after all, had a terrific shock.

"It seems, from what the letter said, that the lawyer who was in charge of filing our divorce papers seven years ago simply failed to do so." She shrugged.

"Well, surely that can't be a major dilemma," Ken said, as if it were a common household problem, easily dealt with, like ants. "I mean, you simply have to send them in now, don't you?"

"I don't know. We didn't discuss it. He just got there right before you did," she added.

Ken looked doubtful. "He certainly looked...right at home. I mean, he was in your kitchen and your dining room and—"

"Falling through my floor," Clea said dryly, but Ken didn't even smile.

"This is the first time I've ever even been through your front door," he reminded her.

"See what you missed?" Clea teased, but she was getting nowhere. Ken still regarded her soberly, a worried frown creasing his forehead.

"Listen." Clea leaned forward earnestly. "Austin *makes* himself at home no matter where he is. And, believe me, this was the first time he's ever been inside my front door, too. Anyway, *he* doesn't matter. You do, and I wanted it to be beautiful when you saw it the first time. I wanted it all fixed up and—"

"Hey, it's okay," Ken said soothingly. "All in good time. You said yourself it would take a while."

"It will take ages," Clea groaned, making a bit more of it than she actually felt, glad at last to be off the topic of Austin. "The longer I live there, the more I see to be done. I must have had blinders on when I bought it."

"Well, don't say I didn't warn you." Ken smiled.

"I know. I know. But you must admit, it will be a perfect advertisement for my work when I get it done. I can have my office downstairs, and a showroom of sorts. And, of course, the kitchen. But we can basically live above it after we're married."

"After you're divorced," Ken pointed out.

"There's plenty of room," Clea went on, ignoring that.

"I know," Ken said dryly. "You told me. It was a brothel, wasn't it?"

"A parlor house," Clea corrected. "Much higher class. And it isn't as if I'm going to restore it to that, you know."

"I hope not," Ken said fervently.

Clea was frankly intrigued by her house's past, but she knew it was a source of embarrassment to Ken. The first time she had mentioned it, he had shushed her promptly.

"What would Mr. Gleason think?" he'd muttered. Mr. Gleason was his supervisor at the bank, and what Mr. Gleason thought meant a lot to Ken. Mr. Gleason was the key to his advancement. A strong recommendation from him could see Ken moving up quickly in one of the several hundred worldwide branches, and Ken had high hopes. Clea shared in those hopes, so she hadn't said any more then. But now, just to tease, she mused, "I wonder what it would be like if I did."

"I shudder to think." Ken scowled, not appreciating the humor of it. "But we won't be living there if you do."

"No. No, of course not," Clea soothed, realizing that she still didn't know quite how to smooth this particular man's ruffled feathers. And how could she be expected to? she asked herself. He was about as different from the previous man in her life as he could get. But she wasn't going to get back on that topic tonight.

And when Ken said, "If I can be of any help with this divorce business," she shook her head, cutting him off, as she exclaimed, "Heavens, look at the time. I really should be getting back."

"You're not meeting with your ex, or your supposed ex, again tonight, are you?"

"Austin? God forbid. No, I expect he'll drop by in the morning so we can sort something out."

"Just be sure you do. We can't have you becoming a bigamist now, can we?" He grinned at her and she found that he didn't quite know how to smooth her ruffled feathers, either. Where Austin was concerned, she had no sense of humor at all.

"No." She got up from the table abruptly. "We certainly can't have that."

Ken paid the check and held the door open for her. "Could make it difficult for our children," he went on.

Clea frowned. "I'll get it settled, Ken. Really I will."

"If you say so." But all the way home she felt a tension between them that had never existed before.

Ken seemed to feel it, too, for he fell silent, not indulging in any of the lighthearted teasing that he sometimes delighted in. Instead he just sighed periodically and tapped his fingers on the steering wheel whenever they were stopped at a red light.

"I'd invite you in," she said when he walked her to her door, "but, well, you know what a mess everything is…and I'm really tired. I have to get up early tomorrow and try to get things sorted out with Mr. Carruthers before I can go forward in this project."

"But it's Saturday," Ken objected.

"I know, but he's going to Chicago, thank heavens, and he won't be back for a week, so he has to get all his dithering in before he leaves." She smiled and shook her head. "And there's Austin, besides."

His name fell into the silence like a boulder into a reflecting pool, sending out ripples into the night.

"You said he'll be by tomorrow morning, too?"

"I told him to come then. But he won't be by early. Austin rarely gets up before noon. Rarely *got* up before noon," she corrected. "He's a night person."

"Unlike you." Ken pulled her into his arms and kissed her forehead, her temple, her cheek. And Clea obligingly looped her arms around him as well, enjoying the soft caress of his lips.

"Well, I was...once." But she didn't want to think about that. *Wouldn't* think about that. Remembering nights wide awake in Austin's arms was not a good idea. Especially not while she was in another man's arms.

She pulled back out of Ken's embrace. "I really do have to go in."

He smiled and bent to kiss her on the lips this time. "All right. You get a reprieve. For tonight. You look like you need it."

Did she ever! Clea thought, leaning back against the door the moment it closed. She kicked off her shoes and padded carefully around the hole in the floor. Her mouth twitched in a reluctant grin as she remembered Austin hoisting himself out of the hole.

He was lucky he didn't plunge all the way to the basement. *She* was lucky he hadn't. He had enough money and enough lawyers now to sue the socks off her. But he wouldn't. Not Austin. He wasn't like that. Not a bit.

"Austin." She said his name aloud, tasting it, rolling it around in her mouth, thinking about it as she said it, the way she hadn't earlier. She hadn't really let herself think about him at all in years.

He had been the bright flaming star of her youth, the instant of passion, the moment of love, enjoyed, savored, and gone.

It had been fun while it lasted, she told herself. Beautiful, in fact. But it had been kid stuff. Cotton candy. Insubstantial as a bit of dust. Not the sort of thing that lasting relationships were made of. And she had known that from the start.

It was a lasting love she wanted now.

A love like Ken's.

Dear Ken. She smiled tenderly. He had taken it rather well. Surprises were not his forte. And he'd got a bigger surprise tonight than many men got in a lifetime. The look on his face when Austin had said he was her husband!

"Well, not for long, Austin, my lad," she said softly as she draped the dish towel over Thurber's cage and put out the light. She climbed the steps slowly. "Not for long."

Theirs had been a bright and shining love. Intense, brilliant and, of necessity, short. Austin couldn't make commitments, didn't want to. And Clea couldn't have forced him to, *wouldn't* have forced him to, no matter what. Loving him the way she had, she'd had no choice.

So she had taken her few short months with him—just two shy of a year—and had gone on as she knew she'd have to when it was over.

And now?

Now she was grown. A woman. With a woman's needs and desires. She wanted—she needed—a home, a family, a stable and loving relationship. That was why she was marrying Ken.

She would make that very clear to Austin when he came tomorrow morning to discuss things. She had given him what he needed once. Now it was her turn.

Feeling much more resolute, she nodded briskly and flicked on the light in her bedroom.

Austin was asleep in her bed.

Chapter Two

"Get up."

Nary a muscle moved.

"Austin, I said get up!"

Nothing.

Clea glared at the inert form outlined under the bed-clothes, then stalked across the room and twitched the comforter off him. He was naked. She twitched it right back on. Damn him.

"Austin!" She reached underneath the bottom edge of the comforter and grabbed his foot, jerking it. "Austin! Get up! Now! You can't sleep there."

At last, a response.

One shoulder flexed, then a head half lifted, and Austin rolled slowly over onto his back, squinting up at her into the light. "Huh?"

"I said," Clea said with the elocution of a primary school teacher, "get up right now. You can't sleep here."

Austin raised himself on one elbow and looked at her, perplexed. "But it's the only bed in the house," he protested.

Clea's teeth clamped together. "I know that. And that is precisely why you can't sleep here. *I'm* sleeping here."

He flopped back down and rolled over onto his stomach once more. "Well, that's all right then, there's room for both of us."

"Austin!" Exasperation vied with rage.

He rolled back over and sat up, awake now and scowling at her with Austin-like irritability. "Clea, don't be a sap. Come to bed. It isn't like we've never slept together."

"That was when we were married."

"We *are* married."

"Don't you be a sap, either, Austin. That's purely a technicality."

Austin shrugged. "Technicalities are nine-tenths of the law." He leaned back, propped on both elbows, and smiled at her engagingly. He looked sleepy and boyish and about a thousand times more handsome and desirable than he had any right to. Clea ground her teeth.

"Austin, why aren't you at a hotel?"

He looked taken aback. "Why should I be?"

"Why shouldn't you be?" she countered. "You don't live here."

"No, but you do."

"Did I invite you to stay?"

"Do I need an invitation?" He looked hurt.

Clea felt as if she'd kicked a puppy. She hardened herself to his pitiful looks. "It is the proper, expected mode of behavior, Austin. In case you hadn't figured that out by now."

"Well, I might have asked," he said as if he really were pondering it, "if we were really divorced. But inasmuch as we're not . . ."

"Don't start that again."

He shrugged. "It's true."

Clea pressed her lips into a thin line. "We'll see about that."

Austin frowned. "What do you mean?"

"I mean, there must be a way to get this thing settled once and for all."

"There is."

She stopped halfway to the closet. "What?"

"Come to bed."

"Austin!"

"You're not really going to throw me out, are you? I mean—" he glanced at his watch "—I'll just have to come right back in the morning. Besides, I'd have to call a cab and find a hotel and . . ."

She sighed. She knew Austin well enough to know that this was an argument she wasn't going to win. When Austin played waiting games, no one else ever won. But she wasn't sleeping with him, and that was that.

"Fine. Consider yourself at home," she told him with sweet sarcasm. Then turning her back, she jerked open the dresser drawer, rooted through it for a nightgown, found one, then, clutching it, she went to the door, switched off the light, and stalked back out of the room.

"Hey!" Austin called after her.

Ignoring him, Clea shut herself in the bathroom and took off her dress. Her jeans and sweatshirt were still there from her hurried changing earlier in the evening. But they were no longer in a heap on the floor. Instead they lay neatly on top of the clothes hamper. He'd folded them.

Clea shut her eyes, fighting down the memories that washed over her. How many times had she done the same for him—picked up the discarded jeans, hung up the sluffed-off shirt, all the while shaking her head and saying, "When are you ever going to learn to pick up your clothes?"

And now he had done it for her.

She tried not to think about it. It was the little things that would get her if she let them. The remembered haircuts, the folded clothes, the creases in his cheeks when he grinned, the boyish flop of his hair across his forehead, the irrepressible enthusiasm. And little things weren't enough.

They had nothing to do with stability, with commitment, with a lifetime sort of love.

"Just you remember that," she said to her reflection in the mirror.

She wished her reflection looked more convinced.

Nightgown on, teeth brushed, face scrubbed, she flicked off the light and padded back down the hall toward the stairs in the dark. She passed her bedroom quickly and stealthily, not wanting another confrontation tonight. But Austin heard the floorboards creak.

"Hey," he called. "Where're you going?"

"To bed." Clea didn't stop walking.

He scrambled out of hers and came after her. "There's no bed down there."

"I know that." She kept going.

"So what're you doing?"

"I am going to sleep on the settee."

He snorted. "You'll break your back."

"And it will be all your fault."

"Not mine," Austin said stoutly. "That's a big bed you have up there, Sunshine."

"Not big enough," Clea said. She had done some foolish things in her life, particularly where Austin Cavanaugh was concerned, but spending a night in bed with him would prove she hadn't wised up one bit.

"Clea—"

"I'll talk to you in the morning, Austin, and we'll get this sorted out. I am not going to sleep with you under any circumstances. So just don't even think it."

"Clea—"

"Good night, Austin." She plucked the afghan off the back of the settee and curled herself up on its horsehair-covered bench. It was a great deal like trying to sleep on a horse itself, Clea thought. It was going to be a very long night. She could see him silhouetted halfway down the stairs, a lean dark shape, hands on his hips, his shaggy blond head silvery in the overhead light as he shook it slowly back and forth.

"You're a stubborn woman, Clea," he muttered.

"A sensible woman," Clea corrected.

He snorted.

She ignored him.

He stood there a full minute more while she feigned comfort and sleepiness. Then with another shake of his head he turned to go back to her room. "Sweet dreams, Sunshine."

With springs poking her back, Clea wriggled down into the settee. Sweet dreams? Fat chance. She'd be lucky if she got any sleep at all.

Dear God, she thought, why now? Why, just when she had finally got her life on track, when she had bought her house and had agreed at last to marry Ken, when she could see her future once more taking shape before her, why now had Austin reappeared in her life?

A divine sense of humor was one thing, she told God irritably. But divine perversity was something else. It would have been bad enough just to have Austin pop up again, but to pop up claiming to still be her husband.

"Gimme a break," she pleaded.

It had most probably been insane to marry him eight years ago. Maybe if, for her, it had been the cut-and-dried business deal between buddies that it had been for Austin, it would have been all right.

Of course it hadn't been. Clea had been in love with Austin for years. Ever since her mother had brought that irritating, obnoxious little boy with the chicken pox into their house twenty-two years ago, she had loved him. He had been a tough, scrappy little boy, very unlike the rich snob she had expected him to be. But not very different, she didn't think, from the man he had become.

Even then Austin had gone after whatever he wanted with fierce and single-minded determination. Whether it was being able to swim fifty lengths of his pool or climbing to the top of the tree in her yard or winning her parents' love and affection, he went after it with a zeal that amazed her.

Of course she had kept up with him. Once she had proved that anything he could do, she would do, too, they became fast friends. He respected her, teased her, liked her. And Clea loved him.

Even so—especially so—she reminded herself now, it had been stupid to marry him. She had wanted so much more from him, from their marriage. Yet she knew from the start that she had no right to expect it.

Still, she'd told herself, she was young and resilient. She might not have Austin forever, but she would take what she could get. And when the time came, she would let him go. And she would survive.

She had. But just barely.

The pain of those months after he'd left her still had the power to leave her with a hollow, bottomless ache. And the memories—far from being the help she'd thought they would be—were, rather, torments. Contrary to the old cliché, Clea knew well that it was worse to have loved and lost than never to have loved at all.

For several months she'd behaved like a zombie, barely eating or sleeping, only just getting by. Her parents worried themselves sick over her. This couldn't go on, they told her. What could Austin have been thinking of?

Since they didn't know the terms of her marriage to Austin, they, of course, had no idea. And Clea wouldn't tell them. They had married for love and it had lasted. She knew they would never understand a marriage that was—to one party, anyway, no more than a business deal.

Finally, when her mother threatened to call him and tell him the shape she was in, Clea at last pulled herself out of her funk. "Don't you dare," she'd commanded with the first real authority in her voice that she'd managed since they'd broken up. "I'll be fine."

And she had set about making her prediction come true.

It hadn't been easy. She had thrown herself into her work, and that had helped. She'd got a job on a museum staff doing cleaning and restoration work, and her boss recommended her to private collectors. She'd taken on any and all commissions. It was experience, it was interesting, and most of all, it filled the empty days of her life.

Before long she had made a name for herself. The private commissions became more lucrative. She kept the job at the museum another year. Then with her supervisor's blessing, she had gone out on her own.

Establishing her business had taken even more time. But it had been worth it. She had gradually moved from doing a piece here and a piece there, to doing whole houses. A man named Jerry Antonelli, who'd had her do work on some old furniture and a medieval tapestry, called her one afternoon and offered her the job of restoring the old house he had just bought. She felt like a roast duck had just flown over and fallen into her mouth.

It was a consolation of sorts. Restoration and renovation became her life. She put her memories out of her head. Tried to forget Austin and, happily, one day last year, she had met Ken.

Tall and blond like Austin, he shared no other similarities. Ken was neither a mover nor a shaker. He was a middle management type, a paper-pusher at one of the big banks. And while he hoped for advancement, he didn't pursue it with all-consuming fervor. He was content to let things happen in their own good time.

And as he behaved in his business, so he behaved with Clea. They had dated casually at first, going to movies, window-shopping, sharing a meal in a restaurant and, later, when they got to know each other better, they'd eat in her apartment or his.

Clea, who had had her share of pushy men trying to put the make on her after her divorce, would have backed off in a hurry if Ken had given even the tiniest shove. He hadn't. He'd moved slowly, catching her with her defenses down, letting her get to know him and appreciate him at her own pace. And it had worked.

There was no grand passion with Ken, no overwhelming desire. What there was, was a calm, steady appreciation, a respect for a man of principles, integrity, steadfastness and common sense. Ken wouldn't set the world on fire. But he wouldn't burn it down, either.

Clea liked that. She liked Ken. In time she learned to love him. And when he'd finally asked her to marry him two weeks ago, she had said yes.

Which was why it was particularly perverse of God to have let Austin show up now. What was He trying to prove? That she was no more immune to Austin than she'd ever been?

Well, that was true enough. She'd only had to see him again and her heart started acting like a jackhammer. It didn't do that with Ken. But, she reminded God crossly, that was something she already knew.

The strings of her heart had already gone zing once. She knew just how painful the experience could be. She didn't want it happening again. She didn't want Austin coming along now and destroying the future she had tried so hard to rebuild.

There was, of course, the possibility, she thought, punching a particularly offensive spring that dug into her back, that he wouldn't even try.

But as she drifted off to sleep, she wished she felt more confident of that.

AUSTIN DIDN'T GO BACK to sleep at all. Couldn't. His mind was running riot with images of Clea.

He'd said she hadn't changed, but she had. She'd become a woman. He'd married a girl with laughing brown eyes and a freckled nose, a good sport who'd played baseball with him, swung from trees with him, climbed around old houses with him, and eventually married him. And he'd expected to find that Clea—the old Clea—when he saw her again.

The old Clea was there, of course, but there was a hell of a lot more to her now. She looked womanly. Curvier, though still slender, as the outline of that pink silk slip had made all too clear. And more experienced, more knowledgeable.

Not surprising, of course. He hadn't seen her in six years, not since he had accidentally run into her in a bank on Market Street one day almost a year after their supposed divorce. The simple sight of her coming through the revolving door had sent his heart hammering and his pulses racing, and he'd been glad that she had been in a hurry and hadn't had time to eat lunch with him or even say more than a few words.

He hadn't realized until then how much he'd missed her. He hadn't had time to realize. But once he did, he knew he wouldn't dare let himself have time to think about it again.

Clea had married him because she was a good sport and she'd wanted to do him a favor. She'd also wanted her tuition. Though honesty compelled him to acknowledge that she probably would have done it anyway if he'd asked her. But he had not just asked. They'd made a deal—a marriage so he could get his inheritance and start his own business and so she could get her tuition and finish school; and then, with no strings attached, they'd get a divorce—and they'd stuck to it.

So Austin had got his business, and one look at Clea told him that she was thriving, too. So, he'd reminded himself, everything had worked out just as they had planned.

Besides that one time when he'd seen her and felt his heart tear, he'd never seen her again. It was pointless. It was past. And Austin always looked to the future.

He'd moved his business dealings to L.A. shortly thereafter. He got back to the Bay area frequently, of course, even building a home in Tiburon a couple of years back. But San Francisco was a big city. He never saw Clea.

Sometimes he thought it would be fun. Sometimes he wanted to share something with someone with more depth than his usual women. And then, for a brief moment, he would think of Clea. But he never thought long, and he almost never let himself look back.

But tonight, lying in her bed, he couldn't help it. He found himself remembering what it had been like being married to Clea, found himself wondering what it would be like to be married to her again.

It wasn't the first time the thought had occurred to him lately. The moment Baxter had brought up the invalid divorce, the wheels began turning in his brain. But he didn't let them turn very far or go very fast. Though Clea cropped up almost constantly after that, there were too many unknowns, too many uncertainties.

The Clea of seven or eight years ago might have vanished forever. The sparks that always ignited between them might have disappeared, the fire might have gone out. It might very well have been just the "kid stuff" that he'd always thought it was. Good fun with a good woman.

But good fun wasn't as much fun anymore. A quality life—one like he had seen his brother Miles settle into over the past year—became more and more tempting. A wife, a child, a sense of future, of purpose. They had been mere abstracts when he had married Clea. And not even abstracts he wanted much part of. But now . . .

Now he found the idea oddly tempting. Being married—sharing his life, his work, his ups and downs—appealed. A lot. So did the idea at least of sharing them with Clea. Of course, Austin had told himself time and again after Baxter imparted his astonishing news, he would have to wait until he saw her again to know.

Now he knew.

He wanted Clea again as badly as he had ever wanted anything in his life.

From the first moment he had seen her, something dead in his heart came back to life. Something revved up, kicked over, and surged inside him. He'd fallen through the floor figuratively as well as literally last night.

He got out of bed and wandered over to the window, staring out at the first pink and gray streaks of dawn. Coit Tower stood like a sentry on the hill. He smiled. When he and Clea had been living in married students' housing they'd played dream games sometimes at night.

Lying in each other's arms they'd whispered to each other what, in their fondest dreams, life would bring them. An architectural design award, Austin would say. A sailboat, a Victorian house with a view of the bay. My own restoration business, Clea would whisper, snuggling closer. Three blond-haired children and a Victorian house.

With a view of the bay? Austin would tease.

And she would laugh, tickling his ribs. Nah, I don't want everything you want. I'll settle for Coit Tower.

Well, she'd got Coit Tower. And her restoration business. He wondered about the three blond kids? Did she still want them? Whose? Ken's?

He leaned his forehead against the cool glass of the window. What did she see in a man like that? With his pale yellow shirt, cream-colored slacks and light blond hair, Ken Hollister made even Baxter look colorful. Dull as dishwater, too, Austin was willing to bet. Probably worked in insurance or a bank. Probably would the rest of his life.

How could Clea honestly think she'd be happy married to him?

Good grief, even if he hadn't wanted her, he'd have had to stay around just to save her from herself!

"SLEEP WELL?"

The words had the effect of a bucket of cold water in her face as she walked through the kitchen door. Clea eased the crick in her neck with one hand, while she buttoned her bathrobe with the other.

"What are you doing here?" She frowned at Austin, who was sitting shirtless at her kitchen table, the remains of a toast and egg breakfast on the blue willow plate in front of him.

"I spent the night here, remember?" He gave her a sunny smile.

She winced. "How could I forget? I don't mean that. I mean here. In the kitchen. At—" she squinted at the clock "—eight-thirty in the morning. Very unlike you."

"I've changed."

"I doubt that." A changed, less predictable Austin she didn't even want to contemplate. Fumbling for the coffeepot, she suddenly found Austin taking it out of her hand and pouring her a cup, then carrying it to the table and solicitously pulling out a chair for her.

"You take it black, don't you?" he asked.

"Yes." She took a tentative sip, then another larger one. "You have changed," she allowed then.

Austin looked at her quizzically.

"You make better coffee."

He grinned. "Had to. You weren't around to make it anymore. Want some toast? Or a bagel? There're some onion bagels in the refrigerator."

"I know," Clea said sourly. "I bought them."

The grin widened. "That's right. I forgot. Remember when we used to say that all the coffee in San Francisco was so uniformly bad that they must brew it all in Coit Tower and pipe it all over the city?"

"Mmm. I'll take a bagel," Clea said. She didn't want to remember. She wanted to forget. She'd had a rotten night. The horsehair settee hadn't been too bad. It was the memories that were doing her in.

She had hoped, regardless of what she'd told Austin about being there, that she would get out of the house and off to work before he even got up this morning. Then, by the time she got home, she would have had several hours of wide-awake sanity and a better perspective on things before she would have to deal with him again.

No such luck.

She raked fingers through her uncombed hair and looked glumly at Austin's smiling face. She didn't want to deal with him before she had her coffee and a bagel, but maybe if she did, he would leave her to eat it in peace. It was worth a try.

"So what about the divorce?" she asked.

Austin shrugged. He had got up and was supervising the toasting of her bagel. It popped up and he tossed it onto a plate, then spread butter on it. "No hurry."

"What's no hurry?"

"Getting it. Talking about it. Either one."

"I disagree. I think we ought to get it settled. I mean, are you sure that we don't just have to take in the papers and that will be that?"

"I'm sure. Baxter checked."

"Who's Baxter?"

"My lawyer." Austin grinned. "You'd love him."

"He isn't a sleazeball like Rawlings?" All Clea could remember about Rawlings were his gravy-stained tie, his greasy hair and the cigarette stains on his fingers. And, now, his incompetence.

"Baxter? He'd make the Prince of Wales look like a commoner."

"He's British?"

"No. He just wishes he were. But he's thorough. And he says we have to refile. Start over. If we want to."

"What do you mean, 'if we want to'? Of course we want to."

Austin set the bagel in front of her, then sat down in the other chair again and propped his elbows on the table, lacing his fingers together, resting his chin on them and regarding her solemnly. "Didn't you like being married to me?"

Oh, God, she wasn't up to guileless honesty so early in the morning. Sighing, Clea shut her eyes. But when she opened them, Austin—and his question—were still there.

"I liked being married to you, Austin," she said finally. "You know that. I won't lie to you about it. But it's over. It's been over for seven years. It was kid stuff, and I'm not a kid any longer."

"Neither one of us is a kid any longer, Clea."

Outside sparrows on the window box chattered, a woman shouted at some children in Italian, then when that didn't quell the noise, Chinese. Once more Clea heard the cable car bell. She tried to close everything out—the sparrows, the children, the bell, but most of all what she thought Austin was hinting at. It had hurt enough the first time she'd loved him. She wasn't going to go through it again.

Austin, for once, seemed inclined not to push things. He got lazily to his feet. Having planted the thought, he changed the subject. "Want another bagel?"

"No. I've got to go to work."

"Where are you working now?"

"I'm restoring a Stick-style house on Haight."

His eyes lit up. "Is it in good shape?"

"Better than this one," she admitted.

"I like this house," Austin told her. "It's got great potential."

"Then you and I are the only ones who can see it," Clea said ruefully. "I had a heck of a time convincing the bank."

Austin shook his head. "It's solid. Good supports. No rot. Lots of cleanup, lots of repair. But the structure is good." His expertise showed.

"You must've checked around a lot," Clea said dryly.

"I had a lot of time last night." There was an accusation and lots of unspoken questions in his eyes.

Clea ignored them.

Finally he sighed. "So tell me about the one you're working on."

She smiled. "It's lovely. The exterior is in fine shape. For some reason the owners took care of that. But the interior has gone to hell. That's what I'm working on, and if I don't get there soon, I'll be at a standstill all next week while Mr. Carruthers is in Chicago. He doesn't know anything, and he wants to approve everything." She finished the bagel, wiped her mouth and carried her dishes to the sink.

"I'd love to see it," Austin said almost wistfully.

It was on the tip of her tongue to give him the address and say, "Drop by."

But she couldn't. If she did, she would be letting him into her life. Worse, she would be *encouraging* him to come back into her life. And she didn't need that. She didn't need it at all.

"Seen one, you've seen 'em all," she said airily. "I have to get dressed." She started out the door, then paused. "Listen, Austin, about the divorce papers..."

"We don't have to talk about them now."

"But—"

"No, you go on. Go to work," Austin said firmly. "There'll be time. I plan to be in the city for a few days."

"Well . . ." One part of her wanted to get it settled right now. Another part reminded her that time was wasting and Mr. Carruthers was going to make her life miserable if she didn't show up by nine-thirty at least. "All right. Give me a call and we can set up a time. I'm in the book." And she vanished up the steps.

Distance restored her equilibrium. But it vanished the moment she came back downstairs. Austin was standing by the door, rumpled and still slightly sleepy. He scratched his bare chest, drawing her gaze. A shaft of pure longing pierced her so strongly that she had to suck in her breath.

Austin's brows drew together. "What's wrong?"

"Nothing," she lied. "Make the door look like it's locked when you leave. It doesn't work. I have to get a new one." Then with a wave of her hand, she bounded down the steps. "Ta ta."

There, she thought as she hopped into her Subaru pickup, she hadn't handled that badly at all. Just the right amount of detachment, just the right blasé air.

She had survived.

And the next time she saw him she would make sure they met on a business footing. Cut-and-dried, pure and simple, and nothing but. In the meantime, she was kicking him straight out of her mind.

"I'D GO WITH THE PUMPKIN ONE."

"Huh? What'd you say?" Clea blinked her way back to the reality of the Carrutherses' dining room and stared blankly at Rosie O'Reilly.

"Honestly, Clea." Rosie shook her black curls in irritation. "Where are you today? You haven't heard a word I've said."

"Of course I have," Clea countered briskly. "You told me Nicky hit a home run in his Little League game last night."

"I told you that at nine forty-five this morning." Rosie shook her head at her friend's distractibility. "Where've you been since? I'm talking about wallpaper. I like the pumpkin one."

The "pumpkin one" was really only minimally concerned with pumpkins. It was basically a stripe intermingling earth-tone verticals with vines and the incidental rust-colored pumpkin, and Rosie, her assistant, was suggesting it for the Carrutherses' dining room. Clea wasn't sure she liked it, but she hadn't been able to concentrate enough to come up with any other viable alternatives to present to Mr. and Mrs. Carruthers for their approval. And this morning's meeting with him had been a farce. Usually her positive attitude was enough to get him to make sensible decisions. Today she hadn't been able to muster any more than vague dithering herself.

Rosie was right—she was somewhere else and had been most of the day. Her mind, regardless of her resolution, was wherever Austin Cavanaugh was at the moment. He had distracted her totally.

She wished she could've asked Rosie what she would've done if her ex-husband had walked back into her life and announced that they were still married and so far seemed to be hinting that he wanted to stay that way.

She didn't because she knew exactly what Rosie would say. Rosie would deliver her polemic on faithless men. Clea had heard it plenty of times before. She knew that Rosie's ex had never even been her husband, and that he had walked out on her when Nicky was born. She would never take him back, she had told Clea countless times. *Never, never, NEVER!*

Well, Clea had no intention of taking Austin back, either. But she didn't need Rosie's lecture on top of all her other negative feelings. And if she even mentioned him briefly, she knew she would get it. Rosie had the truth about life, other people only had opinions.

Still, Clea admitted to herself, Rosie was a fantastic stained-glass artist, and she was coming right along in other areas of restoration since she'd begun working full-time for Clea. Having such a talented assistant made it worth Clea's while to put up with a lot of Rosie's "truths."

But she wasn't going to talk to Rosie about Austin. She tried to concentrate on the wallpaper her assistant was holding up.

"It's not bad," she conceded finally and turned to the man sitting cross-legged on the floor. "What do you think, Devin?"

"What does he know?" Rosie sniffed, barely sparing a glance for the lean brown-haired man who was repairing the bottom of one of the drawers in the built-in buffet.

He looked up and gave Rosie an indulgent, almost tender smile that made her bristle. "I know what I like," he said softly.

Clea saw the beginnings of a dark red blush tinge Rosie's cheekbones and could almost see the retort forming on her friend's lips.

"Do you like the wallpaper?" she asked Devin quickly. She knew what he liked, too. He liked Rosie. But Rosie didn't like him, a sentiment she made frequently and abundantly clear.

Devin shrugged. "'S'all right."

"What d'you mean, 'it's all right'?" Rosie stalked across the dining room and glared down at him. "It's beautiful. Perfect for this room." She turned to Clea. "And if I do the glass over the buffet in the same tones, when the sun comes through it will be gorgeous."

She was right about that. Rosie worked miracles in glass. That was how Clea had found her in the first place. She'd needed a new stained-glass piece for a church window restoration she was involved in, and Devin Flynn, the woodworker restoring the retablo behind the altar, mentioned Rosie O'Reilly.

"She's got the temper of a shrew and the eyes of the devil," he'd warned Clea. "But she does the work of an angel in glass."

Everything he'd said was true, Clea discovered. Black-eyed, black-haired Rosie would argue with a lampshade, would pontificate on everything from men to goldfish to nuclear weapons. But she was tireless, enthusiastic and genuinely talented, and that was enough for Clea.

Rosie worked hard, delighted to have whatever work Clea could send her way. And before long she was Clea's assistant, working at whatever Clea gave her as she could do it while her son, Nicky, was in school. They had been together for two years.

Devin Flynn took all the credit for it.

Clea was delighted to give it to him. But it infuriated Rosie when she found out.

"He's a bum," she said to Clea over and over. "Needs a haircut. Wood shavings all over him." She'd shake her head in distaste at the thought of the lean, hawk-nosed man with the hands that could work magic on wood. "A jerk."

But Clea never let herself get dragged into Rosie's disparagement of Devin. She didn't wholly understand it, but when she'd asked, Rosie had just said, "Let's say, we go back a long way." The negative vibes were almost tangible, and the message was "Don't probe further."

Clea hadn't. She liked Devin a lot. He was quiet, unassuming, and a hard worker. Plus, he was a master at rebuilding and repairing old furniture, woodwork and cabinetry. He seemed to be able to fix anything he set his mind to. Except whatever grudge Rosie had against him.

And that was Devin's problem, not Clea's, thank heavens. She had enough of her own.

"I'll take the wallpaper books home tonight and narrow it down to three or four possibles. If we only come up with one, Mrs. C will be sure to reject it." Picking out wallpaper would be a piece of cake compared with another, weightier decision: What was she going to do about Austin?

SHE WAS LOCKED OUT.

Arms full of the wallpaper books, groceries, as well as her bulging purse, Clea rattled the door, frowned, jiggled the useless lock, then kicked the door.

How could you get locked out by a lock that wouldn't even lock? Damn. She tried one more time, jiggling the doorknob, then backing up and shoving the door with all her might trying to free it up.

As she did so, she heard a rattle from the inside, the door sprang open, and Clea, shoulder first, hurtled straight into Austin's arms.

"What the—" She dropped the wallpaper books, her purse, and the groceries and wrestled her way out of his grasp.

"I fixed your lock." He beamed at her with accomplishment.

Clea stared back, stunned.

"And I fixed your floor." He waved an arm in the direction of the spot where the hole had been. New boards had been fitted in so skillfully that, other than the stain that was missing, they could have been original flooring.

Clea looked from the man to the door to the floor and felt that her life was suddenly spinning out of control. "I thought you'd left," she said slowly. It seemed slightly more polite than saying she'd hoped he had.

Austin looked astonished. "Where would I go?"

"A hotel?" she said hopefully.

He reached for the can of tomato sauce that had rolled under the table. "I'd rather be with you."

Clea bent down and gathered up the wallpaper books, setting them on the table, anger, weariness, despair beginning to simmer within. Austin handed her the purse. She took it and put it on the entry hall table. "Austin, we have got to talk."

"Fine." He followed her into the parlor.

The floor really was well done, she thought grudgingly. The man was a genius when it came to working with wood. Her own expertise lay in other areas. "Complementary areas," Austin had always said. Something else to try not to think about.

She sank down on the horsehair settee, grimacing at the lack of give beneath her weary bones.

"Hard day?" Austin asked sympathetically. He went around behind her and began to knead her shoulders. Clea gave an involuntary purr of satisfaction, then jerked upright.

"I'm all right, Austin!" She pulled forward, trying to get away from the soothing movements of his fingers.

But his fingers followed her, closing on her shoulders, massaging them gently, drawing her back against the settee, working a magic that she was powerless to resist. "Swinging from the rafters, were you?" he asked softly.

She shook her head. His thumbs were easing the tension in the cord of her neck, melting her resistance. "Crawling around on the floor measuring things mostly. And trying to get some sense out of Mr. Carruthers." *Trying to get some sense out of myself.*

"Poor Clea." Something soft and light touched the top of her head. Both his hands continued their gentle soothing, so what had touched her?

She knew the answer to the question before she'd even asked it. And then, shivering, she felt his breath lifting her hair.

"Austin." It was a plea.

"Hmm?" The murmur floated just above her ear.

"Don't."

"Don't what?"

"Don't do this."

"Do what?" His hands stilled. "Do you want me to stop?"

The moment he did, she didn't. His touch had been healing her, taking away the soreness, easing the tiredness, melting her where she sat. And yet she knew she had to make him stop. She sighed.

"Austin, why are you doing this to me?" she asked wearily.

"Massaging your shoulders? Because you look like you need it?"

"No, not massaging my shoulders," Clea said. "Disrupting my life."

"Am I?" He sounded simultaneously hopeful and innocent.

"You know damned well you are."

The fingers squeezed her shoulders comfortingly. "Good."

She turned her head and glared up at him. "You didn't answer my question."

"I didn't think I'd have to." The clear blue eyes were guileless. Then he smiled. "What do you want for dinner?"

"I'm having a can of tuna and some lettuce for dinner," Clea informed him, disconcerted. Every time they got close to discussing what they were going to do about the divorce, he veered off again.

"I'll take you out," he offered now.

She shook her head. "No. I don't want to go out. I want to relax in a hot bath, eat my tuna, and go to sleep. In my own bed tonight. Alone," she added pointedly.

Austin gave a resigned nod. His hands dropped to his sides and he wandered over to the bookcases with the leaded glass doors that separated the front parlor from the back one. Running his finger over the intricate leading, he observed, "You're going to have to get new glass in these."

"Yes, I know. Rosie will do it."

"Who's Rosie?"

"She works for me."

"Tell me about your business."

Clea shook her head. "No. The only thing we have to talk about is the divorce. If you're not going to talk about that, goodbye."

Austin tucked his hands in his back pockets and scowled at her. "When'd you get to be so blunt?"

"When you got to be so devious. Do we talk or do you leave?"

"Let's talk after dinner."

"I'm not eating out."

"I'll eat in."

"I have exactly one can of tuna."

"Don't worry," Austin said. "I'll manage. Go take your bath."

He was gone when she got out and she thought momentarily that he had decided on her second option. But before she had the tuna out of the can, he was back.

The door flew open, and in he came, two bags redolent with the best of Chinese cuisine in his arms.

Hands on her hips, Clea glared at him.

Austin set the bags down on the table and proceeded to empty them, lining up small white paper containers on the table. Then he fetched a plate from the cabinet over the counter, fished a pair of chopsticks out of the bottom of the bag, and began piling his plate.

"Austin," Clea began warningly.

He gave her a benevolent smile. "Don't mind me. You go right ahead and have your tuna."

He had, by this time, a plateful of rice, heaped over with beef and broccoli, almond chicken with water chestnuts, deep-fried prawns, won tons, and moo goo gai pan. Clea picked up her fork and took a mouthful of tuna. Her stomach growled in protest.

Doggedly she chewed on. Her salivary glands ached for the broccoli and beef. Her teeth craved the crunch of the water chestnuts, her stomach wanted it all.

"Damn you, Austin," she muttered.

He grinned and began filling another plate. "I thought I could tempt you."

Clea hoped that wasn't the truth.

She took the plate that he handed her, dumped the remains of her tuna in the garbage, and dug in.

They ate in silence, chopsticks moving swiftly from plate to mouth, and Clea remembered other meals like this. In some ways he still knew how to undermine her, that was certain. Beef and broccoli. Almond chicken. All her favorites. Right down to the fortune cookie he handed her at the end of the meal.

"Remember when I got the one that said, 'You'll be a millionaire'?" He grinned at her.

"And the one you got that said you'd be bald."

Austin rubbed his hand through his still-thick blond thatch. "Well, fifty-fifty isn't too bad. What've you got today?"

Clea unfolded the narrow strip of paper. With luck it would shed some light on her life. " 'Beware of bananas,' " she read.

Austin burst out laughing. "What?"

Clea shrugged. "Probably part of the New Wave School of Fortune Cookie Writing. What about yours?"

Austin cracked his cookie in half and smoothed out the paper. "'You'll have a long and lasting love.'" The blue eyes lifted, meeting hers. "I sincerely hope so," he said.

Clea swallowed. "You getting married, too?" she forced herself to ask brightly.

"I already *am* married."

Oh, God, he couldn't do this to her! "We're getting a divorce, Austin. We've *had* a divorce."

"No," he said implacably, "we haven't. And no, we're not. I've been thinking. A lot. About being divorced, and about being married. About being married to you. I've decided I want to."

"You can't do that!" Clea protested frantically. "You don't even know me anymore."

The blue eyes never left her face. "I want to get to know you again."

"No."

"Clea, be reasonable."

"Be reasonable! You be reasonable for once in your life, Austin Cavanaugh. You cannot just walk in here seven years after the fact, tell me our divorce is over, and that you want to be married again! You can't do it! Especially not when you're the one who wanted the damned divorce in the first place!"

"I changed my mind."

"After seven years?" she said scornfully.

"Better late than never," he said, and he didn't seem to be joking as he said it.

Clea shook her head, slapping her chopsticks down deliberately and pushing herself away from the table. "Sorry," she said. "No. I already have another fiancé."

"You need a divorce first," Austin reminded her.

"I'll get one." She stood up and carried her dishes to the sink, no longer hungry, her heart at war with her mind, her emotions already doing battle with the food in her stomach.

Austin went right on eating. "Be my guest," he said easily. "You'll need a lawyer first."

"We have a lawyer," Clea snapped. "This Baxter person."

"*I* have a lawyer," Austin said mildly.

"So? He can still get us the divorce."

"But *I* don't want a divorce."

"I do!"

Austin broke his fried won ton in half. "Then you'd better get your own lawyer, Clea. Rawlings, perhaps?"

She clenched and unclenched her fists in impotent fury. "Austin, how can you do this? What am I supposed to get a lawyer with? They don't come cheap. The competent ones, at least," she added with a sneer. "And every cent I have is tied up in this house!"

"I know." He took another bite of rice.

Clea stalked back and forth in the kitchen, furious, frantic, her mind whirling. How could he do this? How could he walk in here, turn her life upside down over the divorce, then tell her he didn't want one after all? For how long didn't he want one? she wanted to ask him. Austin Cavanaugh had all the staying power of a fish fly. Was she supposed to believe in a fortune-cookie "long and lasting relationship" with him? Stay married? Ha.

"I'll call legal services."

"They charge on a sliding income scale."

"Precisely."

"Yes, but since we're still married, my income will count too. No, Sunshine, I'm afraid you're up a creek." He got up and came toward her, arms raised to wrap around her. She tried to evade them, but they caught her, pulling her up snugly against him, hugging her into the warm strength of his chest.

Tears brimmed in her eyes. She struggled against him, against herself. "Why, Austin? Why?" she asked him, her voice breaking against his collarbone.

"Why what, Sunshine?" His right arm held her close against him, while his left hand came up and stroked her hair back away from her face.

"Why are you doing this to me?" she asked bitterly. "I thought we were friends?"

His arm tightened. "We are friends, Clea, love. More than friends."

"Then why?"

He kissed her hair. "Because I love you."

She went absolutely stiff in his arms.

He rocked her against him for another long moment, stroking her hair. Then he took a deep breath and gently loosed his hold on her and stepped back. "I'll do the dishes tonight," he said, already moving to clear the table. "You turn in early. You must be beat."

"I . . ." But Clea didn't know what she was going to say. She was totally disoriented, her life spinning upside down.

Austin took her by the shoulders and turned her around, giving her a gentle push toward the doorway. "Go on. Take it easy. Get a good night's sleep. Things will make sense in the morning."

Clea went, but she doubted it.

And she lay awake long after the soft noises downstairs had ceased. Flat on her back, she stared at the crumbling ceiling and, for once, didn't even notice it.

Austin loved her. Or he said he did.

And she didn't know whether she wished she believed him or not.

Chapter Three

When Clea got up in the morning, she found Austin on the settee where she'd spent the previous night.

It was far too short for him, and he lay face up with one leg hooked over the back of it, and the other bent. One arm was folded behind his head, the other trailed on the floor. His hair was tousled and golden stubble lit his jaw and chin. Ridiculously long eyelashes, bleached almost platinum by the sun, fanned delicately against his tanned cheeks which were only faintly grooved now in repose.

He had pulled her afghan over him, but his feet stuck out and it had slipped down to his belly, leaving his bare chest exposed to the cool morning air. He looked beat and vulnerable, and Clea felt a terrible surge of longing to hold him in her arms again.

It wasn't fair for him to come back into her life like this, turn things upside down, make demands, tell her he loved her. What did Austin Cavanaugh know about love?

Making love? Well, yes, he knew a lot about that. He was very good at it. But then he'd had a lot of practice. But honest-to-God caring love—the adult kind that implied commitment, faithfulness, steadfastness, dependability—as far as Clea knew, he'd never given that a try. She wasn't sure he even knew it existed.

Steeling her heart against him, she went into the kitchen and put on the coffee. The smell of it, combined with his uncomfortable sleeping arrangements, had him padding out after her five minutes later. He scratched his chest and yawned, giving her a sleepy smile.

"Good. You're making the coffee this morning."

"Yes," she said briskly. "And you have time to shave before it's done. I'll make you some toast or there's cold cereal . . ."

"No waffles?" He gave her a hopeful look. "We always had waffles on Sundays."

"No waffles. Once you've eaten, you can leave. I'm going out for the day."

He frowned. His jeans were unsnapped and seemed to be defying gravity. She didn't know how much longer they would manage it, either. She wished he'd go shave. Jerking her eyes away, she grabbed two slices of bread and stuffed them into the toaster.

"Where're you going?" He made no move to go up to the bathroom, instead just leaned against the counter and watched her bustle around the kitchen, a look of perplexity on his face.

"I am going out with Ken," she said finally. "Not that it's any of your business."

"Of course it's my business," he said. "You're my wife."

She made a sound of sheer exasperation. "Austin, will you stop that?" The toast popped up. She slathered it with butter and slapped it on a plate.

He took the toast off the plate, dropped a dollop of marmalade on it, spread it, took a bite, and looked up at her curiously. "Stop what?"

"Acting like you're my husband again."

"It's what I am," he said reasonably.

"You never acted this possessively when you had a right to."

He shrugged. "You were never engaged to another man."

"Well, I am now," Clea said, "and I am going out with him in an hour. So you will have to finish your breakfast and get out of my house. And," she added with quiet force, "out of my life."

Austin shook his head slowly and implacably. "Huh-uh."

"What do you mean, huh-uh?"

"I mean I'll get out of your house for the time being, Clea. But I'm back in your life to stay." And the look he gave her with those intense blue eyes said that he meant every word.

They stared at each other, volumes being spoken in the silence, a tension throbbing between them that Clea had never felt with him before. But then, she reminded herself, whatever fights they'd had before had been childish ones. They'd never reached a stalemate like this.

Finally Clea stuffed her hands in the pockets of her robe. "I'm going up to take a shower. When I come down, Austin, I'll expect to find you gone."

THE MIRACLE WAS, she did.

Forty-five minutes later, dressed in a pair of yellow linen pleated pants and a yellow and white bulky-knit cotton sweater, she ventured down the stairs to find not a sign of him. The afghan was folded on the back of the settee, the plate and cup had been washed and returned to the cupboard, the toast crumbs wiped up.

"Austin?"

Nothing.

She opened the door to the cellar and peered down into the darkness. "Austin?"

She looked in the breakfast room, in the pantry, even in the broom closet. He wasn't there.

"He left," she said to Thurber who cocked his head to one side and looked as if she'd lost her mind. She'd never talked to him before.

But the realization was still working its way into her consciousness. The beginnings of a smile were lighting her face. She pirouetted around the dining room.

"He actually left," she chirped. Then, "Well, of course, he left, you dolt," she said to herself. "He could see that you meant what you said."

Obviously that was the way to handle Austin—with firm unwavering adherence to what you knew was right.

If you did, he got the message.

And just in time, too, for less than fifteen minutes later, Ken showed up on her front porch, looking weekend dapper in khaki slacks and a madras sport shirt, his blond hair neatly combed, a smile on his face.

"So, did you sort out your ex-husband then?"

"I . . . I . . . Yes, I think I did."

A tiny crease appeared between Ken's brows. "You think? What's that mean?"

Clea grimaced. "It means exactly that. That I think I did, but with Austin one never knows for sure."

"Well, surely it can't be difficult. If you don't simply re-file, you just get a lawyer and start again, don't you?"

"Yes, er . . . I think . . . I mean, you're probably right."

"Well, then?" Ken was looking at her as if she'd lost her mind. But she had no intention of telling him that she had already suggested that to Austin, nor of telling him the reaction she'd got.

"Let's don't talk about Austin. We spent all Friday night talking about Austin. I want to do something else. Something to take my mind off him."

"Want to go down to my folks?" Ken suggested. "Mother's cooking the usual Sunday dinner."

Ken's parents lived in Santa Cruz. He and Clea went down once a month usually. It was a calm, pleasant sort of family-oriented day, and, as such, Clea thought it sounded like a good tonic for what ailed her. Ken's father would watch whatever sport was seasonal on the television and Ken would watch with him. Ken's mother would regale Clea with stories of his childhood and hopes for his future. The stories wouldn't change, neither would the hopes. But Clea liked Ken's parents. They'd make far better in-laws than Edward Cavanaugh had.

"If you don't think they'd mind on such short notice," she said.

"I'll give them a call." Ken crossed the parlor to pick up the phone. "I see you got your floor fixed."

"Yes."

"Devin Flynn do it?"

"No." A pause. "Austin did it."

Ken's eyebrows lifted speculatively.

Unbidden Clea's cheeks warmed. "Well, he broke it," she said defensively.

Ken managed a laugh. "I guess you could put it that way. Nice of him," he added, but he didn't look too certain. He rang up his mother, got an immediate invitation, held out a hand to Clea and said, "We're on our way."

The afternoon with Ken and his parents was exactly as she'd expected and did everything she hoped it would. Ken helped his father mow the grass, then they watched the Giants game on television. Clea helped Ken's mother polish the silver, while listening gratefully to a recounting of the history of each piece and how long it had been in the Hollister family, as it was brought to gleaming perfection once more. The meal was, as always, wonderful, the conversation undemanding, the drive home soothingly pleasant.

All in all it provided Clea with a sense of returning normality, and it renewed her feeling that she was, indeed, doing the right thing in marrying Ken. Life with him would be easy, comfortable. They were so well suited. They both wanted a home, a family, the simple joys of life.

She lay her head back against the headrest and closed her eyes while Ken drove them back toward the city. "I liked that. I like your parents," she said, opening her eyes and turning her head to smile at him.

Ken's eyes left the road long enough to smile back at her. "And they like you. I hope your parents will like me," he added after a moment.

Clea sat up straighter. "Of course they will," she said firmly.

"We ought to go see your parents one weekend soon. We see mine often enough."

"Well, I enjoy them."

"I might enjoy yours, too. I only met them once. And that was by accident."

"Well, we've been busy and . . ."

Ken shot her a sidelong glance. "I'm beginning to think you're ashamed of me."

"That's ridiculous."

"And that you're keeping us apart for a reason," he went on, teasing her gently.

"Nonsense," Clea said testily, when the truth cut close. "It's just . . ." But she couldn't ever explain to Ken what it was. Sighing, she lay her head back again. "We'll go next week if you like."

"Good." Ken gave her another smile, then pulled out to pass a truck. "I'd like that."

Clea hoped he would. She wasn't at all certain. Ken hadn't been wrong, really—she had had a reason for keeping him and her parents apart. She'd never brought home a man since she'd been married to Austin. She knew comparisons would be inevitable.

Her parents had doted on Austin Cavanaugh. They'd more than made up for his wretched father, loving him like the son they'd never had all the time he and Clea were growing up. They'd been over the moon when Clea had married him, not knowing the reason why. And they'd been distraught a year later when, in their eyes, the most wonderful marriage in the world had come apart.

They couldn't blame Clea, the daughter whom they loved with all their might. And they wouldn't blame Austin whom they cherished equally. All they could do was walk around with anguish in their eyes and hurt in their hearts.

To this day, Clea knew, they held out the hope that the two of them would get back together.

To Austin's credit, he had never presumed on the relationship after they separated. She didn't think he had ever seen them again. It had been hard on her parents, and she was sure it had been hard on Austin, too. She knew he loved her parents, probably as much as she did.

But they had both known that if the break were going to be clean, sentiment couldn't play a part.

Mary and Will Bannister still thought the world of the man who'd been their son-in-law. They followed his career in the newspapers, and Clea sometimes overheard an occasional conversation between them in which his name featured. But, tactfully, they refrained from mentioning him to her. And, tactfully, she refrained from bringing home other men to meet them.

They'd met Ken when Clea had invited them to lunch in the city one afternoon when she hadn't expected Ken to come by. He had, she'd introduced them, and that had been that. So far she hadn't mentioned her engagement to them, preferring just to let things ride.

Now she almost wished she had. She could have got them used to the idea slowly if she'd started sooner. She just hoped they didn't find out that, after all these years, she and

Austin really weren't divorced. She could well imagine what would start going through their heads if they did.

When Ken pulled up in front of her house, she turned to him and smiled. "Thanks for a lovely day. Do you want to come in?"

He grimaced. "Can't. I've got some loan applications to go over before I meet with the people tomorrow. Rain check?"

"Of course." She leaned across the seat and kissed him, getting kissed in return. Then, grabbing her purse, she climbed out.

"Dinner Wednesday?" Ken asked.

"Love to."

"I'll pick you up at six-thirty. And we'll go see your parents next weekend?"

"Of course."

They'd come to terms with him sometime, she told herself. They'd have to. It was doing all of them—Ken, her parents and herself—a disservice to pretend that her love life had ended when she and Austin split.

She stood on the sidewalk, watching Ken drive off, and was glad he'd pressed the issue. It was time to take a step forward, to convince everyone, once and for all, that Austin was no longer a part of her life.

BY SIX O'CLOCK the next evening Austin had moved in across the street.

"You can't!" Clea wailed when he told her as she was getting out of her truck. So much for having found the right way to handle him at last.

"Why not? Mrs. Gianetti had a room for rent." He was smiling at her like a tomcat who'd just swiped a canary out from beneath another cat's nose. Ken's nose.

"That's ridiculous!" she fumed.

"I quite agree," he said. "I should have moved in with you."

Clea gave a snort of rage and slammed the door to the truck.

"Well, I am your husband," he went on in a wounded tone.

It was getting to be a refrain. "Don't start, Austin," she warned him, turning her back.

"Can I give you a hand with your tools?" he offered as she wrestled the box out of the back of her truck.

"No, thank you." If firmness alone didn't work, perhaps stoic indifference would. She brushed past him, heading toward her front steps.

He bounded around her, got to the top first, and filched the house key from her hand, opening the door before she could protest. Jaw clenched, she went in through the open door and dumped the box in the parlor. "Thank you," she said. "Good night."

"Want to go out for dinner?"

"No."

"Have you eaten?"

"No."

"Then—"

So much for stoic indifference. "Austin, I said, no. I will not be bullied. Good night."

"How about a walk? You could show me the neighborhood."

"No."

"You were always very neighborly when we—"

She clenched her fists very tightly. "Austin, go away. Now."

But Austin was walking toward her.

"I mean it! Go!"

Shaking his head, a gentle, wistfully tender smile on his face, he closed in on her. And then he was next to her, so close she could feel his breath touch her cheek. His arms lifted and wrapped around her, pulling her against him.

"Austin," she whispered, stiffening, her voice ragged. "Please. Don't."

He shook his head slowly, his lips brushing her forehead, warm and soft and inviting. His fingers crept up her back. "I still love you, Clea."

"No! You don't. You—" She tried to pull away, but Austin's gentle strength held her fast, melting her resolve. He laughed softly, nuzzling against her hair.

"Ah, Clea. You know that's not true. I've loved you since we were kids."

"That's different. A different kind of love. We're not kids anymore, Austin." She turned her head away from him, but his lips still lingered in her hair. "We're adults."

"So we are," he said mockingly. "And you know damned well I love you that way, too."

"Austin, stop it! That's not what I meant. I don't know— I don't love—"

He jerked back. His fingers caught her upper arm, his hold gentle but firm as he held her a few inches away from him and looked down into her eyes. "Don't say you don't love me, Clea. I know it's not true."

Their eyes battled, fiery brown and blazing blue, until at last Clea pulled out of his grasp, hugging her arms to her breasts, breathing hard. "I don't want to!"

BUT SHE DID.

Austin knew it. Could see it, feel it. And he took all the satisfaction he could get from it. He had left her then, hugging the knowledge to himself, making a strategic retreat, as it were. Not far. Just across the street.

Eight years in business had taught him plenty of things, and foremost among them was that the business never went to the man who wasn't there. Austin could draw a parallel as well as the next man. The same was undoubtedly true about winning Clea back.

But patience wasn't one of Austin's virtues, and simply being there quickly proved to be not enough. Some campaigns could be won by passively waiting until the other product proved inferior. This one, he determined, would have to be won by more active means. He would have to convince Clea that *he*, not Ken, was the one she wanted.

Clea went about her business and obviously did her best to ignore him. Every morning she went to work about eight at the house she was restoring out on Haight St. and every evening about five-thirty she came back. Austin made it a point to be out there when she left and again when she came home. But he never got more than a polite nod, if that.

Wednesday night, while he was sitting on the front porch talking to Mrs. Gianetti, Clea had the audacity to get into Ken's car and drive away with him. She didn't come home until after eleven either, and that was when Austin knew that patience alone wouldn't work.

Thursday morning when she came out to go to work, Clea discovered that her pickup had a flat.

"Need some help?"

She was staring in dismay at the lopsided truck and didn't even turn around. "I have a flat."

He hunkered down and examined his predawn handiwork. "Got a spare? I'll fix it." He gave her an ingenuous grin.

But Clea was glancing at her watch with impatience. "Never mind. I don't have time. Damn. Today of all days. I'm supposed to meet Mrs. Carruthers at nine." She reached in the back and hoisted her tote bag full of cleaning supplies and her toolbox out. "I'll have to catch a bus."

"I'll take you."

"No." She started up the hill, the heavy box and cumbersome bag in her arms.

Austin went after her, determined not to let her get away. He hadn't got up before dawn just to lose her to public transportation now. "Clea, don't be an idiot. They're not going to let you ride the bus with all that crap. Besides, it's already eight-thirty. You're not going to make it out there by nine that way."

Clea kept right on walking. "She'll just have to wait then."

"Damn it, Clea, even when you were a kid you weren't this stubborn!" He was practically running to keep up with her. Grabbing her arm, he hauled her to a stop. "Why won't you let me take you? Chicken?"

The taunt was inspired. It worked on her as well at twenty-nine as it had at nine. A tide of bright red washed over her face. "No, I am not chicken."

"Then come on. I'll give you a ride."

She bit her lip indecisively.

It didn't matter to Austin. Right now he had enough decisiveness for both of them. Before she could protest, he lifted the box out of her arms, lugged it back down the hill and stowed it in the trunk of his car.

"Austin!"

He grinned back at her. "Come on or you're going to be late!"

Clea stood her ground, glaring.

"If you're chicken," he said easily, "I'll promise on Scout's honor that I'll keep my hands to myself."

"You were never a Boy Scout, Austin Cavanaugh, and you know it."

"How about on my honor as a gentleman, then?"

"Or that either." But she began to smile faintly.

"Wolves' honor?" Austin suggested.

"That I believe." Clea took one last look toward Columbus Ave. where the bus ran, glanced again at her watch, and finally made up her mind. "All right. Let's go," she said.

Austin smiled. They went.

He was the soul of circumspection. For the time being, at least. A foot in the door was enough. He wasn't going to push his luck. But he couldn't stop giving her the occasional oblique glance while he drove her across town, thinking how marvelous it would be if they were really together again and he was giving her a ride to work, how it would be if they'd awakened together, warm and sleepy and well-loved in her bed. He'd been thinking that a lot lately, remembering how things had been, how he'd never really appreciated them when he'd had them. He'd appreciate them now, that was certain.

He didn't know what Clea was thinking. She sat stiff and silent as a post and didn't say anything beyond the terse directions she gave him once they got in the immediate neighborhood.

When he finally pulled up in front of the Carrutherses' house, she had hopped out almost before the car had stopped.

"Thanks very much," she called over her shoulder, sprinting up the steps.

"I'll pick you up."

"Don't bother." And the door banged shut after her.

HE WAS DRIVING HER INSANE. Like a personification of the Chinese water torture, he was always there, every moment of the day. And it was getting harder and harder not to give in. The trouble was, she'd had too many years of doing exactly that—giving in to whatever Austin Cavanaugh wanted. Because so often before it had been what she'd wanted herself.

But now she had to resist. Had to wait him out. For herself, for her future, and for Ken.

Forget him, she told herself. *You got over him before. You can do it again. All it takes is good hard work. Something to keep idle hands and idle minds occupied. And you've got a whole house just waiting for you to work on it. So, get to it!*

That was when she discovered that she'd left her toolbox in his car.

"Damnation!"

For another full minute she stood rooted to the spot, uncertain what she ought to do next. No, that wasn't quite true. She knew exactly what she ought to do next. It was just that it was going to be so damned mortifying.

But there was no way around it. If she wanted her idle mind and her idle hands busy today, she'd have to go see if he was still parked at the curb waiting for her to realize what she'd forgotten.

He was.

She gritted her teeth. Inhaling deeply and telling herself that in the larger course of events, feeling like a fool today was not going to harm her, she strode gamefully out to the car. Austin smiled brightly when he saw her coming.

"Forget something?" he inquired gently.

Clea grunted.

He hopped out. "Let me help you with those."

But Clea wasn't letting him do anything else. "I can manage perfectly well, thank you." She snatched the box out of the back seat and stalked back up the walk to the house.

Then, resolutely mixing up the glue and sawdust filler for the wainscoting, Clea put her mind and hands to work.

She did quite well keeping her hands busy. Her mind had a mind of its own.

The visit from Mrs. Carruthers who, in the absence of her husband, could generally be counted on to contradict what he'd just requested, didn't even cause enough problems to distract Clea today.

In fact, Mrs. Carruthers had taken a fifteen-minute tour of the house and had barely noticed the mantel that Clea had slaved over for days. Nor did she deign to comment on the ceiling moldings that Clea had already restored and the work on the buffet that Devin had done. She had simply pronounced it "coming along nicely," and had vanished to keep an appointment with her hairdresser. A little enthusiasm wouldn't have been amiss, Clea thought glumly as she watched Mrs. Carruthers's ample back disappear down the steps.

Then she returned, for yet another day, to filling in the splits and cracks in the dining room wainscoting and thinking about Austin and the shambles her life had become.

She wished for Rosie's chatty presence, but with Clea's earlier blessing, Rosie had gone to Sausalito to discuss doing some stained-glass windows for a new restaurant there, and she was coming in late, if at all. Devin had finished the buffet and was working at home again, restoring an eighteenth-century Dutch highboy for a museum. So Clea was alone.

Unrelieved solitude didn't help her frame of mind.

When the doorbell rang at three-thirty, she was delighted for a chance of a moment's respite. She knew it wasn't Rosie, who would never bother to ring. But even if it was only the UPS man with the light fixture she'd ordered or the Avon Lady, she would still appreciate the sight of another human face.

Austin was standing on the porch. Her Subaru—with four good tires now—was parked in front. Wordlessly he handed her the keys.

Clea gaped. "You didn't have to," she managed finally. "But . . . thanks." The last was grudging, and she knew it.

He obviously did, too. But his "You're welcome" was still polite. He paused, then said almost diffidently, "The outside looks great. Did you work on it?"

"Not much. It wasn't in too bad a shape. But the inside..." she grimaced.

"Can I see the rest?" He looked like a hopeful puppy.

She could hardly turn him away when he'd fixed her flat tire and brought her truck clear across town, could she? Even if he had probably sabotaged it in the first place. "I guess."

If the truth were known, she'd enjoy getting the opinion of someone who knew what he was looking at for once. Rosie's opinions were already indelibly engraved on her brain. And Devin rarely offered any, content simply to do his work and watch Rosie. The Carrutherses themselves were a wealthy but hardly appreciative audience, and while Ken liked the finished products, he had no appreciation at all for what had gone into getting them there.

Austin, on the other hand, whatever his faults, made his living with building and design of one sort or another. He knew about moldings and columns, he worked with sawdust and glue, finishing nails and stripper. He was also unfailingly enthusiastic if he liked something. She could use a bit of that right now.

"Feel free to wander around," she said, leading him into the entry hall and waving her hand toward the front parlor. "Things aren't too bad through there. Both the parlors are pretty well on their way. But the upstairs is still chaos. I'm working in the dining room now."

Austin was already running his fingers down the newly sanded woodwork that arched over the entrance to the parlor, a smile of appreciation lighting his face.

Clea resisted the impulse to follow him around, making her way instead back to the dining room where she tried to concentrate on working the filler into the narrow splits in the wainscoting. But her senses seemed to be following Austin all over the house.

She heard him as he moved through the double parlor living area. She could tell when he stopped to examine the fireplace. The mantel, which she had salvaged from a house being torn down in North Beach, was her pride and joy. Devin had repaired a terrible crack in it, but she had done the rest. She wondered if Austin would notice the way it had been refinished with loving care.

He usually had noticed things like that. She remembered once when they had gone to a flea market in Berkeley during their marriage and she had found a decrepit old dresser painted a gaudy orange. It had been the lines that had attracted her. They reminded her of a dresser her father had refinished once, and she had paid three dollars for it. Austin had groaned when she'd brought it home. But he had been the first to acclaim her talent when it turned out even more lovely than the one her father'd done.

He didn't reappear for more than an hour. After he'd examined the double parlors, she heard him in the kitchen and the breakfast room, then followed the sound of his footsteps down the cellar stairs. No one, not even the Carrutherses, had shown any interest in the basement, but Austin prowled around down there for nearly half an hour before she heard him come back up. Moments later, his footsteps echoed on the back stairs and finally right over her head.

Clea slapped some of her glue and sawdust mixture into the next split in the wainscoting and tried to forget him.

It was almost five when Austin came pounding down the back stairs and appeared in the dining room, a grin on his face. "It's marvelous, Sunshine. You've done a great job."

She smiled, unable not to, defenseless for once. "It wasn't only me. Rosie and Devin did a lot. But . . . thanks."

"Who did the mantel?"

So he had noticed. "I found it. Devin Flynn, a woodworker I know, repaired the horizontal crack. I did the rest."

"You did a fantastic job." He flopped down on the drop sheet beside her. "You mean it wasn't in the house originally?"

She shook her head. "No. Someone had modernized and had got rid of the original. The fireplace was boarded and papered over."

Austin grimaced.

"It was pretty bad," she admitted.

"Well, it's damned good now. Of course, you have a lot to work with. Good structure, lots of potential. But it takes expertise, and you've got it. They're lucky they've got you."

Clea laughed, making a face. "Tell them that," she said. "I don't think they even notice most days. Sometimes I think they'd prefer to simply slap up some fiberboard, flocked wallpaper, and say the hell with it."

"But they won't."

"No, they won't. Because I was recommended to them by Mr. Carruthers's boss whose house I did. And Mr. Carruthers doesn't want to offend him. But sometimes I think that's the only reason."

"Nonsense." Austin shook his shaggy blond head. "Even a nincompoop can appreciate quality. And they got quality when they hired you. You've come a long way, Clea," he said, a serious look complementing the smile that softened his sharp features.

"Not as far as you," Clea said honestly.

"Moneywise, you mean?" Austin shrugged negligently. "It's not everything, believe me. The designing, the constructing, making something out of bits and pieces was the best." His eyes lit with enthusiasm. "The hot tubs and patio furniture and all that—" he shrugged "—it's been a challenge, sure. But it never really touched the heart of me."

"Why didn't you stay with the architecture then?" Clea asked him, interested in spite of herself.

"My dad."

She made a face. "Old Crafty Eddie? What does he have to do with it?"

"He keeps buying me out."

"He should have taken you in with him," she said. "Years ago."

"Yes, well, you couldn't tell him that." Austin pulled his knees up and wrapped his arms around them. She saw again the cynical twist to his smile that she remembered so well every time the subject of his father came up. "So I just kept moving on. And he keeps buying me out. He could still get his hands on one or two things I've hung on to, I guess. But—" a smile lit his face "—he can't buy me out from here on out. Not where it matters."

"Why not?"

"Because in order to be bought out, I'd have to have a commodity I could sell. And now I don't."

Clea turned her head and gave him an assessing look. He was grinning, tossing out bait.

She bit. "What are you doing now, Austin?"

He rested his chin on one knee and gave her a look of supreme satisfaction, smug pleasure grooving his lean cheeks. "I am building sand castles."

Clea's putty knife fell to the floor with a clank. She turned and stared at Austin. "Sand castles?"

He unwound his arms and stretched his legs out in front of him, resting his weight back on his forearms, nodding happily. "It's big business these days."

"Austin." She knew better than to trust that look of his.

"I'm not kidding. It's perfect, Clea, really. Listen. It combines my architecture, elements of construction, a bit of fantasy, and puts it all together." His face was suddenly animated with the enthusiasm she remembered so well. "And then, swoosh—" one hand swept out "—the tide comes in or the convention is over, and it's gone. Neat, huh?" He was grinning again.

Clea shook her head, wonderingly. "You're really serious, aren't you?"

"Yeah, I am. I've been doing it for almost a year now. I got out of the redwood furniture and decking business courtesy of Crafty Eddie long about last July. I've got my finger in a fine furniture company, but it's basically being run by someone else, and I don't want to interfere.

"Anyway, while I was casting around looking for something to do next, I stayed with Miles for a while. He got married, you know," he added as an afterthought.

"Miles?" Clea squeaked. "The ever so reverend Miles?" Austin's brother had been in the seminary the last she knew.

Austin picked up the putty knife and scooped up a bit of Clea's filler, beginning to work it into one of the cracks. "Not so very reverend after all, as it turns out," he told her. "First he got kicked out of the seminary for painting nudes. Then he became a bartender. Then he married the most beautiful woman in southern California and became a terrifically successful portrait artist. And now he's made me an uncle and a godfather, too."

"Miles?"

Austin grinned. "Miles. The baby is called Patrick, by the way. My middle name. He looks remarkably like me, too. Handsome little devil." The smug look appeared again, as if he were somehow responsible for his nephew's features.

Clea laughed.

Austin frowned at her. "Anyway," he went on, "while Miles and Susan were on their honeymoon, I stayed at his place on the beach down in Manhattan. And I didn't have anything else to do, so I started messing around with sand."

He shrugged happily. "Turns out you can make money that way, too. And be creative. And use your talents. And nobody can buy you out at all."

"I don't believe it."

He stuck out his chin and grinned at her. "Believe, oh doubting woman. It's the gospel truth."

Clea shook her head, still amazed. Then quite spontaneously she reached out and tweaked the end of his nose as she had done so many times in their childhood. "Trust you to land on your feet."

Austin captured her hand, holding it in his, his fingers playing over hers, tracing them lightly. "I'm trying to."

What Clea saw in his eyes made her tremble. Unconsciously, instinctively she leaned toward him.

And then rationality hit her between the eyes. She couldn't get involved with him again. He was a sand castle man. Fleeting, insubstantial, here one day, gone with the tide. They summed up his work, they summed up the man.

They were right for him. Perfect, in fact. And she was happy for him. Happy that he had found something that would give him the satisfaction he deserved. Happy, but that was all.

She pulled her hand away, slowly, deliberately, and took the putty knife out of his other hand. "I'd better get back to work," she said, and she was already facing the wainscoting as she spoke.

He reached out again, tentatively almost, his fingers tangling in a lock of hair beside her ear. "Clea?"

"What?" She kept right on shoving glop in the crack.

"We had something once...together...didn't we?"

She licked her lips, then drew a long unsteady breath. "Yes, Austin, we did. Once."

"Why won't you give us another chance?" His knuckle was grazing her cheekbone in soft persuasion. "What can it hurt?"

She turned her head and met his eyes, serious now, not a spark of laughter in them. "Me, Austin," she said softly. "It can hurt me."

He blinked, then shook his head uncomprehendingly. "Would I ever hurt you, Clea?"

But how could she answer that? He would hurt her this time the same way he had last time, whether he meant to or not.

Chapter Four

But even with the wisdom of past experience, it wasn't easy to turn one's back on Austin—especially not an Austin determined to be noticed, and especially not for Clea who had loved him most all her life.

He didn't seem to be going away. On the contrary, judging from the way Mrs. Gianetti talked when Clea saw her at the laundromat last night, he was digging in for the long haul. And that made Clea decidedly nervous.

She went to the house on Haight St. even earlier than usual, hoping that it would give her the sanctuary she sought. But it wasn't easy to lose herself in it anymore. Since Austin had gone through it, she could no longer escape him there.

She finished filling in the splits in the dining room that afternoon. But while she did so, her eyes kept drifting to where she'd been sitting when he'd come and sat down beside her. More than once she found her fingers running lightly over the cracks Austin had filled.

When she took a midmorning break and went into the front parlor to sit and have a cup of tea with Rosie, it was Austin's smile as he ran his fingers over the mantelpiece that she saw in her mind and not Rosie's cheerful grin.

At lunch while she was heating a can of soup on the hot plate in the kitchen, her eyes drifted to the dumbwaiter that went up into the master bedroom, and she almost found herself telling Rosie that Austin had poked his head in it and called in a sepulchral voice, "Hello, up there!"

Then he had pulled his head back out and grinned at her. "Wouldn't that have been a great thing to have had when we were kids. We could've scared the daylights out of Crafty Eddie."

"Crafty Eddie would've blistered your bottom," Clea had replied, laughing.

Austin had shrugged. "He usually did. It was worth it."

Clea smiled now, remembering. Then she forced her mind back to the conversation at hand—a Rosie polemic about Cow Hollow zoning ordinances. But wherever her mind went, the memories followed, haunting her whatever she did.

She was still there past six, continuing long after Rosie had gone to pick Nicky up from school. Sometimes she quit then, too, and ran the errands she didn't take time for earlier in the day. But today she didn't want to.

And there was no point in going home earlier, she told herself. Ken worked late on Fridays, and Thurber was singularly poor company. He never kept up his end of the conversation. So she kept right on working, and didn't stop until she heard the front door open and footsteps in the entry hall.

"Rosie?" she called.

But the tread was heavier, male.

"Mr. Carruthers?" He'd been in Chicago all week. He must've got back and decided to drop in and see how things were going. Good, she thought, glad now that she'd stayed and that she'd worked like a demon all week, even if it was just to avoid her own problems.

"I thought I'd find you here."

She spun around. Austin stood leaning against the doorway into the dining room, his hands tucked into his pockets, a gentle smile on his face, real now and not the daydream she'd been encountering at every turn for days.

"You work too damned hard, d'you know that?"

Off balanced, Clea wiped a dirty hand through her straggling hair. "I . . . have a lot to do."

He looked around the room appraisingly. To an untrained eye, it wouldn't look as if she'd done much. But Austin saw all the filling, all the sanding, all the stripping of wallpaper that had gone on just since yesterday. "And you've done it," he pronounced. "Time to quit now."

"I . . ."

"Come on, Clea. They aren't planning to move in over the weekend surely."

"Of course not."

"Well, then . . ."

"I . . . I can't. I've . . ." She cast around for something she needed to do. Austin wouldn't buy that sizing the walls was immediately imperative. He knew restoration better than that. "I've got to hang that door," she said, indicating the one she and Rosie had horsed up from the cellar earlier in the day.

"Fine, I'll help you," he said automatically.

"Austin, you don't—"

"Clea," he said patiently in the same tone of voice, "I know I don't. But I'm going to. So if you've got to hang the door, get your butt over here and help me do it."

Biting her tongue, she did. She ought to be glad, she told herself. It was made of solid oak cross pieces and thin, albeit solid, oak panels, and it was so heavy, it had very nearly killed them just dragging it up the steps.

"*We're* not hanging it," Rosie had declared when they finally got it into the kitchen.

"I'll ask Devin to help when he comes to fix the cabinet upstairs."

Rosie'd looked down her nose. "Might as well have him be good for something."

Clea had let that pass. She thought Devin was good for quite a lot. She knew that recently he had taken Rosie's son to a Little League game when Rosie had another commitment, and she was tempted to remind her friend. But she didn't.

In any case, now she wouldn't have to wait until Devin came. "Fair enough," she said to Austin. "Heave ho."

Austin heaved, anticipating Clea's every move, lifting the door and swinging it at just the precise moment to allow her to slide the bolts home. Once it was hung and he was leaning against the doorjamb rubbing his back, he demanded, "How the hell were you going to hang that by yourself?"

"Well, actually..." she said guiltily.

"You weren't going to hang it at all."

"Er, I..." She spread her hands, palms up, hoping honesty would disarm him. "No, I wasn't. I thought you'd leave."

"I didn't." Glinting blue eyes challenged her. "And since I was such a big help, I figure you owe me."

"Owe you?" Clea took a step backward. "Owe you what?"

"Dinner."

"But—"

"And you don't even have to cook," he told her as he took her by the shoulders, spun her around and headed her toward the kitchen where he turned on the water tap, stuck her hands under it and said, "Wash."

Her hands were dirty. That was positively the only reason that Clea washed them. Austin held out a towel. They were wet, so she took it from him and dried them. "Austin, I—"

"Don't argue. You have to eat. And you're going to eat with me. Did you bring a jacket? You left at the crack of dawn this morning, you should have."

"No, I— How did you know when I left?"

"I heard your truck," he said. "Woke me up. What the hell were you trying to do?"

"Avoid you," she said as he steered her out of the house, flicking off the lights on the way.

"Figures," he muttered. "Didn't work." He took the key out of her hands and locked the door. "Come on," he said, "we're taking my car."

"Austin, I—"

"We're taking my car," he said implacably. "I'll drive you over tomorrow morning for yours or we can get it later tonight." There was a stubborn set to his jaw that Clea had no trouble in recognizing.

"We'll eat," Clea conceded as he hustled her out to his car. "But then you'll bring me back. I've got work on my own place I want to do tonight."

"Of course," he said all amiability now, and Clea knew she'd just been bulldozed by a smile.

IT WORKED OUT BETTER than he'd dared hope. Taking Clea by surprise seemed to be the only way to get under her guard. Coming right out and asking her to have dinner with him would have got him exactly nowhere, and he knew it. It was good something worked.

She had defenses five miles wide and three miles thick. She'd acted yesterday like he'd spent his life stomping her feelings into the dirt. Hurt her? He'd hurt her the last time? How? By giving her the divorce they'd agreed at the outset was necessary? No. He couldn't see it. It didn't make sense.

Clea had wanted the divorce as much as he had. She'd had plans of her own, goals of her own to accomplish. She couldn't have wanted to stay married to him, could she?

Could she?

The question had kept him awake most of the night.

In the morning the answer was no more obvious. The only obvious thing was waking up at the crack of dawn to hear the Subaru pickup grinding its way noisily up the street.

He had scrambled out of bed, thrown on his clothes and raced out the door after her. Then he'd jumped in his car and followed her.

The relief he felt when he saw her truck turn onto the street in front of the Carrutherses' house was palpable. It was only then that he admitted to himself what he had really been afraid of—that she wasn't simply avoiding him but actually had had an early-morning assignation with Ken.

That she hadn't had made him thankful enough to pull over to the curb and rest his head on the steering wheel, breathing great gusting sighs of relief. Then, still almost giddy, he'd turned the car around and headed home.

He spent the rest of the day on the phone with Baxter getting things set up for the sand castle he had to build for the competition. He should have gone down to Ventura this week to make the arrangements instead of getting Baxter to do it over the phone. And he should have gone to Seal Beach and practiced again the sculpture he was going to enter. Leaving things to chance like this wasn't his style, but he didn't want to leave Clea either.

He had no choice.

Baxter, not for the first time, had thought he'd lost his mind. The young man's usually unflappable demeanor had sounded in danger of cracking when Austin opened the conversation with the command, "Don't refile."

"What do you mean, don't refile?"

"Just what I said. Don't file for the divorce."

"But— Haven't you found her yet? Talked to her? Explained?" Baxter had neither seen nor heard from Austin since they'd gone their separate ways in Logan International a week ago.

"Yes, Baxter," Austin said patiently. "That's exactly what I have done. I've found her. I've talked to her. And I've explained to her—that I don't want the divorce."

"Don't want it?" Baxter practically yelped. "But you haven't seen this woman in years! You don't know her. You—"

"You want to work for her, Baxter?"

There was total silence on the other end of the line. Then, "Pardon me, sir?"

"I said, you sound just like Clea. Maybe you'd rather work for her."

"N-no, sir."

"Good," Austin said. "Then don't file for the divorce."

"Yes, sir." There was a pause during which Austin could hear Baxter mentally shifting gears. "Now then," he said, clearing his throat, "when will you be back in L.A.? There are some papers for you to sign. And your father seems to have found Houston's furniture."

"Oh, hell." Dennis Houston's on-the-edge-of-bankruptcy fine furniture business was the last thing Austin still had a share in, trying to pull it out of the red. He was doing it, too. His own way. Dennis would get out his father's way, too, of course. There was no doubt about that. But he'd end up by being swallowed by Cavanaugh Corporation at the same time. "Have Dennis lie low. And send the papers to me here."

"In San Francisco?"

"Of course in San Francisco."

"Er, all right, sir. Will you be staying at the Mark Hopkins as usual?"

"No, I'm staying with a Mrs. Gianetti." He gave Baxter the street and house number.

"I beg your pardon, sir?"

"Gianetti," Austin repeated.

"Not a hotel, sir?"

"Not a hotel, Baxter." Not even close.

"Er...very well, sir."

"And, Bax, would you do me a favor?"

"Certainly, sir."

"Would you call Lacey's in Ventura and see about getting me a boat for the sand castle competition?"

"Me, sir?"

"You." Austin outlined his needs specifically and carefully, leaving nothing to chance. And Baxter wrote it all down. In detail.

"Is that everything?" he asked twenty minutes later.

"Everything you can get for me," Austin told him. "Thanks."

He wished he could get Clea to come along with him.

It was exactly what they needed, he thought. A chance to be alone together without anyone else around to cloud the issue. Right now the only way he seemed to be assured of that was to pop in at the Carrutherses' place after her assistant had gone home.

It wasn't much, but it was all he had, and he wasn't giving up on it. Not even for first prize and two weeks in Hawaii.

Twice during the day he drove back over to Haight St. just to check and make sure Clea was still there. He didn't know what he'd have done if she weren't. But his peace of mind told him that he had to be sure.

The last time he went it was close to four o'clock. The rust-pocked old Ford that had been parked behind hers and which he figured must belong to this Rosie he'd never met had left. He thought he might run into Clea just leaving, too, but her truck was still there when he arrived, and as long as he sat, it stayed there.

Finally just past six-thirty he could stand it no longer. His stomach was growling. His patience was shot. He needed to see Clea, to talk to her, to touch her again. He couldn't hold out another minute.

So he'd barged in, not even knocking this time, and taken her by surprise, thank God. She'd looked exhausted, and he'd wanted to go to her and take her in his arms, but common sense told him he shouldn't. But lounging nonchalantly against the doorjamb and just looking at her was almost the hardest thing he'd ever done. Next to hanging that damned door.

Still, having hung it, he'd achieved his immediate aim. He'd got some time with her.

HE TOOK HER to a little seafood restaurant on Geary. She ordered shrimp and he ordered calamari.

Clea wrinkled her nose.

"It's good," he told her, laughing.

"Maybe," Clea allowed. They'd had this argument before. "But it still looks like rubber washers fried in batter."

"How come you always ate mine when I wasn't looking then?"

"Me?" She tried to look affronted and failed miserably.

"You. Or someone who looked remarkably like you. Someone with thick brown hair and big brown eyes. Someone with a gorgeous smile, a kiss of freckles, a cute nose—" his catalog of her features was making her squirm "—and no boobs to speak of."

"Austin!"

He laughed, eyes dancing as he shrugged his shoulders. "Not my fault nature neglected you."

"Nor mine that you didn't get any manners," Clea retorted.

"It is," he insisted stoutly. "You should've raised me better."

"I didn't raise you."

"You damned near did. You and your parents." He looked suddenly serious. The waitress brought their dinners, and he waited until she left again to ask, "How are they, by the way?"

Clea speared a shrimp. "My parents? They're fine."

Austin smiled wistfully. "Your father got any hair left?"

"Some. I don't think he lost any more after you left." She had meant her words to sound flip and funny, but instead found the memory they provoked wrenching.

His grin changed, becoming rueful. "I wouldn't be surprised. I'd ... like to see them again sometime."

Clea felt like a heel. *Go ahead,* she should say. *They'd love to see you, too,* she should say. But she couldn't.

She chewed her shrimp slowly. And Austin, seeing that he wasn't going to get the response he wanted, changed the subject to the work she was doing on the Carrutherses' house.

They talked about that for the rest of the meal, and Clea felt herself relaxing gradually, opening up even under his skillful, interested questioning. He got her to expound on her plans for it, offered his own suggestions, then, over a piece of cherry cheesecake, asked her, "What about your own?"

"Mine?" No one ever asked her about her own place. No one cared. But Austin seemed to.

"Tell me," he urged.

She must have gone on for hours. The waitress brought them countless cups of coffee, Austin ate another piece of cheesecake, Clea drew diagrams on napkins and Austin, taking the pencil away from her, showed her how to do it better. It was past nine and the waitress was muttering things about closing time, when Clea finally looked up.

"I think she wants to get rid of us," Austin said.

"I don't blame her." Clea waited while he paid the bill, then went out the door he held open for her. "Thank you," she said quietly when he joined her on the curb. "I enjoyed that."

"I did, too," he said sincerely. "The company as well as the food."

"The company was far less than scintillating," Clea protested.

"The company," he insisted, "was just right."

The eye contact they hadn't made all evening they made now. "Well, the company has to go," Clea said, feeling suddenly awkward. "Could you please drive me back and let me get my truck?"

"I could take you home. We're halfway there."

"We're not. We're far closer to the Carrutherses and you know it. No. Please, Austin. Take me back."

He grimaced. "If you insist."

"I do."

He took her back. He walked her to her truck. He held the door for her and shut it carefully when she climbed in. He bade her a tender good night.

Then he followed her all the way home.

CLEA HAD BEEN UP SINCE SEVEN. Actually she'd hardly been to bed. Or at least she'd hardly been to sleep. She'd lain awake for hours replaying the evening in her mind. Nothing had happened, really, she told herself. Nothing at all. She'd had dinner with her ex or almost-ex-husband, and for once they hadn't been at each other's throats. So what? It didn't mean a thing.

Except that the ground was eroding beneath her feet.

She needed some stability, something—*someone*—solid to hang on to. Thank God Ken was coming.

When the knock came at eight-thirty, Clea practically flew to answer it. Today was the day they were going to visit her parents, and since it had been his idea, he surely would be prompt.

But it wasn't Ken.

Austin was standing on her porch, looking for all the world like an overgrown eight-year-old in his old blue jeans, ratty sneakers and a white T-shirt with a surfer on it. He gave her one of his melting grins. "Can you come out to play?"

It was so like the Austin she had grown up with, that Clea simply stood there, shaking her head, a reluctant smile on her face.

He cocked his head at her lack of reply. The grin became a leer. "Well, if you can't, can I come in and play, then?"

"Austin..." Talk about dangerous ideas.

"Come on, Sunshine," he coaxed.

She shook her head, gathering her willpower. "I can't."

He frowned. "Why not?"

"I'm going out with Ken."

"Where?"

"Well, I..." she floundered, not wanting to tell him that she was taking Ken to her parents' house, especially after their conversation last night. She knew it would hurt him. And she might not be married to him anymore—except in name—but she didn't want to cause him pain either. She scowled, unsure how to phrase it. Finally she simply said ungraciously. "It's none of your business."

Austin scowled back at her, unmoving. She waited for him to get mad at her ungracious behavior and stomp off. He had every right to.

Instead he just stood there, looking at her.

Damn. Clea shut her eyes.

"I'll see you later, Clea," he said quietly. And she heard him turn and walk softly back down the stairs.

KEN ARRIVED at nine-thirty, looking bright-eyed and handsome. His fair hair, still damp from the shower, was neatly combed, and he was wearing a pair of gray twill slacks and an awning-striped sport shirt, very much the fashionable young up-and-coming executive.

"Will I do?" he asked her. "I didn't quite know what to wear to impress your parents."

"You're very impressive," Clea assured him with a smile. "Can we take my truck? I want to pick up a wallpaper steamer on the way home."

Ken looked momentarily doubtful, then shrugged. "Why not?" He held the door of the cab for her just as Austin had done the night before. Then he went around and got in beside her, leaning across and kissing her cheek. Clea started.

"What's wrong?" Ken asked her.

She shook her head. "Nothing. I—you just surprised me."

"You must be nervous. Maybe it's because we're going to see your folks."

"Maybe." But Clea really thought that if hair could have split ends, so could nerves, and that was what had happened to hers. From the moment Ken had arrived, she had sensed Austin watching them. She didn't know where he was, she only knew that he was. It made her feel oddly guilty. And the feeling disconcerted her more than she wanted to admit.

It shouldn't be that way, she told herself. She should be looking forward to the day, to introducing her parents to her fiancé. Her parents were casual people who liked most everyone, and Ken was a genial man. They would get on well together, liking each other fine, Clea was sure of it.

But it was the marrying part that she was worried about, because Ken wouldn't be the Austin they adored, no matter what.

"You look apprehensive," Ken said to her during the brunch they stopped downtown to share before they drove across the bay to her parents' house. "Does my meeting them worry you?"

"No," Clea said. "It's not that."

"What is it, then?" Ken's kind face looked concerned.

"I'm just . . . just thinking about a problem at the Carrutherses' place," she mumbled, biting into a blueberry muffin. It wasn't a lie really. The problem had come up because of Austin's arrival there. If he hadn't, if she hadn't eaten with him last night, shared her restoration plans with him, let him share his enthusiasm with her—in other words, let him get a toehold in her life—she wouldn't be so anxious today.

Ken reached across the table and squeezed her hand. "I'll be on my best behavior," he assured her.

Clea gave him a wan smile. "You always are."

She hoped her parents would be, too.

They were. In fact, they were quite welcoming.

"How nice that you brought one of your friends over to meet us," her mother said as she brought Ken a glass of iced tea out on their patio where he sat discussing the stock market with her dad.

"He's . . . uh, more than just a friend, Mom," Clea said. She carried the sugar bowl and a plate with slices of lemon and followed her mother out onto the porch.

Mary Bannister stopped halfway between the screen door and the umbrella table where Ken and her husband were sitting. "Oh?"

Clea licked her lips. "He's . . . we're . . . getting married."

Her mother's eyes widened. "Married?"

Clea smiled encouragingly. "Yes."

Mrs. Bannister didn't seem to be able to move for a moment. Then she turned her head and considered the lean fair-haired man who was sitting in the webbed deck chair, laughing at something her husband said. "He . . . seems . . . nice," she ventured at last.

"He *is* nice, Mom." Clea would have given her a hug if the tray of iced tea hadn't prevented it.

Mrs. Bannister looked at her daughter, a tiny worried frown on her forehead. "Don't you think he . . . looks . . . a lot like Austin, darling?"

Clea blinked. Her head whipped around. "Austin?"

"Yes," her mother said more firmly now. "The same blond hair, lean build. The same . . ." She stopped. "Are you sure you aren't just trying to replace—"

"No, Mother, I'm not." Clea's jaw came together with a snap. "He's not a thing like Austin. I don't know how you can say that. It's precisely because he's so different from Austin that I'd marry him!"

Her mother looked taken aback at her vehemence. "Well, I only thought . . . of course, you're right, dear." But she gave Clea an appraising look over her shoulder as she went back to the kitchen for the plate of breads and cookies.

Clea stood watching her, stung by her mother's obvious supposition about her impending marriage. Did Ken really resemble Austin?

Of course they were both blond, slender men with thick straight hair. They were both pleasant, with ready smiles and senses of humor. But that was the extent of the similarity.

In fundamentals they weren't a thing alike.

Mrs. Bannister settled herself into one of the redwood chairs. "Clea told me your news."

Ken looked over at her questioningly. "You did?" He seemed almost surprised.

"Shouldn't I have?" Clea was surprised now. He was the one who'd been pressing to meet them.

"Well, I thought you might not want to . . . that business with your ex . . . er, your husband, you know."

Both Clea's parents stopped mid-movement and looked at their daughter inquiringly.

Clea gave a hollow little laugh. "It's not a big deal," she told them quickly. "Just a bureaucratic hassle really."

"What is it?" her father asked, his warm brown eyes concerned.

"Nothing much. It seems that the lawyer Austin hired all those years ago, the one who did the divorce papers, well—" she laughed again "—he didn't file the final ones."

Mrs. Bannister frowned. "Didn't file them?"

"No, apparently not." Clea gave an awkward shrug. "Stupid of him. But we can get it sorted out," she added quickly.

"But what does it mean in the meantime?" her father wanted to know.

Clea made a face. "It means…it means that…legally…we're still married, I suppose. Which is the stupidest thing I ever heard," she added with a snap, shaking her head, her brown hair flying in her face.

"Still married to Austin?" Her mother sounded as if she'd won the lottery.

Clea gritted her teeth. "It's a technicality, Mom."

"I know, dear, but—"

"Mom, I just told you, I'm marrying Ken."

Mrs. Bannister looked momentarily abashed and slightly sheepish. She gave Ken an apologetic nod. "Of course you did, dear. I'm sorry," she said to Ken. "It's just that Austin was very dear to us, too, you know. I worked for his parents. I knew him as a boy. He was—"

"Mom," Clea began in strangled tones, "Ken doesn't care about Austin."

Her mother's face was wreathed with chagrin. "Oh, of course not. I'm sorry. Some more iced tea, dear? How about a piece of banana bread?"

"No, thank you, Mrs. Bannister," Ken said, smiling gently. "I understand your concern. Really, I do."

Mrs. Bannister beamed at him. "I thought you would. You seem to be a very nice young man. I told Clea what a nice man you were," she added. "It's just that..." Her hands fluttered ineffectually.

Don't say it, Mom.

"Oh, dear. I hope you'll both be very happy," she finished lamely.

"Damned with faint congratulations," Clea muttered.

Her mother blinked. "What, dear?"

"Nothing." Clea cracked an ice cube between her teeth.

Ken, bless him, had better manners than she did. He smoothed over her mother's awkwardness with a few well-chosen words, he ate a cookie, then he went out to her father's workshop and was properly appreciative of the rocking chair Mr. Bannister was building at the same time that he confessed to being all thumbs when it came to such things himself.

Clea heard her mother tsk-tsking in the background at the admission, but when Clea gave her a sharp look, she subsided without a word.

In fact things improved for the rest of the afternoon. Once the surprise of Clea's announcement had worn off, they went rather well actually, and Clea began to feel as if the worst of it was over.

Her parents had had a shock, she reminded herself. For years Austin had been the apple of their eye, the son-in-law of their dreams, and Clea hadn't helped things by never bringing home anyone to replace him.

But now that she had, they would adjust.

"I've had a wonderful time," Ken was saying to her father as they were leaving, walking down the flagstone path to the truck. "I'm so glad to have finally met you both."

"We've enjoyed it, too," Will Bannister told him, shaking the younger man's hand. "You come back again."

"I will," Ken promised.

"Of course he will," Clea chipped in. "You'll be seeing a lot of him in the coming years."

"Of course," her father said. But Clea didn't hear the heartiness she'd hoped for.

And her mother caught her hand just as she was getting into the truck. "He is a nice man," she admitted. "But will he make you happy, my dear?"

"I wouldn't be marrying him if he didn't," Clea said firmly. And then impulsively she gave her mother a hug. "It'll be fine, Mom, really. You should be asking if I'll make him happy, too."

Mary Bannister returned her daughter's hug, then held her out at arm's length, brushed a stray lock of hair off Clea's cheek and looked deeply into eyes as brown as her own. "I'm concerned about all three of you, dear."

There was no need to ask who the third person was.

Chapter Five

Austin was jealous. Jealousy ate at his guts, tormented his soul, haunted his heart. He stood looking out his bedroom window and watched Clea drive away with Ken and felt a pain so fierce, so fundamental, that Mrs. Gianetti, coming up the sidewalk with her shopping, hurried up the steps to his side.

"You are hurt?" she demanded, putting a chubby hand on his forehead, her dark eyes probing his face anxiously. "You look so pale. So white."

Austin shook his head. "I'm okay." He brushed her concern off gently, giving her the best smile he could manage. "I'm fine. Really."

Mrs. Gianetti clucked her disagreement. "No, no. I don't think so. You come in and sit down. I'll make some chicken soup for lunch."

"Chicken soup?" He hadn't had chicken soup in years. "The universal panacea?" he teased.

Mrs. Gianetti scowled at him, shaking her head and shooing him toward the front door. "You laugh. But you are wrong. Chicken soup is always good for what ails you. Didn't your mother ever teach you that?"

"Not my mother, no," Austin said.

His mother hadn't done much cooking. She'd been a vague, gentle, highly religious woman whom he remembered best reading or praying or playing the piano. That she could actually have willingly married his obnoxious, rough-hewn father, let alone have borne him three sons, had always been a source of amazement to Austin. She'd seemed too delicate for any of it. And he guessed she had been. He'd never had a lot of mothering from her, beyond hugs and kisses at bedtime anyway.

What chicken soup he'd got had come from Mary Bannister. Clea's mother had deluged him with it. He remembered having the chicken pox when he was eight. His own mother, who hadn't been well herself, wasn't allowed to take care of him. His father couldn't be bothered, so Clea's mother had. In fact she'd bundled him up and taken him home with her.

"No sense leaving him here to fret by himself," she'd said. "You don't mind, do you, Mr. Cavanaugh?"

Of course, Austin's father hadn't. He'd had little use for Austin even then. If the boy wasn't underfoot, so much the better. Then he wouldn't be a bother to either his mother or his father.

Austin wasn't a stupid child. He had figured all this out at a very early age, and it hurt. It made him angry. He knew he was merely tolerated at the best of times, but he'd never been outright ostracized before.

He didn't want to go. But there had been no arguing with his father. What Edward Cavanaugh said, everyone else did.

So Austin had gone home with Mrs. Bannister. It was the best thing that had ever happened to him.

He'd met Clea. He'd never spent time with any girls before that. His experience of them was sadly limited. He thought they were all fragile, frail wisps like his mother. Clea proved how wrong he was.

She was a year younger than Austin, but determined that the age difference shouldn't matter. She vowed to read everything he read, to do everything he did. She vowed to be as good as he was at gin rummy, at Monopoly, at playing cowboys and Indians, at anything else he set his mind to. An only child, Clea was as lonely as he was. He quickly became her hero—idolized, emulated, revered. And for a boy who had two teasing older brothers, a frail mother and a disparaging father, she was a gift from the gods indeed.

Austin, who hadn't wanted to come, at the end of a week and a half, didn't want to go home. Clea became his best friend—the only person who mattered in his life who didn't try to improve him, change him, or otherwise try to dictate what he should do. She let him be and loved him for who he was. He thought he did the same with her.

He supposed, he thought now as he leaned against the kitchen table and watched Mrs. Gianetti heat her soup, that he had always taken Clea for granted. He had basked in her approval for so long that he didn't ever expect things would change. And, indeed, for years they hadn't.

She had married him when he'd suggested it, just as he'd expected she would. And he'd never doubted that she would divorce him when the time came. She did whatever he wanted. It was the way she was.

And now?

Now she wasn't playing by the same rules anymore. Now she wouldn't even play the game. She had someone else. And Austin found that it hurt. A lot.

He ate Mrs. Gianetti's chicken soup. He tolerated her soft maternal cluckings and pats on the arm, but he shook his head when she told him he probably needed a nap.

"No," he said, carrying his bowl to the sink, washing it, drying it, and putting it away on the shelf. Going to bed was the last thing he needed. In bed there was nothing to distract his thoughts from Clea. "No. I've got some work to do." He gave her a smile. "Thanks for the soup, though. It was great."

The compliment mollified her. "I told you it'd help."

It hadn't, really. Work had always been the real panacea in his life. Whenever he had felt lost and unloved, he'd thrown himself into his work, letting it consume him. On the whole he was successful. He had money and a reputation as an innovative architect and clever entrepreneur to show for it. And usually it filled in the gaps.

But when he sat down at the worktable in his room, trying to get his mind on some of the papers Baxter had express mailed him, and thereby fill the hollowness that his jealousy had dug into his life, he couldn't do it.

His eyes kept lifting to stare out past the lace curtains that blew gently in the breeze that came in through the bay window. They kept being drawn inexorably to the house across the street. Clea's house.

A house like the one he'd often said he wanted, yet with all his money had never bought. Clea's house. With its inadequate plumbing, its substandard wiring, its million flaws and its fantastic potential. Clea's house.

He wished it were his. Wished she were his.

"She *is* mine," he said aloud, and his fingers clenched so tightly that he snapped the pencil in his hand.

"HIKE UP MOUNT DIABLO? In this heat? Have you lost your mind?"

No, just my cool, Clea thought. "All right. Forget Mount Diablo." She didn't want to hike there anyway, she just didn't want to go home. Her parents had invited them to stay for dinner, but she had declined. Accepting would have subjected both Ken and herself to three or four more hours of her parents' veiled worries and unexpressed doubts about their engagement and her divorce. Not a cheerful prospect.

But going home meant the possibility of running into Austin on her doorstep again. And in her present mental quandary, that wasn't much of a prospect either.

"We could get on the BART and ride from one end to the other," Ken teased.

Clea felt faint warmth in her face. "Well, I just thought it would be fun to do something else," she said. "I don't want to go home and face my half-stripped wallpaper and my leaky plumbing yet." That wasn't all she didn't want to go home and face, but she wasn't bringing Austin up unless she had to.

"Having second thoughts?"

"No. But there are days when I don't want to work on it. And this is one of them."

"We can always go to my place." Ken's eyebrows waggled hopefully.

"I don't think so." She knew what they would do—or what Ken would like them to do—if they went to his place. And she wasn't in the mood. In fact, her mood for that sort of thing seemed to have vanished the instant Austin had reappeared in her life.

It seemed like an unnecessary complication in a life that was becoming increasingly complicated enough.

Ken gave her a rueful smile. "Well, let's go for a walk then. How about Golden Gate Park?"

Clea smiled. "I'd like that. We can pick up my wallpaper steamer first. It's on the way."

"You sure you want to? What about your not even wanting to go home?"

"That's right now. I can't avoid it forever. By tomorrow I'm sure I'll be raring to go."

"I thought we were having brunch together at Ricco's."

"Well, of course. But brunch doesn't last the whole day. I'll wallpaper after." She would have added, "You can help me," but she knew that house renovation wasn't high on Ken's list of priorities. When he wasn't at work, he liked to relax by playing golf or swimming. He didn't find anything remotely relaxing about messing around a house.

But he did fetch the steamer with her, and then he drove them to Golden Gate Park, where they walked from the panhandle all the way to Stow Lake and back, stopping for tea and cookies at the Japanese Tea garden and then to watch the seals being fed in the Steinhart Aquarium.

It was lovely, leisurely, and nondemanding, and another day Clea would have enjoyed it thoroughly. Today, however, she was distracted. She had hoped that her parents would accept Ken, welcome him, put their seal of approval on their daughter's decision. They hadn't, and Clea knew it.

She also knew she could put off going home no longer. Ken's feet were dragging, he was consulting his watch. "It's half past seven, you know," he told her once, and then later, squinting at his watch in the near darkness, "Now it's nearly nine."

Finally, with great reluctance, Clea said, "I guess I'm ready to go."

Ken looped an arm around her shoulders and gave her a squeeze. "Think we've exorcised the wallpaper and plumbing demons now?"

"I think so." She gave him a wan smile in return.

He wasn't fooled, though. And when they were unloading the steamer and carrying it into the house, Ken said, "It isn't the wallpaper, really, is it? That's not what's bothering you."

She paused on the threshold. "No," she admitted. "Not really."

"Is it the business with your...your...with Austin?"

Clea ran a hand through her hair. "Yes." Her gaze flickered across the street where Austin might, at this very moment, be lurking.

"Can I help?" Ken's blue eyes were serious, concerned.

Clea shook her head. There was nothing he could do. Nothing anyone could do. Austin and their marriage were her problems. She would have to sort them out herself.

Ken bent his head and kissed her gently on the lips. "Don't worry. Everything will be fine."

Clea sighed. "I hope so."

"You told me yourself he was impetuous."

"Yes."

"Well, then..." He smiled crookedly at her. "Maybe he'll forget all about this in a day or two. You know, move on."

"Maybe," Clea said, trying for more assurance than she felt. She gave Ken a quick peck on the cheek. "I'll see you in the morning."

"Yes." He wrapped her in his arms and gave her more than just a peck. "Sleep well," he breathed in her ear.

Clea stared over his shoulders at the light in the upstairs bedroom across the street. "I'll try."

Ken might be right, she tried to tell herself as she watched him drive away. Maybe Austin would forget.

But the trouble was only half Austin forgetting or not forgetting.

More important was whether Clea would forget. And she was beginning to suspect now that she wouldn't. Ever.

IT WAS ALREADY HALF PAST NINE when Clea woke up out of sorts and grumpy. Stumbling into the shower, she shivered her way through another icy drenching. Then, teeth still chattering, she scurried back to her bedroom to dress.

Ken had said they would go to church and then have brunch at Ricco's. So Clea put on a blue shirtwaist dress with a woven red belt and a pair of red open-toed heels. She was just adding a red ribbon to hold back her fall of shoulder-length hair, when a knock came on the door.

"Hi," Austin said when she opened it. "I was going to church. Will you come with me?"

Clea stared. Austin standing there wasn't such a shock. She was almost getting used to that. But Austin going to church? That was a new one.

He'd been there at best half a dozen times during their brief marriage.

"I let Miles take care of that end of things," he'd once told her blithely.

She gave him a tiny smile now. "Has Miles stopped taking care of that end of things?"

He looked slightly sheepish. "Well, I . . ."

She shook her head. "I can't," she said with a gentleness that surprised even her. "I'm sorry. I'm...waiting for Ken."

Austin's jaw tightened, his lips pressed together. She saw his fists clench. But before he could reply, the phone rang.

"Excuse me." She started to shut the door, but his foot was firmly wedged against it. She gave it an experimental shove. It stuck fast.

Austin smiled innocently at her. "I'll wait."

Clea's gentler thoughts vanished. *So, wait. See what it gets you,* she thought and stomped off to answer the phone.

"Clea?" It was Ken.

"Hi, Ken," she said brightly, noting Austin's narrowing eyes.

"Bad news. Gleason just called. He wants me to make up a foursome at his Country Club and I don't dare say no."

Clea looked away from Austin's interested eavesdropping. "No, of course you don't."

"We don't tee off until eleven," Ken went on. "I don't know when I'll be done. There will probably be lunch after."

"If you're lucky." She knew that Gleason's recommendation would help Ken's future at the bank.

"I'd rather be with you."

"You have to be there, though. It's all right," she assured him. "I understand."

"You're sure? You could meet me..."

"No. I'll be fine. I can do that much more wallpapering."

"Ugh."

Clea laughed. "Really. See, we'll both be doing something important."

"It is, really." Ken sounded more cheerful. "Maybe they'll notice me. One of the men is from the Río branch."

"You want to go to Río?"

"A promotion's a promotion."

Clea laughed. "If you say so. Do well then, but don't beat them."

"No fear there," Ken laughed. "I'll call you later. I am sorry."

"Don't worry about it. Have fun." She blew him a kiss on the phone, and hung up.

Austin gave her a bright smile. "Do I take it you're free?"

"I'm working."

"But..."

"If Ken can't go out, I'll have that much more time to strip wallpaper."

"I'll help."

"No, thank you."

"What about church?"

"Well, I..."

"Or don't you go anymore?"

"Of course I go."

"But you won't go with me?" His lower lip jutted out. "How Christian is that?"

"I...oh, damn it, all right." Bulldozed again. "But once church is over, I'm working," she told him firmly.

Austin nodded his head. "Of course."

Clea gave him a suspicious look, wondering where the usual argument was.

But all Austin said was, "You'll want a sweater. It's still cool out."

They walked to church. It was only four blocks to the nearest one, and neither of them spoke on the way. Clea couldn't think of a thing to say, and Austin for once seemed content to keep the silence. When they entered, Clea walked up the left side of the nave and took her place in the pew where she always sat. When they were children and her mother had sent them to church together, Austin wouldn't sit with her. He did now.

Kneeling beside her, his head bowed, he distracted her completely. An unforgiving God would have despaired of her. She could think of nothing but the man beside her. The subtle hint of citrus after-shave on the morning breeze tantalized her. The readings might as well have been in Greek and the sermon in Latin. She muddled them far worse than the priest did.

For some reason all she could remember was that all her life she had wanted a church wedding. They hadn't had one.

It was perfectly understandable, of course. There was less compunction to stay married that way. Would they have stayed married had they wed in church? she wondered.

A ridiculous question. It was with no intention of staying married that they had wed in the first place. That hadn't been the purpose of the exercise. It was a marriage of expediency, not of love. Wasn't it?

Having Austin sit next to her, hearing his deep strong voice during the hymns, and feeling the rough calluses of his hand at the peace greeting filled her head with thoughts better left buried. He confused her. With Ken she felt secure, in command, certain of her fate. With Austin she felt caught in a maelstrom, buffeted about by emotions she failed to understand.

Church usually brought her peace, tranquility, a sense of purpose and well-being. Today it sent her back into the world more torn than ever. She practically ran the four blocks home.

"Are you sure I can't help you?" Austin asked when they reached her front steps.

"I'm positive."

He gave her a doubtful look, opened his mouth as if he would have said more.

Please, no, she thought. And the thought must have communicated itself to Austin, for he seemed to think better of the idea, merely shrugging as he said, "Suit yourself."

Then he turned and sauntered across the street to Mrs. Gianetti's.

Clea stared after him, amazed. No argument either before or after. No argument at all.

Perversely, within an hour Clea wished there had been.

After a cool morning, the day got progressively warmer and muggier, an oddity for San Francisco. It felt more like July in Chicago than July by the Bay. And the steamer she rented didn't help matters a bit. It was faster, of course, but far more taxing. The steam heat had her drenched in no time. Her shorts felt damp, her halter top clung like a wet bandana to her breasts. Sweat sluiced down the valley between them, it coursed down her cheeks, and made streaky, pasty lines down her neck whenever she swiped at the sweat with her hand.

Two people could have done everything four times as fast. As it was she had to steam, then scrape, steam, then scrape. If Austin had been there, one of them could've steamed while the other scraped.

But Austin wasn't there. He was, she discovered to her envy and chagrin when she glanced out the window, standing in the street wearing only a pair of cutoffs while he washed his car.

He looked cool and gorgeous, and Clea couldn't tear her eyes away. Instead she hovered behind the bedroom curtains, peeking out at him, drinking in the view of the flex and stretch of his muscular back, of his hair which was turning dark blond with sweat, and of the way his cutoffs rode low on his lean hips.

Money and success hadn't softened him, that was certain. He looked as if he spent as much time climbing around rooftops and swinging a hammer as he had ever done. But now it was lugging and shaping loads of sand, she supposed. Still, she didn't doubt that he did it all himself. The physical Austin Cavanaugh was still a sight to behold.

And not a healthy one for a woman whose heart was already doing overtime simply from stripping wallpaper. Damn it all, she had to stop this. Wiping a sweaty palm across her face, she ventured one last glance at the man crouched beside the fender of his car. He was no different from any other man, she told herself. It could as easily be Ken down there, cool and tempting—her reaction would be exactly the same. She closed her eyes and tried to form a mental image of Ken in Austin's place. She failed so miserably that she frightened herself into getting back to work.

It was three o'clock when she, not the steamer, ran out of steam. She simply couldn't scrape another inch, no matter how much she knew she ought to. Her arms ached, her back throbbed, her fingers seemed to stick together from the steamy glue. Sagging, she slumped against the windowsill, the spatula she'd been scraping with in one hand, the steamer nozzle dangling from the other. She felt as if she'd run a marathon through equatorial quicksand, and she still had half of one wall to go.

"My turn," Austin said, and Clea's head whipped around. He was standing in the doorway, still wearing nothing but the scandalous cutoffs, and looking cool and deliciously desirable. The quicksand seemed to swallow her right up.

Before she could say or do anything, he crossed the room, took the steamer nozzle and scraper out of her hands, turned up the jet on the steamer and set to work.

Numbly, wordlessly, Clea watched him. He was within touching distance now. A sheen of perspiration built up on his back, and she could watch the rivulets of sweat trickle down his spine and disappear into the waistband of his shorts. She could see the way the steamy pasty residue from the paper clung to his golden furred legs, could watch the tiny beat of the pulse in his neck. And there was no way she could pretend he was Ken at all.

She didn't move, just sat there against the windowsill mesmerized, until at last he finished and turned the jet down, looking over at her. "Go take a shower," he said. "Then we'll get something to eat."

She knew she ought to protest. He was taking over again, coming in and running things, bulldozing her. But what sort of protest could she make? Was she supposed to say she didn't want to?

God knew she needed a shower. She was grimy, sticky and smelly. Could she sit here and say she was fine just the way she was? She could try, of course. But she could see right off that Austin wasn't going to have any.

"Go on, Clea. We can argue later."

She gave him a narrow look. "Promise?" she asked after a moment.

He grinned and winked at her. "I wouldn't miss it for the world."

She went, showered and washed her hair, feeling one hundred percent more human when she'd finished. When she came out, clean and dressed in a pair of blue chambray slacks and a bright blue-and-white-striped tank top, she found that the steamer was shut off, the wall finished, the floor swept and the job done. Austin was nowhere around.

She called his name, went down the steps and peered in every room, but apparently he'd gone.

"Where'd he go, Thurber?" she asked, feeling oddly bereft.

If Thurber knew, he wasn't telling. But Clea didn't have to wonder long. In less than ten minutes Austin was back.

"Ah good, you're ready. I had to get cleaned up, too." Dressed now in a pair of jeans, a red polo shirt, and a pair of huaraches, he was rubbing his hands together briskly and smiling at her. "Ready to go?"

Clea demurred. "I really don't think..."

He gave her an exasperated look. "Clea, when you think we never do anything. Come on. You need a break. You can't tell me that if Ken were here asking you, you wouldn't come?"

"Well, I—"

"See?" He fixed her with a hard, narrow-eyed stare, then reached out a hand and grasped hers, hauling her toward the door.

"But—"

"Don't tell me you never go out and have a good time anymore." He was lacing his fingers through hers, drawing her inexorably onward, locking the door after them, and tugging her down the stairs.

"But if Ken calls—"

Austin gritted his teeth. "So what?"

"Well, I—"

"You're not married to him yet, Clea."

"No, but—"

Austin stopped dead right in the middle of the sidewalk and took hold of her arms, staring intently down into her face. "Do you really think he's going to call?"

"I...well...no, probably not," she answered finally, honestly. "He...probably got involved with the people he was playing golf with. It's not a crime, you know," she added with some asperity.

"Of course it isn't," Austin said with calm reasonableness. "And neither is your going out for a while, don't you see?"

Clea's mind wavered, her resolve swayed. Did she really want to sit home and wait for an unlikely phone call? Of course not.

Did she really want to go out with Austin? Yes, perversely enough, she did.

But should she? And to that question, she had no answer.

"A meal, a walk, a look in some shops. How's that sound?" Austin tempted her.

It sounded innocuous enough. And it wasn't as if he were going to jump her bones in the middle of Fisherman's Wharf, Clea reminded herself. Even Austin had more finesse than that. Clea took a deep breath.

"All right," she said. "Let's go."

It was a picture-book day. The wind whipped across the sunlit bay, dotting the water with whitecaps, clearing the air, outlining Alcatraz Island and the Marin County hills in sharp detail.

The weather, which had been too warm for steaming wallpaper, was perfect for meandering along The Embarcadero. It would cool off later, Clea knew, so she looped her blue sweater in a loose knot over her shoulders, and Austin lifted her flyaway hair out from beneath it, then brushed it away from her face. His touch was gentle, like the softest of summer breezes, and Clea threw away her caution and smiled at him. It was hard not to smile at Austin. He smiled back and took her hand.

They went first to Pier 39, wandering among the crowds of tourists and shoppers, poking through specialty shops vending Victoriana, chocolate of every description, pretzels, cookies, movie memorabilia.

"Don't you think I have more charisma than Cary Grant?" Austin asked as they poked through old black-and-white stills of thirties and forties movies.

Clea looked at him dubiously, though privately she suspected he probably did. "He wasn't blond," she said, smiling.

"Blonds have more fun," Austin claimed, tweaking her nose.

Clea didn't know about that. But they were having fun today. Austin was easy to be with, undemanding, witty, always ready to stop and look at something, always prepared with a suitable quip. He made her laugh, he made her sing. He made her ride the Pier 39 merry-go-round.

"Austin, I can't," she protested when he dragged her toward it. "It's for kids."

"Nonsense," he said. "Is there a sign somewhere? And anyway, what makes a kid?"

He bought two tickets and tugged her on. "I bet you don't even remember the last time you rode a merry-go-round, do you?" he prodded her, weaving through the rows of prancing horses until he found just the right one.

Clea shook her head. "It's been years."

"Disgusting. Here," Austin said, giving her a hand onto a striding white charger with a gaudily painted saddle. Then he leaped onto the black one next to her. The horses began to move, the music began to play, and Clea, forgetting her objections, began to smile.

"Told you so," Austin said and leaned across, as he went up and she went down, and stole a kiss.

"Hey!"

He grinned wickedly. "Better than a brass ring any day." And to prove his point, he did it again.

Clea took a playful swipe at him, then leaned away, the music singing inside her now, the wind and the movement of the carousel lifting her hair. It was almost disappointing when the tune came to an end and the merry-go-round slowed to a stop.

"How about another ride?"

Clea didn't even hesitate this time. "Yes."

"Wait here." Austin hopped down and bought two more tickets.

"Come on," Clea called as he wove his way back to her. "They're starting."

"Yep." He leaped up behind her just as the music started again.

"Austin!" The hard warmth of his body against hers was a shock.

"It's as close as I'm ever going to get to carrying off m'lady on a white charger," he said in her ear, then his arms slipped around her and held her fast against him. "Humor me."

Clea could do nothing else. She tried telling herself she didn't want him to, tried telling herself that he was being presumptuous, pushy, and that she found it offensive in the extreme. But even she didn't believe it.

The fact was, she liked him there and didn't know what to do about it.

When the carousel ended this time, the two of them remained motionless for a long moment. Then Austin slid off slowly and held his arms out for her to jump down into. He put them on her waist to help her, lifting his face so their gazes met. Hers was subdued, troubled, his hot with desire.

They'd never had any secrets from each other before. They had none now.

Austin sucked in a harsh breath. Clea shut her eyes for a split second's prayer for guidance. Then she slid down into his arms, and followed him on wobbly legs down off the carousel.

Neither of them spoke. Austin took her arm and walked her away through the crowds. People shouted, babies cried, horns honked, a helicopter buzzed overhead. But Clea only heard her own heart beating, only felt the warm grip of the man by her side.

The awareness between them built like a thunderstorm for the rest of the day. They left Pier 39 and walked toward Fisherman's Wharf; they bought shrimp and crab cocktails from sidewalk vendors, trading bites as they walked. They wandered through the Cannery, through Ghirardelli Square. They sat in the park at the foot of the Hyde St. cable car line and watched the sailboats on the bay. And every time their eyes met or their bodies brushed, lightning seemed to crackle in the air.

The sun began to go down out beyond the bridge, gilding the city with golden light. They got up and began to walk again, weaving in and out past clumps of gawking tourists, not a word passing between them, yet with every moment of silence awareness grew.

"D'you want to get something to eat?" Austin asked her finally.

Clea shook her head. "I'm not hungry."

"Me either," he said in a low, rough voice. "Not for food." His thumb rested against the tendon on her inner wrist, rubbing gently, sending shivers right up her arm.

"Remember Arnie's?" Austin asked suddenly.

Clea did. "Wasn't it . . . ?" she began.

He grinned. "About seven, eight blocks from here. Up on Russian Hill. Want to see if it's still there? We could have an Irish Coffee at least."

"Why not?" Arnie's was a local watering hole cum restaurant, frequented by students, artists, and sundry other low-income types. Whenever they had come over from Berkeley in their student days, one way or another they had ended up at Arnie's. It was nostalgia for college that made her agree to it, Clea told herself as they climbed the steep blocks one after another. It was curiosity and fond memories, nothing else.

Arnie's was still there, huddled into the side of the hill just a block off Hyde. It had had a new paint job, but that was about all. Still dark, crowded, resounding with tin whistle and banjo music, and redolent with garlic, onion rings and foreign beers, it made them turn to one another and smile.

Austin held the door for her as they went in. There was a table just being cleaned off near one of the tiny leaded glass windows, and he led her to it, then sat down across from her and said, "What'll you have?"

Clea smiled. "An Irish coffee, of course."

Austin ordered two, then sat quietly, smiling at her, holding her hand between his. Clea tried to pretend she didn't notice. She couldn't. All the nerves in her body were centered in that hand. She looked down at the graffiti-scarred table, and tried to think of something irrelevant to say.

"D'you suppose our names are still here?" Austin asked.

And then Clea remembered that once when service was nonexistent and they'd had time to kill, he had added their names to the hundreds carved in the soft pine planks. She looked down. It would have been too much of a coincidence to find their names, but it didn't stop her looking. Or remembering.

She remembered another, even earlier, time. They had been eight and nine years old, sitting in the treehouse that Austin's older brother, Edward, had built in the backyard. And Austin had carved their names there, too. AUSTIN + CLEA = TRUE LOVE, it had read.

"Do you remember the treehouse?" she asked him suddenly.

He grinned, tossing a lock of hair off his forehead. "Only one thing's changed," he said quite seriously.

"What?" Clea asked.

"Now I spell better."

They were still grinning at each other when the Irish coffees arrived and were set between them. Austin raised his and waited until Clea lifted hers to her lips. Then he met her eyes over the tops of the mugs. "To the future," he said.

By the time they had finished, the wind had shifted, bringing with it an early-evening fog that came rolling in like a layer of cotton batting to blanket them in dampness. Clea slipped her arms inside her sweater.

"Cold?" she asked Austin, for he only had the polo shirt.

"Only on the outside." He looped an arm over her shoulder. "You'll have to keep me warm."

They walked back home by way of the twists and turns of Lombard Street, his arm over her shoulders, hers around his waist, hips hard against each other, thighs brushing at every pace. Clea didn't think, just let herself go, for once not planning the present or trying to assure the future. Instead she just let herself float on the sensations and the alcohol and the heady perfection of the whole afternoon. At the moment it felt right, and whatever would come after she neither knew nor cared.

Austin walked her up the steps to her house, took her key and opened the door. Clea simply smiled, in a fog both inside and out. Austin shut the door behind them, then turned her and wrapped her in his arms. And to Clea it felt just like coming home—the satisfaction of a desire that had been building all day.

"God, Clea..." Austin's breath was hot against her neck. "I want you. I need you. I've been dying for you the whole afternoon!" His lips fastened on hers, his tongue seeking entrance, his hands knotting in the luxuriant softness of her hair.

And Clea wanted it, too. Wanted Austin. Needed him. The years of aching loneliness seemed at last to have disappeared. Unthinking she accepted him, burrowing against him, seeking warmth.

He dragged himself bare inches away from her. "Touch me, too," he muttered. "God, Clea! Love me. Love me the way you used to."

And the words brought Clea to her senses at last.

She shuddered, then stiffened, an arrow of pain piercing her. "I can't!" And it was more a wail than anything else.

"You *can't*?" Austin was taken aback, incredulous. "What d'you mean, you can't?" He took hold of her chin and tipped it up so he could look right down into her eyes.

She knew what they would look like—wide, frantic, like an animal in pain. "I can't," she repeated, her heart tearing under his gaze.

"You want me, Clea, damn it. You know you do."

She tried to turn her head away but he wouldn't let her.

"Don't you?" he persisted. The press of his arousal was still hard against her abdomen.

She shut her eyes, tried to shut her heart, but couldn't, quite. "Yes, damn it," she said roughly. "I do."

"Well, then...?" His voice was gentler now, confused but triumphant.

"I... I can't," she said again.

He frowned. "Damn it, why not?"

"It... it wouldn't... be fair. To... to Ken!"

"Ken?" It was a yelp of outrage. "What the hell does this have to do with Ken?"

"Everything," Clea tried to explain. "How can I betray his trust. How can I go to bed with you when I'm engaged to Ken?"

Austin looked almost apoplectic. "Engaged to Ken?" he bellowed. "Betray Ken? How the hell can you even be engaged to Ken when you're married to me?"

Chapter Six

It wasn't easy, Clea could have told him that.

In fact it kept her awake all night, and by morning she was no nearer sorting things out. It was no use pretending now that Austin was no more than a fond, but better forgotten memory. He was very much a part of her life.

But what part?

Could she really, once again, be his wife?

Stay married to Austin?

Once...twice...a thousand times over the past seven years she would have jumped at the chance. It had been the stuff her dreams were made of, the most sublime resolution of her youthful fantasies. But, like free run of a candy store, it had its drawbacks.

Austin was wealthy now, as handsome as ever, as personable as anyone could ever be. He was ambitious, determined, irreverent, charming. On the surface at least, everything a woman could ask. But deep down inside, Clea wondered if he knew any better what marriage was about now than the first time he'd asked her.

Granted, that had been a stopgap measure at best, a marriage of convenience in the truest sense of the words. But this time, although he didn't seem to be proposing that, she wasn't at all sure what he was proposing.

If he intended a "till death do us part" arrangement, she wondered if he had given any thought to what that entailed. She doubted it. Forethought was not one of Austin's long suits. He just plunged in, blithely confident that whatever arose, he would be able to handle it.

Well, he might. But she didn't see how or where he'd learned it, as far as marriage was concerned anyway. He certainly had no personal experience of good, long-lasting marriages.

His own parents had never been a model of wedded bliss. His hard-driving father had been totally preoccupied with making his millions to the exclusion of any interest in his wife or sons whatsoever. And his mother, a lonely, beautiful woman as Clea remembered her, had been no more than the ornament on Edward Cavanaugh's arm.

She had died when Austin was twelve. After that there had been a succession of women in his father's life, none of them the sort to settle down; none, obviously, that Edward Cavanaugh wanted to settle down with. The man had gone through women the way Clea's woodworker father went through sandpaper. No positive role model there.

Even worse from Clea's viewpoint was the fact Austin had clearly used his father as a role model in other areas. He had spent the better part of his life trying to get his father's love by emulation. He'd gone after things with the same single-minded intensity that his father had. And, she knew from reading the society pages that after their supposed divorce, he'd emulated the womanizing part of Edward, Sr.'s life, too.

All of which left her where?

Just as confused as ever. And fairly certain that when you came right down to it, Austin was probably just as confused as she was.

They would have to talk. She would have to try to sort out what he thought he wanted, and why he thought he wanted it, and then, knowing, she would have to decide what to do next. But she wasn't going to do it this morning.

She'd made a life of her own before Austin had made his ill-timed reentry into it. And she needed to get on with it. She needed time and space and at least some perspective to help her evaluate if he belonged there or not.

Chances were, he didn't. Chances were his interest in getting back with her again was a momentary whim, like a mountain to be climbed just because it was there or a business to save from bankruptcy just to prove that he could. And in that case, she couldn't—wouldn't—let him destroy what she already had—Ken.

So it was life as usual, she told herself as she started up the Subaru and headed over to the Carrutherses' house. But "life as usual" anymore meant that sooner or later, Austin would show up.

All she had to do was wait.

She got an amazing amount of work done that day. Driven by the demons of confusion and indecision in her love life, her work life seemed to flourish. She convinced an originally reluctant Mrs. Carruthers that the light fixtures she had chosen—and not the imitation brass hurricane lamps that her client thought were so "cute"—were exactly what the dining room and double parlor demanded—no mean feat. She got the wallpaper in the dining room hung, and she started stripping the woodwork in the stairwell.

Rosie had brought in sketches of the stained glass she wanted to do for the dining room windows. Clea approved them enthusiastically and sent Rosie home to work on them.

That was the only reason she sent Rosie away, Clea told herself. It had nothing to do with the fact that she expected Austin to appear about two o'clock.

That was about how long she suspected he would be able to hold out. Angry or not, offended or not, Austin had always been a man of action, and she couldn't imagine him simply walking away for long, even after the way things had ended between them yesterday. Especially after the way things had ended between them yesterday.

She felt both smug and apprehensive when she heard a car pull up at a quarter after. She went upstairs to glance out the window, the better to prepare herself for the coming confrontation. She was astonished to see Mr. Carruthers getting out of his car.

Frowning, she wiped her damp palms on her jeans. A vague, unsettling disappointment assailed her. Thrusting it aside, she hurried down the stairway where she continued to concentrate on the wood she was stripping while she waited for Mr. Carruthers to make his appearance.

"Just passing in the neighborhood," he told her. "Thought I'd see how things were coming along."

Clea buried her disappointment and gave him a bright smile. "Come see," she suggested, and led him into the dining room.

She had finished the wainscoting and the wallpapering since he'd been there last, so there was plenty for him to see. She'd decided against Rosie's pumpkins, so the wallpaper was muted climbing roses and soft green vines. There was just enough of a vertical design to make the lines clean, though the soft tones brought a light airiness to the room that it had lacked before.

He stopped in the doorway and glanced around briefly, his hands clasped behind his back. "Ah," he said, nodding his head. "Yes. Very nice." And he walked back out.

Nice? Just *nice*? It was gorgeous, stupendous, marvelous. It was everything she would want her own dining room to be if she had the time and money to make it that way. Nice? Clea gritted her teeth.

He paused in the entryway and gave her a perfunctory smile. She half expected him to pat her on the head. "Very good. Carry on, Miss Bannister.'' And with another nod, he vanished out the door.

Clea stared after him, nonplussed. She shouldn't have expected more. The Carruthers were not the ideal clients. Ordinarily she didn't expect anything from them. It was only that some renegade part of her had been expecting Austin to show up. He would've appreciated it, exclaimed over it. She knew that. It was right for this sort of house, and Austin would have known it, too.

He will know it, she corrected herself. For soon enough, she was convinced, Austin would show up, too.

She went back up the steps and started to work with the stripper again, half her mind on what she was doing, half on what she would say to Austin when he arrived.

But he never arrived at all.

She worked until past six, waiting more than working, climbing the stairs every quarter hour or so to stare out at the street as if in doing so she could conjure up his car. But she couldn't. And eventually she had to admit that he wasn't coming.

Maybe he'd been so angry after the way the day had ended yesterday that he'd left town. His fury was obvious and, she had to admit, partly justified.

But it wasn't her fault that she was still married to him. He had picked the attorney, after all.

She continued to fume while she cleaned up and prepared to leave. She kept right on fuming all the way across town. And she was still fuming as she went up her front steps. She'd tell him a thing or two if he was standing there.

Of course, he wasn't. He wasn't on Mrs. Gianetti's front porch either. Damn. When she didn't want to see him, he popped up everywhere. Now that she wanted to talk to him, he had vanished into thin air.

Well, if he didn't show up by the time she'd finished showering and cooking supper, she'd go across the street and seek him out. Things had gone far enough. They had to talk.

She was just getting out of the shower when the phone rang. Pulling a towel around her, she raced into the bedroom to answer it. It would be Austin, she was certain. How like him to get her out of the shower.

"So, how's my girl?" Ken asked her.

"Er, wet," Clea stammered, her heart doing odd flip-flops at this unexpected voice. "I was in the shower."

Ken groaned. "Don't tell me you're wearing nothing."

"All right, I won't," she said briskly. She dried herself off while they talked, then groped through her dresser for some clean shorts and a T-shirt. "How was the golf game?"

That elicited another groan. "Don't ask."

"You didn't hit three holes-in-one or something else that would have you winning, did you?" Clea teased.

"Not a chance. I'm lucky I'm still not out on the fourteenth fairway trying to get out of the sand trap."

"That bad?" She made sympathetic clucking noises.

"Worse. I can't stand another weekend like this one. Let's go away somewhere."

Clea's eyes widened. Ken hadn't suggested anything like that before. What had brought it on now? The golf game? Or was he reflecting on her parents' preoccupation with Austin and on her own mixed-up relationship with the man?

"Well, I..."

"Maybe go up to the wine country," Ken suggested musingly. "I understand there are great little weekend packages. A bed and breakfast, a wine-tasting tour of the vineyards. What do you think?"

"Well, I..."

"I'll check into it, okay?"

"Well...okay." She wasn't sure, really. Getting away for a weekend sounded like a great idea, on the one hand. On the other, given the way her life seemed to be going lately, there was always the possibility it could get a whole lot worse.

"Weekend after this okay with you?"

"Er..."

"I'll set it up," Ken said. "Now what about supper? Want to go out?"

"Uh, no...no, thanks. Not tonight," Clea declined quickly. "I'm really bushed. I worked like a demon today, got all the wallpapering done in the dining room and started stripping the stairway. And, I think I'd just like a...like a nice quiet evening at home."

That was nothing but the truth. It was exactly what she would like. It was her bad luck that she wouldn't get it because she would have to track Austin down instead.

"Well, okay. If you're sure, I'll toss in a Lean Cuisine instead," Ken sulked.

"Sounds good," Clea said brightly. "I'll talk to you tomorrow." And before he could say another word, she hung up.

FOR A MAN who could take a failing business and turn it around in less than a year, for a man who could see a building in his mind's eye and make it a reality in less than three months, for a man who could imagine virtually anything and sculpt it in sand in a few days, Austin didn't think he'd understand Clea in a million years.

How could she share a day with him like the one they had shared yesterday, and then turn around at the end of the day and act as if he were some sort of lecher determined to break up her engagement?

He was the one who was married to her, damn it.

He was the one who had rights, not Ken.

She still loved him—or at least felt something for him— he was sure of that.

He'd caught hints of it before in her voice, in quick little oblique glances she'd give him, in her defensiveness. But after yesterday he couldn't doubt it.

He'd seen the way she'd looked at him. He'd felt the warm softness of her body against his on the merry-go-round. He'd held her hand in his, had touched her lips with his own, and tasted fire—a fire that he remembered all too well. And knew that she remembered, too.

So, what was her problem?

They were meant for each other. It was obvious.

Why didn't she just tell Ken to bug off?

She couldn't seriously still be considering marrying him, could she? But if she couldn't, she sure as hell seemed to be scrupulous about upholding her engagement to him even while she was still legally Austin's wife!

Damn it! He had not been able to believe it when she'd stiffened in his arms and pulled away. He'd needed her so badly, wanted her so desperately. And she had wanted him, too.

But she had rejected him just the same.

It didn't make sense.

He'd told himself all day to be patient, to wait her out, that she would turn to him in the long run. But it almost killed him. Waiting was as inclined to give him ulcers as going after what he wanted.

Besides, he told himself a hundred times, he couldn't simply sit and wait forever. He had obligations, responsibilities. He had a sand sculpture to build, and he had to get going on it. He should have left already. Instead he was still here pacing back and forth in this damned room trying to decide what to do next.

Maybe he should have gone back over to the house where she was working. He'd seen her leave bright and early, and he'd consciously had to force himself not to follow her. He'd managed it only because he didn't know what he would say if he did. The violence of his emotions hadn't calmed a lot since she had pushed him away yesterday. And Austin did know better than to go after things when he was at his most emotional.

But now? Should he go over now? He'd seen her come home almost an hour ago. She'd looked exhausted and grubby. She'd be in a better mood if she got to take a shower first.

And anyway, by then he might have decided on something to say, how to convince her once and for all that she was his wife and she was going to stay that way.

He hadn't, though, and he was considering what other alternatives he had—kidnapping being the only thing that came to mind—when he heard Mrs. Gianetti's tread on the stairs and her calling, "Austin, you have a visitor."

He frowned and got up off the bed where he'd been lying and staring at the ceiling. A visitor?

No one knew he was living here except Clea. And Baxter. Given the way she was acting toward him, it was a foregone conclusion which of them it would be. He steeled himself to deal with his zealous young lawyer, who must have decided that express mail wasn't even good enough. Striding down the stairs, he began, "Listen to me, Baxter. I do not have to be in L.A. to sign your bloody papers. I can do it just as well from right—"

Clea was standing just inside the door.

He stopped dead halfway down, feeling as if he'd taken a sudden blow to the chest. He couldn't breathe. His ears buzzed. He swallowed, then cleared his throat. Hope was floundering upward, choking him.

"C-Clea?"

She gave a tight little nod. "Can we talk?"

Wordlessly, he came down the rest of the way. She was barely five feet from him then, close enough so he could smell her perfume, close enough so he could remember the feel of her in his arms. He swallowed an involuntary groan.

Clea took a nervous step backward. "Talk, Austin," she repeated, as if he hadn't heard her the first time. "Just...talk."

"Sure. Of course. Now?"

She glanced around the room as if assessing its suitability. Mrs. Gianetti was banging pots with unusual fervor right behind the kitchen door. "How about forty-five minutes? At my place. I haven't eaten."

"Me neither," he said quickly, ignoring the fact that he had already told Mrs. Gianetti he would eat there. "We could go out and—"

"No." Clea was already stepping out onto the porch. "I... No, thank you."

"But..."

"Just talk, Austin. Not eat."

He closed his eyes and prayed for patience. "All right," he said when he opened them. "Forty-five minutes."

She nodded once more, then gave him another stiff little nod, and closed the door behind her.

He stood watching through the glass as she crossed the street, noting the rigidity of her spine, the deliberateness of her walk. He wondered what she wanted to talk about.

There were any number of possibilities, and forty-five minutes gave him the opportunity to run through several hundred of them as he paced the length of his room. The one he liked the best ended when she flung herself into his arms and told him she couldn't live without him. The worst was the one in which she said she'd gone to Tijuana last night to get a divorce and tonight she was going to Las Vegas and marrying Ken.

"You walk so much, you wear my floor out." Mrs. Gianetti stuck her head in and complained.

Austin grimaced. "Sorry."

"Dinner's ready."

"I'm not hungry after all." He gave her a smile, albeit a bleak one. "I think I'll go out for a while."

Down the hill and back, consulting his watch and raking his fingers through his hair, he went. It was like waiting for a dentist's appointment or, worse, a confrontation with his father.

No, a confrontation with Clea couldn't be described in the same sentence with those he'd had with his dad. But, he realized for the first time, this one might very well be worse. He had learned long ago to steel himself against whatever his father said or did. Edward Cavanaugh could scarcely touch him now. But Clea had the power to hurt.

If it was any consolation, Austin told himself when Clea opened the door to his knock three-quarters of an hour later, she looked as apprehensive as he felt.

She was wearing a pair of white midlength shorts and a scoop-necked rose-and-white-striped shirt. It was an outfit designed for casual, easy living. Clea looked as if she had an appointment with a firing squad. As she ushered him into the front parlor, Austin thought that she seemed more nervous than she had on their wedding day.

And why not? he asked himself. That had been a lark. God knew what this was going to be.

"Please sit down," she said formally, nodding toward the settee he had slept on.

Austin sat. It was no more comfortable for sitting than for sleeping. But he made an effort, leaning against the back and stretching one arm along it while he rested his left ankle on his right knee. He gave her a smile to show her that he was waiting.

Clea took the straight back chair opposite him. God forbid they should share the sofa, he thought bitterly. And she perched on it as if she were facing a firing squad, too.

But she didn't flinch. She fired the first shot herself. "When you showed up here that day, Austin, what did you really want?"

"Want?" He frowned slightly, then flexed his shoulders. "You mean when I . . ." he began slowly, not sure exactly what she meant.

"I mean, when you arrived on my doorstep—er, through my floor," she corrected wryly. "Just what did you have in mind?"

"Well, I . . ." He ran his tongue over his lips. They felt dry, cracked, the same way they felt when he'd been out too long in the sun. He tried to form into words exactly what he had wanted that day. He remembered how he'd anticipated finding her again, how he'd looked forward to sharing the great joke of their "divorce" with her. But beyond that . . . "I . . . wanted to see you."

"Why?"

"Why not? I'd just found out we thought we'd been divorced and now we weren't!"

"You could have sent a letter."

"I didn't want to send a letter."

"Why not?" she pressed.

He shifted, laying the right ankle on the left knee this time. "I don't know why not. I— Hell, Clea, it'd been years since I'd seen you. I thought . . . I thought it'd be fun." He spread his palms.

"Fun?" she muttered. Her lips pressed together and she shut her eyes for a moment, drawing in a deep breath, then letting it out slowly. Austin had the feeling a judgment was taking place, and he wasn't getting the right verdict.

"Well, it was sort of funny," he pointed out.

Clea made a noncommittal noise.

"So when did you decide you didn't want the divorce?" she went on quietly when she'd opened her eyes once more.

"The minute I saw you again."

Look what we've got for you:

Get 4 FREE full-length Harlequin American Romance® novels.

Plus this handy compact manicure set

Plus a surprise free gift

▼ **PLUS LOTS MORE! MAIL THIS CARD TODAY** ▼

Harlequin's Best-Ever "Get Acquainted" Offer

Yes, I'll try the Harlequin Reader Service under the terms outlined on the opposite page. Send me 4 free Harlequin American Romance® novels, a free compact manicure set and a free mystery gift.

154 CIH NA9W

PLACE STICKER FOR 6 FREE GIFTS HERE

NAME _____

ADDRESS _____ APT. ___

CITY _____

STATE _____ ZIP CODE _____

PRINTED IN U.S.A.

Don't forget...

...Return this card today to receive your 4 free books, free compact manicure set and free mystery gift.

...You will receive books before they're available in stores and at a discount off retail prices.

...No obligation. Keep only the books you want, cancel anytime.

If offer card is missing, write to: Harlequin Reader Service,
901 Fuhrmann Blvd., P.O. Box 1867, Buffalo, NY 14269-1867

Postage will be paid by addressee

BUSINESS REPLY CARD

First Class   Permit No. 717   Buffalo, NY

Harlequin Reader Service®
901 Fuhrmann Blvd.
P.O. Box 1867
Buffalo, NY 14240-9952

No Postage
Necessary
If Mailed
In The
United States

"Oh cripes, Austin, you're crazy."

He scowled, affronted. "It's crazy to want to stay married to the woman I've loved for years?"

"Loved me for years? You've been divorced from me for years."

"I thought I had. I hadn't. Lucky me." He grinned at her.

She shot him an exasperated look. He could see her gearing up for another assault and he decided it was his turn.

"Listen, Clea." He gathered himself together, put both feet flat on the floor now, and leaned forward, resting his elbows on his knees. "We've always been honest with each other, haven't we?"

She didn't answer for a minute, as if she were assessing the question, looking for the trick. Finally she nodded slowly. "Yes, I think so."

"Okay, then. I'm being absolutely straight with you now." He felt as if he were fighting for his life. "I didn't know when I first came back that I wanted to still be married to you. How could I? I hadn't seen you in years. I didn't know if you might have changed—"

"I have changed," Clea cut in.

Austin shook his head adamantly. "No, you haven't. Not fundamentally."

She snorted. "Thank you very much." Her tone was sarcastic.

"You're more lovely than you ever were, but you're the same woman," he persisted.

"I thought we were being honest." Her voice was scathing.

"We are. And when I saw you again, talked to you again...felt the way you made me feel again," he added with a grin, "I knew there was no way I was going through with that divorce."

"So you just unilaterally decided we were going to stay married."

"Why not? You're sure as hell not indifferent to me."

"No, as a matter of fact I'm mad as hell at you."

"You're not," Austin said mildly. "Except insofar as I'm mucking up your well-thought-out little life."

"Well, it may not seem like much to you, but it's *my* 'well-thought-out little life' and I happen to like it," Clea snapped.

"I know you do. But it isn't what you really want, Clea."

"Oh?" Her voice dripped scorn. "And what do I want?"

"Me."

"You haven't changed either," she told him. "You've got an ego as big as all outdoors."

"Be honest, Clea." He wouldn't let her look away.

She sighed, shifting, twisting her hands. "Marriages are made of more than feelings, Austin," Clea argued finally.

He shrugged. "But you've got to have those feelings to make it work."

Clea didn't say anything. She did break the contact between them then, staring out the window behind his head, seeing God knew what.

"You have those feelings, too, Clea, don't you?"

She gave an impatient flick of her head and got up from the chair, pacing around the room. "I don't know why you're doing this."

"Because I love you."

"Oh, Austin..."

"Come on, Clea, we're being honest, remember? Don't you have those feelings for me?" Why the hell couldn't she admit it? Unless she really didn't feel anything...unless he'd imagined her responses...unless it was only wishful thinking. He felt an ache deep in his gut.

Clea jammed her hands into the pockets of her shorts, still pacing the room, making the floor squeak with every step.

His jaw tightened. He wanted to shake her, to make her admit it. He had to make her admit it. "Don't you?"

"Another way you haven't changed!" She'd got to the end of the parlor and flung herself around, glaring at him, her feet planted solidly, her chin thrust out. "You're just as damnably persistent as you ever were. Just as stubborn."

Thank God. He waited, one eyebrow lifted.

"All right, damn it," she snarled. "Yes, I do."

"Ah." He breathed again.

"There's no 'ah' about it! It doesn't mean anything."

"It damned well does! Do you feel that way about what's-his-name?"

"Ken. His name is Ken," Clea said sharply.

Austin nodded with more complacency than he felt. "Do you?" A sweat was breaking out on his back. The nape of his neck felt clammy. "Does he make you feel the way I do?"

"No."

He smiled.

Then she smiled back. Smugly. "He makes me feel things you don't!"

She might as well have slapped him. His head jerked back. He blinked. His jaw snapped together so hard his teeth hurt. "Like what?" he snarled.

"Like cherished...like more than a possession... like..." Clea's eyes were flashing.

"I cherish you," Austin insisted.

Clea shook her head.

Austin stood up, walking toward her. She backed away, moving into the rear parlor. "I do. I can show you."

"No, Austin."

"Yes."

She had backed as far as the room would allow and was up against the marble fireplace now, staring up at him, her nostrils flaring, her breath coming in quick gasps through parted lips. He wanted to taste those lips, wanted to seek inside them, and knew he couldn't, knew that this time a kiss wasn't the way to Clea's heart.

Instead he lifted his hand and touched her cheek very lightly, stroking it. His fingers trembled. "I do, Clea" was all he said.

For an eternity everything seemed to stop, and they stood there bare inches apart, the only contact between them his fingertips on her flushed face, but their eyes saw into the depths of each other's heart.

"Remember how it was?" Austin urged her softly.

A tiny shudder ran through Clea and she dropped her eyes. Then she took a deep breath and shook her head. "Love is more than memories, Austin. It needs a future."

"I'll give it a future," he swore. "Give me a chance."

"I have Ken."

"You have me, damn it."

She pressed her hands against the sides of her head, closing her eyes as she shook it slowly.

"Break your engagement," Austin coaxed softly.

"No."

"Clea..."

"No. Ken's done nothing to deserve that."

"And I have?"

"You divorced me."

"Well, besides that..."

She blinked, then stifled a laugh. "You're incorrigible."

Austin grinned, grateful to see a smile on her face at last. "I always have been."

"I know." The grin faded and seriousness took over again. "I'm going away with Ken," she told him slowly.

"What!"

She nodded her head, at first cautiously, then with more enthusiasm. "Next weekend," she told him, making up her mind as she spoke. "To the wine country."

"You're going to spend the weekend with him when you're still married to me?"

"I'm not going to sleep with him," Clea said sharply.

Somehow that still didn't make things all right. Austin scowled fiercely, dropping his hand and stalking away from her, thinking furiously.

"I don't want you to go," he said finally, turning and scowling at her.

Clea shrugged. She gave him a bland look that told him as well as anything that she didn't care what he wanted. Sometimes she was like that, Austin remembered. Stubborn, and you couldn't budge her, couldn't argue with her. But, he remembered as well, sometimes you could bargain with her.

"If you're going with him someplace, and if I have to compete with him, I think you should go somewhere with me." It was his turn to thrust his chin out and glare at her.

"Don't be silly." Clea looked nervous again.

"Nothing silly about it. You're telling me that he's the stumbling block between us, right?"

"Not exactly..."

"I'd say he is," Austin insisted. "Wouldn't you be more inclined to stay married to me if he weren't in the wings?"

"I don't think—"

"Wouldn't you? Honestly?"

"It's...possible," was as much as she'd say.

"Well, fair's fair." Austin spread his hands. "You give him a weekend, you give me time, too."

"I..." She paused, frowning, obviously trying to second-guess him. One thing he liked about Clea was her innate sense of fairness. Another was that she'd never been much of a chess player.

"Like what?" she asked finally and with great caution.

Austin took a careful breath, then stared off out toward the front parlor as if what he was going to suggest weren't the most important thing in the world to him. "Nothing much. Just build a sand castle with me."

"What?"

He shifted his gaze, bringing it back to her for a moment, allowing himself to smile just once, a small, hopeful smile. "I'm entered in a contest. Actually it's for me and my immediate family, which is, I suppose, you." The smile broadened for an instant, then faded again. "I'd like you to help me build it."

"Build a sand castle?" He could almost see her poking at the words as she spoke them, testing them, probing them as if they were a verbal mine field that might explode in her face.

"Uh-huh." He permitted his smile to get a bit more hopeful.

"When?"

"I have to start at least by Wednesday."

"This Wednesday?"

"Next Wednesday." It would take some time to organize things, and so far he hadn't. He'd been too preoccupied here. He should've left already, but now he was glad he'd waited. He couldn't believe this was happening. It was better than his wildest dreams. If he could only convince her...

"Is it a big sand castle?"

"Sort of."

"How big?"

"Uh, about twelve feet."

"Twelve feet? High?"

Austin nodded. He hadn't wanted to get into it too deeply. The deeper he got, the more reasons she would find to turn him down. Then he remembered his chiding her about honesty and plunged ahead. "It's twelve feet high, about six feet square at the base. It'll take me three days to build it."

"Three days?"

"We're talking about eleven tons of sand here."

Clea's jaw dropped. "Can you do that in three days?" The cause of her astonishment seemed to have shifted.

"I hope so." He looked at her squarely then. "I know I can if you help."

Clea opened her mouth, as if she were about to say something, then obviously thought better of it. She frowned and ran her fingers through her hair. "I'm supposed to be going with Ken," she ventured at last.

"The wine country will still be there a month from now."

"Ken's already made plans."

"I'll have you back on Saturday morning."

"I didn't say I was going yet," Clea reminded him.

Austin gave her a rueful look.

"Don't do your woebegone puppy face for me."

"Come on, Clea." He was so close now. Damn it, she couldn't turn him down. "It's only three days."

"But Ken would only get two."

"But with Ken he'd be spending the whole time courting." Austin made a horrible face. "With me I'd be sixteen hours a day shoveling sand."

"And the other eight hours?" Clea said archly.

"And the other eight hours," Austin said more truthfully than he wished, "I'll be too damned tired to do more than breathe." He gave her one more beseeching look.

"What about my job?"

"What about it?"

"I have one, you recall."

"You've got help. I bet you that Rosie could handle it."

Clea chewed her lip indecisively, then walked the length of both parlors and stared out through the lace curtains at the sunset reflected in Mrs. Gianetti's windows across the street.

Austin stayed where he was, chewing his own lip. "Come on, Clea. At least think about it."

She turned her head and looked at him over her shoulder, her hazel eyes light and fathomless. Her fist tightened reflexively on the curtains, then slowly relaxed, and she inclined her head. "All right. I'll think."

Chapter Seven

He called himself seven kinds of a fool all night long. How could he have tossed out the invitation and then let her walk away undecided?

What kind of an idiot was he? He should have known better, should have pressed his advantage while he had it, should have used every subtle damned trick in the book to get her to say yes.

Now that he had let her get away, he would never have the power to influence her decision that he'd had in those few moments in her living room. Now she would be prey to every anti-Cavanaugh idea that she could muster. She would think of fifty reasons why she shouldn't go with him.

If she could break out of his embrace because of the mere thought of Ken, God only knew how well she would resist his invitation to come build a sand castle. But Austin had a pretty good idea.

He had half a mind to charge over there first thing in the morning and restate his case, using every big gun he could muster. Only an early-morning phone call from Baxter stopped him. By the time he'd got another maneuver of his father's analyzed and sorted out to Baxter's satisfaction, Clea's pickup was no longer in front of her house.

He considered following her over to the house on Haight St. He didn't only because he didn't want to confront her in front of her friend, Rosie. He had no idea whether Rosie would be sympathetic or not. But if she worked for Clea, he didn't want to take the chance. Better, he decided, to wait and pounce on her when she got home after work.

If, he thought, biting his thumbnail down to the quick, he lasted that long.

"Lunch?" Clea was dismayed. "Today? Oh, Mother, I don't think—"

"I think it would be marvelous, dear," Mary Bannister interrupted. "Just the two of us. We hardly got a chance to talk on Saturday. And it's not as if we don't have a lot to talk about," she chided her daughter gently.

Clea knew exactly what they had to talk about. That was the source of her reluctance. It would be easier to meet her mother with equanimity if she were as staunchly anti-Austin as she had been on Saturday. But Sunday had raked up a lot of feelings she was still exploring. And so had her "talk" with him yesterday. She felt that things were less sorted out than ever. And all the while she tried so hard to sort them, she wondered at the wisdom of doing so. It might be best just to forget him, to leave well enough alone.

"But if you really are too busy..." her mother went on, and Clea heard not-quite-masked hurt in her voice.

"No. Not really," she confessed, as unable as ever to reject her mother's concern. "It's just that..." Her voice trailed off.

Her mother waited, knowing, Clea was certain, exactly what it was that her daughter couldn't bring herself to say.

Finally, when her mother didn't offer a word of encouragement or even a helpful murmur, Clea took a deep breath. "All right. Where shall I meet you?"

"I'll pick you up at the Carrutherses' place," her mother said. "I've been wanting to see the progress you've made. About noon, all right?"

"I'll be ready."

She'd planned to be. But the morning conspired against her and she didn't have much time to think about lunch or her mother or to plan her defenses against maternal concern. Within the first half hour she discovered that the built-in cabinet in one of the bedrooms had been much more seriously gnawed by rats than she had first thought. There would be no refinishing it as it was. It would need considerable repair and possibly reconstruction.

"Call Devin, will you, Rosie?" she hollered down the stairs.

"Not me," Rosie hollered up.

Taken aback, Clea ventured halfway down. "Why not?"

"There are other carpenters." Rosie was standing in the dining room doorway, looking up at Clea with a mulish expression on her face.

"Yes. But I want Devin."

"I don't," Clea thought she heard Rosie mutter under her breath.

"I beg your pardon?" she said.

"Nothing." Rosie scowled.

"Well, then . . ." Clea waited for an explanation in vain.

Rosie glowered, but when Clea didn't react, finally she shrugged. "I'll call," she gave in ungraciously. Turning on her heel, she stalked back into the kitchen. Clea could hear her punching out the number.

What was it with Rosie and Devin?

Shaking her head, Clea went back to the bedroom to see how much repair she thought would be necessary on the cabinet. But while she did so, her mind was playing with Rosie's antagonism. It was oddly reminiscent of her own toward Austin. But without the same reasons. Without any reason as far as Clea knew. Rosie just didn't like the man.

But then, with Rosie that was not necessarily surprising. She was a woman of strong feelings and definite opinions, and once roused, she was roused for-or-against for life. Devin had probably spoken out against one of her causes, thereby incurring her everlasting wrath.

Poor Devin, Clea thought. Personally, she thought he was pretty nice. She wondered if her mother would have liked Devin. Probably no more than she liked Ken. He would be "all right," but he wasn't Austin. Mary Bannister had never got over Austin.

Neither, Clea thought glumly, had her daughter.

"He wants to talk to you," came a bellow from the kitchen.

Groaning, Clea went back down the stairs. Rosie had left the portable phone on the newel post and had retreated into the kitchen again.

"You wanted to talk to me?" Devin said when she picked it up.

"I thought you wanted to talk to me," Clea said.

"Huh-uh. Rosie just said . . ." His voice trailed off.

It didn't take a genius to figure out what Rosie had said. The rat. "I need you to repair a cabinet," Clea told him. "Have you got time?"

"Today?"

"If you can."

"I can come take a look at it. If it's not too bad, I could get started at least."

"Would you?"

"Sure. I've got to put a coat of sealer on this altar I'm working on first, though. Be there in about an hour."

"I'll be out to lunch with my mother," Clea told him. "But Rosie can show you where it is."

Devin snorted. "All Rosie will show me is the door."

Clea laughed. "Seems like it, doesn't it? What on earth did you ever do to her?"

There was total silence on the other end of the line.

Clea wondered if he'd hung up. Then he cleared his throat. "Don't worry about it," he said. "I'll find the cabinet myself."

Curiouser and curiouser, Clea thought. "All right," she said, because she didn't have time to consider it further. Her mother had just appeared at the front door. "Call me later, Dev," she said and hung up. Then, to her mother, "Come on, let me give you the grand tour."

"I heard of a wonderful little Ukrainian place not far from here," Mary said after she had oohed and aahed over the miracles of restoration Clea had wrought and was chivvying her daughter into her Honda. "Is that all right?"

"Fine." It didn't matter to Clea where they went. Or to her mother, either, she was positive. While her mother had made all the appropriate murmurings of appreciation about the house, the house wasn't what she had come for. And neither was the meal. What mattered was what would be said, not the food it was said over.

This fact was borne out almost as soon as they were seated and had ordered, for Clea's mother stirred sugar into her tea and said with studied casualness, "The restoration is really lovely, dear. Has Austin seen it?"

Not even a preliminary skirmish, Clea thought. They were in with a vengeance already. "Thank you." She took refuge behind her own cup, burying her face in the steam from the hot, sweet tea. "As a matter of fact, he has."

Mary smiled fondly. "I'll bet he was impressed."

"He liked it."

Mary Bannister searched her daughter's face, a myriad of maternal concerns lining her own. Then she leaned forward, her voice dropping. "How is he, Clea?"

A wealth of questions lurked in those four words, in that intent, worried gaze. Clea pressed her lips together, trying for a steadiness that was at best precarious. "He...he's fine."

She groped for the right words, focusing on the stem vase filled with daisies that sat on the window ledge next to their table. "He's . . . the same Austin." The man, God help her, that, deep down, she still loved.

She took a quick swallow of the scalding liquid, blinking back sudden tears that owed more to her emotions than the temperature of the tea.

"What's he doing now?" her mother asked. "Still building?"

Clea grinned, swiping at her eyes with her napkin. "Building sand castles."

Her mother didn't bat an eyelash. "God love him."

The waitress came with their order, setting wide bowls of Ukrainian stewlike borscht in front of them. *"Priyatneve appitita,"* she said, smiling. "Good appetite."

Mary dug in with gusto. Clea couldn't eat a thing. Lilting balalaika music wove in and out of the dining room clatter.

"I do like Ken," Mary said between bites.

Clea looked at her mother. The older woman's expression was guileless. "I'm glad." She poked at a bit of cabbage in the borscht.

"He seems a lovely sort of man. Kind. Gentle. Loving."

"Yes."

"Just what you've always wanted."

"Yes."

"Do you love *him* though?"

Subtlety was not Mary's forte. And Clea couldn't help smiling wanly at her mother's blunt concern. Her eyes drifted back to the daisies. If only the answer were that easy. Would that simple love were all it took. But "I love him, I love him not" didn't guarantee happiness, didn't promise the right spouse, or assure everlasting commitment. Love alone did not always make a marriage.

"The way I loved Austin, you mean?"

Her mother looked slightly abashed at Clea's own forthrightness. "Yes, I guess that's what I do mean."

"No." Clea stirred her soup, steering a piece of beef from one side of the bowl to the other. "I love him differently."

"Enough?"

Clea traced a pattern on the bowl's edge with her spoon. "I thought so."

Mary looked up, her wide blue eyes searching her daughter's face. She hadn't missed the past tense. "And now?"

"Now..." Clea reached for a roll and began crumbling it into bits, lining her bread plate with tiny crumb fortifications. "Now I don't know what to think."

"You are married to Austin still," her mother ventured. "At least that's what Ken said. So, I mean, couldn't you just..."

"No," Clea said sharply. "The marriage is over."

"But Ken said—"

"Officially, I admit, there's been a hang-up. But what Austin and I had then is gone. Finished. It's insane to think we can just pick up where we left off seven years ago. Things have changed."

"How much?" Mary asked her gently.

Clea stacked the bread pellets in a neat pile. "I don't know."

"How does Austin feel?"

"About me, you mean?"

"Mmm-mm. And about your marriage."

Clea shrugged. "Now he wants it. He says he loves me."

Mary brightened. "Well, then..."

Clea slapped her spoon down with a clank. "He says three words and I'm just supposed to welcome him back with open arms? Hail the prodigal husband? Is that what you want?"

"Well, I never understood—"

"No. You didn't." Clea inhaled deeply. And she wasn't ever going to. "I don't know, Mom," she sighed. "It's just that for all that I've changed, that circumstances have changed, I'm not at all sure Austin has."

"What do you mean?"

"I mean, I don't know what he means by love. I don't know what he means by wanting to stay married."

"Have you asked him?"

Had she? She couldn't remember. Probably. Or she had tried to. But if she had, she knew she hadn't got an answer. One rarely did with Austin. One simply got driving emotion, intensity, desire. "It's like talking to a steamroller."

Mary Bannister smiled fondly. "Maybe you just need to give him some time."

Clea eyed her mother warily. "That's what he says."

"Really?"

"Have you been talking to him?"

Mary sat back, affronted. "I haven't talked to Austin in years, and well you know it. He hasn't called," she added wistfully.

"I knew he hadn't," Clea allowed, pricked with guilt. "I thought he might've changed his tactics."

Her mother shook her head. "We haven't heard a word. Not that we wouldn't have liked to, mind you. Such a young scamp he was." Her expression betrayed her fondness. "And me practically raising the boy..."

"I know. I know." More guilt.

"So what did Austin say?" her mother pressed.

Clea wrinkled her nose. "He said I should give him and Ken equal time."

Her mother nodded sagely. "And what's wrong with that?"

Clea's chin jutted out. "What right has he—"

"Maybe none, Clea," Mary said calmly. "Maybe none at all. But don't *you* have a right, darling? Don't you have a right to a life with the right man for you? Don't jump into a life with Ken just because once upon a time Austin hurt you. You said yourself, seven years is a long time. Give him a chance. Give yourself a chance." She leaned forward, her voice, her whole being taut with urgency. "It won't be fair to anyone, darling, least of all Ken, if you don't."

ROSIE DISAGREED.

"The schmuck divorced you seven years ago, walked out of your life, and now he wants you back?" She stared at Clea, incredulous. If she'd been a cat, Clea thought, her back would've arched and her fur stood on end.

"Well, we're not exactly divorced. That's the problem," Clea explained, wondering why she should feel as if Austin needed defending when she'd spent most of her time lately attacking him.

"He left you, didn't he?"

"Well, yes, but—"

Rosie shrugged. "So, there's your answer. He's a jerk. Ken's not. Tell old Austin to bug off."

Another simplistic solution. Why was it always so easy to cope with other people's problems?

Clea sighed and leaned against the newel post. She shouldn't have even brought it up. But when she'd got back from lunch with her mother, she'd been in more of a muddle than when she'd left.

Her mother made sense, of course. Her mother usually did. But Clea couldn't live her life by her mother's designs alone. If she was going to go with Austin to build his sand castle, the decision had to be hers, not her mother's. But she'd been distracted enough, trying to make up her mind, for Rosie to have lots of questions.

"I thought the idea was for you to go out and come back refreshed," Rosie had said. "What happened?"

So Clea had told her the dilemma.

Rosie didn't see it as a dilemma at all. "He had his chance. He blew it, didn't he?" she said, hands on her hips, as Clea wearily shoved herself away from the newel post and climbed the stairs to the bedroom where Devin was working. "How many chances should he get?"

"How many chances should he get?" Clea mused as she walked into the bedroom where Devin Flynn was sitting cross-legged on the floor sanding the piece of wood he held in his hand.

"Huh?" Devin looked up and blinked, his warm brown eyes confused.

"Nothing," Clea said. "Just muttering. Trying to sort out my life. How many chances do you think a man should get, Devin?"

A wistful, weary look flickered across Devin's face. "In an ideal world?" he asked, his callused fingers absently stroking the wood he was working on. "As many as he needs to get it right."

AUSTIN THOUGHT it would be Baxter when Mrs. Gianetti called him to the phone. Clattering down the stairs to pick up the receiver off the table in the kitchen, he was prepared to hear about his lawyer's latest legal maneuverings on his behalf or to be informed of his father's latest attempt to take over Houston's furniture business.

He was completely unprepared to hear Clea's soft voice on the other end of the line. "Austin?"

"Yeah?"

And he was absolutely astonished at the words that reached his ears next. "I just wanted to tell you . . . I've decided to come with you."

"YOU'RE GOING TO *what*?" Ken's voice rose a full octave when she told him.

"Going to help Austin build a sand castle," she repeated though she knew he'd heard every word. The noise in the bar wasn't that horrendous.

Ken scowled. He was sitting across from her at a minuscule table in a tiny posh pub just off Union Square where she had told him she'd like to meet him after work.

Now she was thinking she could have made a better choice. She'd picked the pub because she thought he wouldn't make a scene there. Ken was circumspect in public.

Not as circumspect as she'd hoped, though. Half a dozen tables full of patrons turned at his outraged response.

"It's what he does for a living," Clea began.

She had rehearsed this explanation all last night and for the entire day today, practicing it all the while she was stripping the stairway, all the time she was driving to and from the Carrutherses' place, all the time she was eating, drinking, and most of all, all the time she didn't sleep last night.

She wasn't any better at it than she thought she'd be.

"He builds *sand castles*?" Ken was repeating indulgently, as if she were a little girl who had just said she was going to go off and marry a cowboy when she grew up.

"Yes," Clea said firmly. "He does. Austin is . . . well, eccentric, I guess you'd say."

"I guess," Ken concurred with rather more emphasis than Clea thought was entirely necessary. He pasted a bright smile on his face. "Go on," he suggested, stabbing his olive with a toothpick. "Explain. Do."

"He is an architect, you know," Clea said, getting annoyed now at his patronizing.

"So you said. But I know plenty of architects, and none of them builds sand castles for a living."

"Neither did Austin until recently." She'd never talked much about Austin to Ken.

What could she have said? She'd never wanted to mention the reason she had married him in the first place. It seemed somehow disloyal, though whether Austin would think so, she didn't know. He might not even care. He was close-mouthed because she wanted him to be, not because he cared himself.

So she went on to sketch out some of the things he had done, concentrating on the construction, the office buildings he'd designed, the businesses he'd rescued from near bankruptcy. And when Ken asked how Austin had got started in the first place, she just told him that Austin had inherited some money from his mother.

"And he parlayed it into a fortune," Ken finished for her.

"Yes, I guess you could say so. Anyway, he can afford to take some time and get started on this sand castle building business."

"But is he serious about it?" Ken asked, still disbelieving, though not as obviously now.

"Oh, yes. It's perfect for him really." The absolute rightness of it could still make Clea smile.

"But what about you?" Ken zeroed right back in on the issue at hand. "How do you fit in?"

Trust Ken to get to the heart of the matter.

"He needs his immediate family to help," Clea explained, "and I'm it."

"I don't mean in the sand castle building. I mean in his life."

"I'm just building a sand castle," Clea said quickly. She'd debated telling Ken that Austin had demanded his fair share of time with her, and she'd decided against it. She was engaged to Ken, after all. It didn't seem fair to plague him with her second thoughts.

Whether she wanted him to or not, he picked them up. "I don't like it," he said, exactly the same way Austin had said he didn't like her going to the wine country with Ken. "How

can you be his immediate family when you're engaged to
me?''

Shades of Austin's own question, turned upside down.
Damn it, Clea thought. *Why do they both make it sound
like it's my fault?* "Legally I am," she hedged.

The waiter arrived just then with a second round of drinks
and she gave him a grateful smile, taking her margarita and
sipping rather more rapidly than she normally would have.

Ken scowled. "I still don't like it. What about our weekend? I've made plans."

"We can still go. He'll have me back by Saturday morning. He promised."

Ken's scowl deepened. "He'll have you back? Sounds like
he thinks he's 'letting' you come with me."

Clea suspected that wasn't far wrong, but she wasn't
confirming Ken's fears.

"That's ridiculous," she said sharply. "It's got nothing
to do with him 'letting' me. I make the decisions in my life.
It's just . . . well, he's in a bit of a jam. He should have gone
earlier this week to work on it, and he didn't . . ."

"Because he was hanging around you," Ken inserted.

"Because he was hanging around me," Clea admitted.
"*Not* with my encouragement, I might add. And now he
needs to get on with his life. I think I ought to help him do
it."

It sounded less than convincing, and Clea knew it.

If she'd been Ken she'd have been examining it with a
microscope, too. But she didn't like all this possessiveness,
whether it was Austin's or Ken's. The two of them were
acting like she was a favorite bone that they had every right
to fight over.

It was her decision, damn it. She wasn't just going to go
by default to the most stubborn of two jerks.

"I am going with him, Ken," she said with every ounce
of firmness she could muster. Standing up, she met his gaze

squarely, then picked up her glass and drained her drink in one long gulp. "I'll call you Saturday as soon as I get back. Trust me."

She spun around and marched out with far more confidence than she felt.

Chapter Eight

She almost backed out every minute on the minute until the plane left San Francisco. She had reasons to. Plenty of them.

But when the PSA jet took off at 5:47 Monday evening of the following week, Clea was sitting in seat 11A. And when she got off, Austin was there to meet her.

He looked almost as surprised to see her walk out of the tunnel into the terminal as she was to actually be there.

Perhaps he was, Clea thought, pleased. Perhaps he wasn't as all-fired confident as he seemed.

In fact, besides surprised, he appeared nervous as he waited for her, shifting from one foot to the other, his fists bunching in his pockets, a frown creasing his face until he spotted her.

The moment he did, his relief was almost comical. He exhaled sharply, and a grin split his tanned face, grooving his cheeks and making tiny lines fan out from his eyes. Jerking his hands out of the pockets of his jeans, he wiped them on his thighs, then strode toward her.

"You came."

Clea nodded. Her knees quivered. She swallowed hard and tried to sound blasé. "So I did."

"I'm glad."

She looked up at him warily, the fervency she heard in those two words making her a bit fearful.

He laughed unevenly and ran a hand through his hair, which looked as if he'd run his hand through it a dozen times before. "It's just that I thought you might've had second thoughts."

"I did," Clea admitted.

Austin took her duffel bag and they walked together down the long corridor toward the parking area.

"But you came anyway."

"Yes."

"Why?"

"I said I would come. So here I am." Her jaw tilted stubbornly, daring him to make something of it.

He smiled, then his face grew grave again. "What about Ken?"

"I told Ken I'd call him Saturday morning."

"So it's still on?" he asked.

"It's still on."

Austin grunted, shifting her bag to his other hand so that it was no longer between them.

"He isn't any happier about this than you are about that," Clea reminded him.

"*He's* not married to you," Austin growled.

Clea didn't reply to that. She had made up her mind to spend this time with Austin getting to know him again, not arguing with him. "Why did you want me to come a day early?"

He had gone down south almost as soon as he'd got her commitment to accompany him, and she hadn't expected to hear from him until she arrived in Los Angeles. But the next night he had called and asked her to come on Monday night instead of Tuesday.

"I thought you might like to see Miles again," he said now. "Meet his wife. We're going to stay with them tonight."

Since Clea thought that had been the plan in the first place, she felt a bit confused. "I thought I'd see him anyway. He lives right on the beach, didn't you say?"

"Yes, but we're not building there."

"Why not?"

"Mediocre sand."

Clea blinked, but decided he must know what he was talking about. "So where are we building it?"

"Up near Ventura."

"Where?"

He hesitated a moment. "An, uh, an island."

"An island?"

He shrugged irritably. "It's got good sand."

"Oh."

He was striding on ahead now, and Clea almost had to run to keep up with his long legs. She had a thousand questions, but before she could ask him any of them he went on, "Did you eat dinner?"

"No. There wasn't time. Rosie drove me right to the airport from the Carrutherses'."

"Come on, then. Let's get you something to eat."

Clea followed along willingly, enjoying the southern California breeze in her hair and the warmth of the setting sun on her back. She had expected to feel apprehensive, on her toes the moment she met him again, and oddly enough she didn't. She felt lighter somehow, just slightly elated, though she wasn't quite sure why and didn't want to probe the feeling too deeply. She decided to save her questions about the sand castle expedition for later. Right now she said, "Tell me more about Miles and his wife. Where did they meet?"

It was the right question to ask. Austin couldn't find enough wonderful things to say about his new sister-in-law.

Miles, according to Austin, had married the most marvelous, beautiful, understanding, sweet, kind, lovely woman in the world.

He went on so long that Clea found herself getting decidedly jealous.

"She's a regular paragon, is she?" Clea said as she trailed him past row upon row of parked cars.

"Yes," Austin said quite seriously. "She is. Besides, I owe her."

Clea's brows lifted. She'd never known Austin to admit owing anyone, besides possibly herself for their marriage. "Really?" she asked, her tone skeptical.

"Really." And he proceeded to tell her why, describing his first encounter with her on Miles's front porch, his subsequent friendship with her, and the night he thought he had probably destroyed that friendship forever.

"You gave a nude drawing of her to one of her co-workers?" Clea was aghast.

Austin was obviously still contrite. He raked his fingers through his hair and bent his head, staring at his toes. "Yeah. It was one of a series of sketches that Miles had done. I was pissed off at Miles really, and I wasn't thinking straight." He lifted his eyes and met her gaze as if beseeching her to understand. "I thought it would set him on his ear to have it get out, him being such a saint and all. Instead it damned near wrecked her career."

Clea could hear the pain in his voice. "But it didn't?" she asked hopefully.

"No. Miles saw to that."

"How?"

Austin smiled wryly. "He found me at Aunt Grace's and got me to tell all. He hit me in the mouth." He rubbed his face now thoughtfully after he said it.

"Miles?" It didn't sound like the Miles that Clea remembered.

"He did a lot worse to Slaughter, the guy I gave the pictures to."

"I'd have killed you both."

"Yes," Austin reflected. "You probably would have." He stopped beside an older model black Ferrari and flicked out his key. "Thank God Susan didn't."

"She *must* be a saint," Clea said emphatically.

"Married to Miles, what else could she be?" He grinned, then opened the door and tossed her duffel bag in, then gave her a sweeping bow and waited for her to climb in the car.

Clea did. The car suited Austin. She hadn't known what he was driving these days. When they had been married—really married—he had driven an old Karmann Ghia that he had found in a junkyard and had brought home, it seemed to Clea, in pieces. When he wasn't trying to make something of his business, he was out in back of married student housing, lying in a puddle of grease and oil underneath the Karmann Ghia, whispering sweet nothings to its drive shaft and its brake drums, and otherwise exhorting it to run.

Eventually it did. It was a tribute to Austin's stamina, perseverance, and dedication. The Ferrari looked equally well loved.

"Mexican suit you?" Austin asked, sliding in behind the wheel. "I know a good place."

"Whatever."

He cocked his head and grinned at her. "God, you're amenable. Is it going to last?"

"As long as we're talking about food, anyway," Clea assured him.

They talked about food and about wines and about good southern California eating places. They talked some more about Miles and his wife and new son. They talked about Clea's restoration work. In short, they talked about anything and everything that wouldn't provoke a confrontation or upset the precariousness of the situation. And the dinner came off perfectly marvelously.

If they could only manage it for the next three days, Clea thought, everything would be fine.

Or would it? If it came off perfectly fine, where would she be then?

What would she do then?

She gave herself a little shake. Now was not the time to think about that.

MILES AND SUSAN CAVANAUGH lived in one half of a duplex right on the beach. They were sitting on the porch in canvas chairs, Susan rocking a tiny blue-wrapped bundle and Miles conversing with a tall, spare man in a sport shirt and black slacks, when they arrived.

Miles jumped to his feet, grinning from ear to ear, when Clea and Austin came up The Strand. "Clea?" He sounded as if he really didn't believe it.

She smiled back at him, a lump lodging in her throat as she wondered how she could have gone so many years without seeing him. "Hello, Miles. Yes, it's really me."

But she'd scarcely got the words out before she was enveloped in a bear hug that left her breathless. And even when he'd loosened his grip on her, he still kept an arm looped almost protectively around her shoulders. "I want you to meet some people," he said. "My wife, Susan." The pride and love he felt fairly sang in his voice as he introduced her to the slender dark-haired woman who eased one hand out from beneath the child she cradled against her and held it out.

Clea shook it, her earlier jealousy vanishing under the brunt of Susan's smiling welcome. "Hi," she said softly.

"I'm so glad to meet you," Susan said. She shook her head at Austin. "He's been keeping you from me, you know."

Clea felt herself flush and was glad it was now almost dark enough to make anything anyone saw look like reflected sunset. "He . . . well . . . it's been a bit of a shock."

"I can imagine," Susan said dryly.

"And this is Patrick." Miles gestured at the bundle in his wife's arms.

Austin reached out and pulled the receiving blanket away from his nephew's face. "See?" he pointed out proudly. "Doesn't he look like me?"

Clea looked at the baby, most of his features obscured by the dim twilight. "He might have your nose," she ventured.

Miles groaned. "God forbid." Then he turned her to meet the other man. "Clea, this is Father Jack Morrisey. He was everything to me my father never was."

And that, Clea was sure, said it all. Miles had been no more fortunate in his dealings with his father than Austin had, though for different reasons. The senior Cavanaugh had decreed that Miles was going to be a priest, and when that hadn't worked out, his second son had come to mean as little to him as his third. She was glad Miles had found someone to fill the role for him that her own father had for Austin. At least until the divorce.

She pulled back from that thought instinctively. She smiled instead at Jack Morrisey. "I'm pleased to meet you," she said.

"Come sit down," Susan invited. "Austin, you put Clea's bag in Patrick's bedroom. Then get her a beer. Get one for yourself while you're at it." She smiled up cheekily at him.

Austin grinned at her. "Sure thing." And he bounded up the stairs and disappeared into the apartment.

Everyone else settled back down on the porch, Miles giving Clea his chair and perching sideways on the railing, his back against one of the end pillars, his knees bent. Clea sank into the canvas chair, beginning to relax.

Moments later Austin reappeared carrying two beer bottles. He handed one to Clea and kept the other for himself. Then he sat down on the porch and leaned his head back against Clea's knees, and all her relaxation ceased. She sat up straight, her whole body stiffening in response to the touch of his hair against her kneecaps, the firm press of his shoulders against her calves. But Austin didn't even turn around to see if she minded. He just asked Jack Morrisey a question, and Jack answered, and then Miles got into the discussion, and, ignored, Clea once more began to relax.

She had been afraid that Miles would ask a lot of unanswerable questions about their marriage, had been afraid that Austin would presume too much. But her fears seemed to have come to naught. Whatever questions lurked in Miles's mind, they lurked there silently. He and Susan had made her feel welcome without focusing deliberately on her. She blessed them both for that.

Before long Susan carried Patrick into the house to put him to bed. Then she returned, offering more beers. All the men took one. Clea declined.

Austin tilted his head back against her knees to gaze up at her. "You sure? Can I get you something else instead?"

She shook her head. "No. I'm fine." It was all she could do not to reach out and stroke the silky hair that rested against her legs. She was feeling muzzily marvelous as it was, just sitting there in the cool darkness, listening to Austin and his brother trade anecdotes and barbs the way she had so many times long ago. It made her feel warm and comfortable and secure, the way she had as a child. The way she would if she were still Austin's wife.

The thought crept into her heart and mind before she could stop it. It teased her, tormented her, tempted her. And she couldn't fight it off. Not entirely. Especially as the evening wore on and they were joined by more friends of Miles and Susan—the neighbor who owned the duplex, whose name was Chase Whitelaw, and two other couples, Brendan and Cassie Craig and Griff and Lainie Tucker.

More beers and more laughter arrived with them. The porch got more and more crowded. There weren't enough chairs to go around, and Clea got up to offer hers to Lainie Tucker who was extremely pregnant.

"Are you sure?" But Lainie looked grateful for the offer, and at Clea's nod, she readily sat down.

Austin had shoved himself over against the stucco wall of the apartment when Clea got up, and as she looked around for another place to sit, she felt him grab her hand and haul her down onto his lap.

"Austin!"

His arms tightened more firmly around her. "I don't bite," he murmured into her ear.

He didn't need to. He was lethal just holding her. "Really, I—"

"Come on, Clea," he coaxed softly. "What can I do with damned near a dozen people on top of us?"

She didn't answer that. She remembered quite well times eight years ago when he'd not been at all circumspect.

"Please?" he added. "You wouldn't embarrass me in front of all these people, would you?"

Clea turned her head and looked directly into the eyes that were a mere inch from her own. They were silvery blue, like a moonlit sea, warm and sincere and deep enough to drown in. She scowled at him. One of his hands started smoothing slowly across one of hers. She wondered who would embarrass whom.

"You'll have to stop that then," she said.

His hand stilled, but the gentle smile on his face mirrored his satisfaction. Clea leaned back in his arms and tried to pretend it didn't make any difference at all.

It made all the difference in the world.

A few square inches of contact between her kneecaps and his scalp were nothing compared to the feel of the hard warmth of his lap beneath her, the strong arms that drew her back against his chest, the gentle heat of his breath as it tickled her ear.

She could barely make herself concentrate when Jack Morrisey turned to her and asked, "I know Austin is building castles these days, but what do you do?"

"I do restoration and renovation work," Clea told him, and, because he was genuinely interested, she went on to tell him a bit about the Carruthers place and some others that she'd done.

"In San Francisco, you say?"

"Yes."

"Whereabouts?"

She told him, explaining that she'd just bought a house.

He was smiling at her, teeth glinting whitely in the dark. "We're practically neighbors, then. I'm the new pastor at St. Adelbert's."

Clea knew it. He was right. They were less than a mile apart.

"You'll have to drop by and take a look at our place," Jack said. "Talk about potential renovation projects."

They spent the next few minutes talking about what restoring St. Adelbert's would entail. Clea offered suggestions, Jack asked questions. He was helping her immensely, had he but known it. He was managing to keep her mind off the sensations Austin was creating as he held her so close.

"You really ought to come over and take a look at it one day," Jack said. "If we could come up with some money, maybe you could even put some of those good ideas into practice."

"I'd like that," Clea told him.

"What sort of structure?" Austin asked. Clea had been aware that he'd been following the conversation. And now he got into it in earnest, his architect's interest coming to the fore as he listened to Jack's answer. She could feel vibrations of excitement and interest emanating from him. She could feel her own.

So far after her museum work, she'd done mostly private dwellings. Wouldn't she love to get her hands on a church! To restore a public building that so many more people could see and contemplate. And, she admitted honestly, to have her work on display for that many more people to appreciate.

Austin's interest seemed to equal hers. The two of them plagued Jack with questions for the rest of his visit, and when he finally got up to go, he told them both, "Drop over anytime. I'll be happy to show you around."

"You should," Austin said to her later when they had said good-night to Miles and Susan's departing friends and were going into the apartment.

"Maybe I will." God knew it was tempting. But even more tempting was to suggest that Austin look at it with her. She knew the old church interested him, knew they would work well together on it if they were ever given the chance, knew...knew that she should stop thinking this way right now.

She turned away from him and said to Miles and Susan, "I'm really bushed. If you don't mind, I think I'll turn in."

"Be our guest," Susan said. The baby started to whimper in their room and she headed for the door. "Austin can show you where. Clean towels in the hall closet. Help yourself."

"Me, too, if you don't mind," Austin said to her. Then he turned to Clea. "Come on."

Clea gave Susan a grateful smile and a little wave, then followed Austin down the short hall to the door he opened. "Thank you," she said and went in, then turned around to discover that the door was closing and he was right behind her.

"I'm bushed too," he said easily as he began to unbutton his polo shirt.

Clea stared—first at him, then wildly around the room. It was clearly Patrick's room. There was a crib in one corner, which he wasn't going to be sleeping in, Susan had assured her earlier, pointing out the portable crib set up in the living room. Also she spotted a chest of drawers and a changing table. Less prominently, but now very obviously, she spotted a folded up futon. One futon. Her eyes zeroed back in on Austin.

"Just a minute," she said.

His hands paused only momentarily before easing the shirt over his head. When he reappeared one blond brow hiked into the fringe of tousled hair on his forehead. "Hmm?"

"I said I'd build a sand castle with you, Austin. I never said I'd go to bed with you."

"I know that," he said bluntly. "You've made it all too clear." His accusing gaze nailed her where she stood. "But I think you've seen my manly chest before, and I'd rather undress in here than in the living room with Susan."

"You're...not sleeping here, though," she ventured, her cheeks still warm.

"It isn't that I wouldn't like to," he said pointedly, "but no, I'm not. I'll make do with the futon in the living room. Me and Patrick."

"Er...good." She found his willingness to accommodate astonishing. But he met her hard, narrow-eyed stare with equanimity. Finally she shrugged. "Just overly suspicious, I guess."

Or overly susceptible. He was standing there bare from the waist up, the dusting of golden hair on his chest drawing her eyes, making her palms damp and her mouth dry.

Clea, whose mind had been plagued by second thoughts for days, had them again. A serious case of them this time. How was she going to spend three days in the company of this man without succumbing to him again?

Miles tapped on the door. "I'm through. Whoever wants can use the bathroom next."

Austin gestured toward the door. "Be my guest."

"I can wait."

"No. I'll go last. It'll give Susan a chance to get Patrick settled in his bed before I go out there."

So Clea went first, taking her time, trying to get back her equilibrium, trying to remind herself that all this was just in the manner of a test. It might not be her future. Chances were, in fact, that it wouldn't be.

She came back to the bedroom to find that Austin had rolled out the futon for her, had made it up with sheets and a thin cotton blanket, then had fallen asleep in the middle of it.

She stopped dead just inside the door, drinking in the sight of the lean, muscular body sprawled across the light blue blanket. He lay on his stomach, one knee pulled up, the other foot hanging over the edge. One arm was looped around the pillow, hugging it close. His back rose and fell slowly and evenly, and Clea's eyes followed the length of his spine to the spot where it disappeared beneath the denim of the jeans he still wore.

She crossed the room quietly and put her clothes away in her duffel bag, then pulled her seersucker robe more closely around her and thought about what to do next. Susan was still in the living room crooning softly to Patrick. There was no going out there, unless she wanted to disrupt mother and son. So her options were limited. Indeed, as far as she could see, she had only one.

She shut off the light and lay down gingerly next to him. She wasn't planning on staying. No, sir. But she wasn't going to stand there while he took over the bed either. She would simply lie there quietly and wait until Susan had got Patrick back to sleep. Then she would go into the living room.

As a theoretical plan, it was commendable in the extreme. In actual fact, Clea had never been less comfortable in her life. Nor more aware. She could hear every breath he took. Every millimeter he moved seemed to vibrate through her body, and the light breeze from the open window carried the hint of citrusy soap to her nose.

She lay flat, folded her hands below her breasts and tried to will herself into a beatific trance. It was impossible. Everything was impossible except remembering the times that she had lain beside him before.

She remembered the first night of their marriage, the first night they had shared a bed. She remembered how she had marveled at the beauty of this man, at his strength, his gentleness, his care. He had been a miracle to her. And she had told herself then that even one night with him would be enough, that she should never expect anything that perfect to last.

She remembered the last night they'd shared, too—the last night before his agreed-upon departure, the night before their legal separation began. Austin had started to make love with her almost cavalierly, saying, "One for the road," only to lose control almost immediately and take her with an urgency and a desperation that made a lie of the lightness of his words.

Oh, yes, she remembered. Remembered all too well. Remembered the joys, remembered the tears, remembered the laughter, and the pain. She remembered all of it.

And she lay there listening to the soft soughing of his breathing until at last she saw the night light go out in the living room and heard Susan's footsteps pad softly back to the bedroom she shared with her husband. Then, with utmost caution, Clea eased herself off the futon and out of the room.

It wasn't as simple to ease the memories out of her mind.

"I'M SORRY ABOUT LAST NIGHT. Falling asleep and all." Austin apologized when he came dripping in the door from an early-morning swim.

Clea, who had got up while he was out and was sharing breakfast with Susan and Miles, shook her head. "Don't worry about it. I just came out here as soon as Susan had got Patrick settled down."

"It couldn't have been very pleasant. Patrick's a noisy roommate."

"It was fine." Better than lying awake all night beside him, wrapped in memories. That she was sure she couldn't have survived. Besides, talking about whether or not she slept with him seemed somehow too intimate for such a public conversation. Miles and Susan were understandably interested, although so far they'd been restraint personified when it came to asking just what was going on between Miles's brother and his not-so-ex wife.

"So," she said briskly, rubbing her hands together. "Just let me help Miles with the dishes and we can get going."

It turned out to be far more of a project that she had envisioned. They didn't take the Ferrari, first of all. Austin, grinning, had shaken his head. "No way," he'd said and had led her instead to a pickup in Miles's garage that had seen about as many miles as her own.

"This?" Clea asked, doubtful.

"This. Hop in," he invited, and bemused, Clea had done just that. It reminded her once more of the days of their marriage, when the Karmann Ghia was finally running, and he would appear unannounced just when she was getting off her shift at the UCB library and spirit her off down unknown roads to some unlikely destination. He'd sung exuberantly and off-key then, the same way he was singing now. And like now, he'd exhorted her to join in.

"I don't know the words," she protested. Song lyrics weren't her forte.

"So hum," Austin commanded, and he hummed, too, because he'd forgotten them as well.

They hummed their way all the way up the coast to Ventura, Austin's lighthearted conversation making her smile between songs. And it wasn't until they pulled into the marina that Clea remembered she had piles of questions to ask.

But before she could start, Austin parked the truck. "Come on," he said. "We've gotta load my gear."

"Gear?"

"To build the castle," he explained patiently, jerking his head toward the back of the truck.

Clea turned and stared. She'd noticed it before, of course, but she'd just thought it was some of his construction stuff left over from a contracting job. All that was to build a sand castle? Good grief.

Her eyes swiveled to look at Austin again, expecting he would be laughing at her. But he wasn't. He was obviously perfectly serious. In fact he was starting to unload the first bit.

Clea hadn't paid any attention to any of it heretofore. She paid close attention now.

There were four wooden forms, sixty five-gallon buckets—she counted them in disbelief—a 55-gallon casting bucket, a seven-gallon casting bucket, several shovels, ceramic and plaster sculpting tools, a portable ice box, two sleeping bags and a tent.

A tent?

"What do we need a tent for?"

He was hauling one of the forms out of the truck. "To sleep in, of course."

"But—"

But she was talking to his back. He was already halfway down the ramp to the dock where two young men were readying an old Navy U-boat. She followed him quickly.

"We're going to sleep in the tent?" she demanded when he came back past her.

"Unless you want to sleep on the beach. But," he said over his shoulder, "it gets pretty cool out there."

He grabbed another form and started back, meeting her coming the other way. "Listen, Clea," he said on his way past her. "It would help a lot if you would carry something if you're gonna follow me around."

Clea stared after him, flatfooted, hands on her hips. A tent, huh? She took a deep breath, then reminded herself that he hadn't lied to her. He was just being selective with the truth.

And maybe she wouldn't even have to share his tent. If this was a contest, there would be other contestants. That meant other people and presumably other tents.

He was coming back up again for another load. "It's going to take us an hour at least to get all this loaded," he said, "especially if you watch."

She stopped watching and began to help. It was what she had come for, after all. And despite her misgivings, the notion of the island and the boat ride intrigued her, seeing Austin at work intrigued her. Besides, when Clea made a commitment she kept it. When she made a promise, she followed through.

She also, in the interests of self-preservation, asked him a lot of questions.

"What kind of contest is this? How many competitors?"

"It's run by a magazine. I don't know how many."

"Do they all spend three days?"

"They can spend as long as they want."

"Will they all spend three days?"

"Some of 'em. Some of 'em maybe more." They had most of the heavy stuff loaded now. Only the buckets and tools were left.

"Are they good?"

"A few."

"Better than you?"

He grinned. "I hope not. There," he said, wiping his hands on his cutoffs and grinning at her. "That's the last of it. Let's split."

Clea scanned the horizon. "Where are we going?"

"There." He pointed out toward one of the Channel Islands.

"How on earth did they pick that?"

"I picked it. It has good sand." He shoved the sleeping bags below with his toe.

They let Austin pick the spot for the contest? "Will there be room enough for everyone?"

"Of course. Cast off for me, will you?" He was fiddling with the engine now, getting it to sputter and cough, then roar to life.

The sudden throb of the boat beneath her feet made her smile, made her glad she came. Clea cast off.

Two and a half hours later she discovered the answer to the one question she'd forgotten to ask.

There was no one else on the island.

Chapter Nine

The way Austin figured it, he was damned if he did and damned if he didn't. So he hadn't.

Of course, if she'd asked him if it would be just the two of them on the island for three days, he'd have told her. But Clea hadn't asked. And Austin couldn't see any sense in jeopardizing her agreement to come in the first place by volunteering the information. There were already enough obstacles in the way of their reunion without creating more while she could still back out.

She couldn't back out now. Not unless she wanted to swim twenty-plus miles to shore. She didn't, he could tell. He could also tell she wasn't pleased.

He debated trying to soothe her and decided against it. He hadn't been notoriously successful at smoothing ruffled feathers where Clea was concerned of late. So he thought that perhaps the best idea was to let her alone and hope that distance would remedy what persuasion would not. So he made himself as scarce as possible once he'd put her ashore.

He didn't ask her to help him load everything onto the raft that he would have to ferry into the beach from where he'd anchored the boat in the shelter of the cove. He didn't ask her to help him unload it at the other end. He didn't ask her to help set up the tent, roll out the sleeping bags or fix supper.

Given time, she would come around. He hoped.

But by nine o'clock when he was ready to turn in so he could get up at dawn, she was still sitting on the tiny promontory where she had gone the moment he'd set her ashore.

He'd taken her supper out to her—a plateful of canned spaghetti and meatballs, an apple and a candy bar. She had looked at him, then at it, then at him again. He had given her a hesitant smile.

She didn't return it, but at least she took the plate. He didn't wait around to see what she did with it. She might have wanted it for ammunition, and he didn't want to be anywhere close. He hadn't gone back to collect it either.

Probably he should have, he thought now, standing beside the tent, staring at her dark form hunched on the rock and silhouetted against the last streaks of orange in the almost dark sky. Probably he should have tried talking to her, reasoning with her. God knew what she was thinking. Damn it, why did it have to be like this?

They used to have such a terrific time together. There was no one on earth he would rather be stranded on an island with than Clea. He wanted to tell her so, but he didn't think that right now she'd really want to hear it.

But he had to tell her something. His patience was shot.

"Clea?" he called, walking across the sandy beach toward her. "Clea, aren't you getting cold?"

Her answer was to hunch her shoulders more closely inside the lightweight jacket she wore.

"Clea. It's past nine. I've got to get up at dawn to get started on the pound-up. I want to go to bed."

"Go."

It was the first word she'd spoken to him since she'd surveyed the deserted beach as they arrived.

He couldn't. Not and leave her sitting there like that. Irritated now, he scrambled out on the rocks and sat down next to her. "What do you want me to say?"

She turned and gave him a look that was quite discernibly scathing even in the dark. "Say? How about the truth, Austin? I thought you were big on that."

"I never lied to you!"

"No, but—"

"All right, I didn't say we'd be alone. But you didn't ask."

"I didn't imagine I had to. You said it was a contest, for heaven's sake. A contest implies other contestants."

"In this one we compete through photographs."

"Photographs?"

"Yeah. We pick a spot, we build the castle or whatever, photograph it, then submit the photos. That way we can go wherever we like, build whatever we like, and not get in each other's way."

"And wherever you liked was a deserted island?"

"Because of the sand," he explained. "I already told you, it's got great sand."

"Great sand?" Clea scoffed, eyeing him narrowly.

"Yeah, great sand. It's not all alike you know. The stuff where Miles lives is mediocre at best."

"And the only good sand is out here?"

"No, not the only. There's a beach in British Columbia at White Rock where the sand is terrific. I've no doubt it's being well used, too. Lots of people know about it. And there's one area in Seal Beach. It's not exactly a secret either. There are others with lesser quality. I can enumerate them in descending order of quality if you want me to."

She was looking at him carefully, the cool night wind whipping the hair across her face. "You're serious," she ventured finally.

"Yeah, I am. I was coming here anyway. I found this place in the spring when I wanted to get away for a while. It's got incredible sand, packs beautifully, not the least bit coarse or grainy. The best sand is dredged sand. But this . . . Look." He scrambled down off the rocks and grabbed two handfuls of wet sand, then came back, packing it together with his hands. "See, even like this it holds together fantastically. And if I get it tamped down, it's amazing the detail I can— What are you laughing about? What'd I do now?"

"Nothing," Clea said, shaking her head. "I've just been sitting here thinking this was all a big trick. Another Austin Cavanaugh manipulation."

He sighed. "So I blew it?"

"No," she said slowly. "No, you didn't. But you could have told me. Prepared me."

"I was afraid you wouldn't come if you knew." He shifted around so he could see her face. She didn't look angry anymore, but he couldn't discern her feelings either. "You wouldn't have, would you?"

Clea sighed. "Probably not."

"That's why I didn't say anything. It's just that I wanted you to come along so bad—"

Clea touched his lips, silencing him. Her smile was rueful. "All right. I believe you. Now," she said getting to her feet and stretching languidly, "if you're really getting up at dawn I suppose we'd better go to sleep."

She clambered down off the rocks and headed straight for the tent he had pitched near the overhang.

He hurried after her, suddenly afraid that they might have another minor skirmish over her having to share a tent with him. He tried to forestall it by offering, "I could sleep on the boat."

She paused at the flap of the tent. "Do you want to?"

"Hell, no." He grinned.

"Then sleep here," she said simply. "I've slept beside you before. I can do it again."

"But last night—"

"Last night I hadn't come to terms with things yet," Clea said. She crawled into the tent and snuggled down into one of the sleeping bags.

He crawled in after her, looking at her doubtfully. "And now you have?"

"Yes." She tucked her hands under her head and closed her eyes.

He stared at her. *Yes?* A simple straightforward word. Clear-cut and concise. And he hadn't the foggiest notion what she meant by it or whether he ought to be glad about it or not.

AUSTIN WASN'T THERE when she woke up.

She wasn't surprised.

It was, according to her watch, just past five-thirty in the morning, but at the height of summer he'd probably already had an hour or more of visibility. He was taking advantage of it.

And he hadn't taken advantage of her.

She hadn't gone to sleep right away, even though she'd allowed him to think she had. And she had heard him shifting around restlessly as he undressed, then slipped into the bag next to her. She had heard him sigh and thump his pillow. She'd been minutely aware of every move he made, every breath he took. And she would have known if he had so much as laid a finger on her.

He hadn't. Not, she was sure, because he hadn't wanted to. But because, for once, it seemed, he was willing to give her space. Maybe, she thought, he had done some growing up. Maybe he wasn't quite so consumed only with his own goals now. Maybe he had learned what loving really meant.

She lay back in her sleeping bag and folded her hands under her head, smiling slightly, glad now that she hadn't kicked up an enormous fuss over her discovery that they would be alone on the island. It had been a shock, granted. Her immediate reaction was that he had contrived the whole thing just to get her alone. Obviously he hadn't.

"Good sand," she muttered, shaking her head. Only Austin could come up with a reason like that. It was so unlikely that you had to believe it.

"Well, let's see how you're doing with this good sand," she said and scrambled out of her sleeping bag, shivering in the cool morning air. Tugging on a sweatshirt over her T-shirt, she unzipped the tent opening and poked her head out to see where Austin was.

He was walking up from the water, a plastic bucket filled with sea water in each hand. As she watched, he carried them to the spot he had chosen the night before as the building site, and he pyramided them on top of others that he'd already brought. Then, without even glancing at the tent, he turned and headed back for another pair. He was wearing only a pair of faded red cotton swim trunks like lifeguards wore, and the early morning sun made his hair gleam golden and his tan look bronze. It was a treat just to look at him, to feast her eyes on his muscular body and to enjoy his loose-limbed gait. But it made her heart beat faster and her legs feel trembly. So she crawled quickly out of the tent, ran her comb through her hair, and went down the beach to help him.

He'd scooped out two more buckets full of water and was just straightening up with them in his hands when he spotted her coming toward him.

"Hi." She gave him a bright smile. "Want some help?" She held out a hand to take one of them from him.

"Hi." His smile was warm and boyish. "You're up early."

"Well, I came to help." She held out her hand again.

He shook his head. "No thanks. I'm balanced."

"I'll get my own then," Clea said.

"They're pretty heavy."

It was the understatement of the year. Clea got a bucket and waded into the chilly ocean far enough to scoop it full of water. When it was, she just managed to stagger back to the shore with it. She set it on the sand, then picked up another and contemplated filling it, then trying to carry them both. A daunting prospect.

Austin had stacked the previous two and was coming back for another load. Clea looked with new appreciation at the muscles in his arms. "You're right. How much do they weigh?"

"About forty pounds apiece, full," he said cheerfully, filling a bucket, then picking up the one she had filled with his other hand and marching back up the beach.

Clea watched him go. Obviously she wasn't going to be much help carrying. "I'll fill them," she called after him, and he yelled back.

"Thanks."

It was a matter of teamwork after that. Clea dipped and filled, managing to get two done and waiting for him on the sand between each of the trips Austin made to the building site.

By the time they were done, she was already sweating and ready for a break. "Swim?" she asked when he came back to her, offering her a cold drink from the jug.

"Temptress," Austin grumbled. "I don't have time really. I—" But he stopped whatever he'd been going to say, his eyes skating over her with sudden hunger. "Swim," he said firmly, and before she could speak he had grabbed her hand and hauled her into the water.

It was freezing and refreshing. And it lasted all of ten minutes. Then Austin floundered ashore and said, "You can stay in if you want. But I've got to get to work."

And work it was.

"Glorified ditchdigging," Austin called it when she followed him up the beach, drying off as she watched him begin to shovel sand into the first wooden form. He was right.

"Want some help?"

"Absolutely. You don't think I brought you along to cheerlead, do you?"

Clea laughed. "You mean I can't stand here, waving pompoms, yelling 'Hip hip hooray! Shovel away!' while you work?"

"Not on your sweet life," Austin said, grinning. "You want to tamp or shovel?"

"Tamp?"

"Tamp." He held out what looked like an axle with a flat steel disk welded to the bottom of it.

"That looks like a truck axle," Clea said.

"It is."

She took it. If it didn't weigh what the buckets of water weighed, it came close.

"You smash the sand with it," he explained.

"I'll shovel," she said.

So Austin stood inside the largest of the forms, adding buckets of water, and then instructing Clea on where to dump the shovelfuls of sand while he tamped it down. It was, she decided, like making granite by hand.

They'd only been at it fifteen minutes when her palms were beginning to hurt and she was thinking that the calluses she'd developed working on the Carruthers house wouldn't protect her half an hour here. She grimaced and wiped them on her shorts.

"Hey!" Austin sounded horrified. "You don't have gloves."

"No, I—"

"You have to have gloves. Just a sec." He dropped the tamper and loped over to the tent, disappearing inside and coming back moments later with another pair of brown cotton yard gloves like his own. "Sorry," he said quickly. "Let me see your hands."

Without giving her a chance to demur, he caught them and held them out. The palms were already red. He touched the pads at the base of her fingers, his touch gentle against incipient soreness. Clea tried not to wince.

Grimacing, he shook his head. "I hope these aren't too late." He slipped first one on, then the other, then looked up. "I really am sorry. I should have realized you wouldn't know. Sand tears up your hands something terrible. Maybe you should quit."

Clea shook her head. "No, I don't want to. Not at all."

And the fact was, she didn't.

It was tedious, of course. Shoveling and tamping, dumping water, then sand, then more tamping. Her muscles ached, and she acknowledged quickly that she wasn't in near the shape she'd fondly thought she was in. But she still liked it—liked it because as the sun rose higher, it warmed her face, liked it because she felt a growing sense of companionship and sharing. It reminded her of the times they had made forts in the woods behind his father's house and had dug tunnels at her parents'. It called to mind the warm summer nights when they had sat companionably in the hideout they'd built in the fork of the old oak tree.

Back then they'd talked of plans, of dreams, of destinies. And now she learned what had become of those childhood dreams. As they talked, she learned more about this man and what he had done in the years since she had seen him.

"Basically," she summed up after they had been shoveling, tamping and talking for quite a while, "you've done it all."

Austin paused, leaning on the tamper, a faint grin lifting one corner of his mouth. "I hope not."

Clea rested on the shovel. "Well, everything you said you'd do, you did."

"I never got my dad to come around."

She searched his eyes for the pain she always remembered seeing there, but all she saw was the matter-of-fact acceptance that she heard in his voice. "Are you still trying?"

He smacked the tamper down hard on the loose sand, packing it tight. "No. It isn't worth it."

"Was all the rest worth it?"

He stopped once more and got a faraway look in his eyes. "I don't know. I know it isn't everything," he said slowly at last. His gaze moved back across the water and settled on her. "I think I may have missed something." His blue eyes caressed her. "Someone," he corrected softly.

There was no doubt whom he meant.

When they'd filled the first form, they took a break, drinking cans of Coke that Austin ferreted out of the portable icebox, and eating sandwiches that Susan had packed for them.

"Bless Susan," Clea said fervently, taking a bite and washing it down with a swig of Coke.

"Amen," Austin concurred. "She's a great lady."

"I agree. I liked her a lot."

He was sprawled on the sand, leaning against the cliff wall, the can of Coke balanced on his belly, and he looked at her out of hooded eyes. "She liked you, too. Everyone did."

Clea smiled. "The feeling was mutual. Miles has nice friends."

"Yeah. I find myself spending quite a bit of time there. Brendan Craig is as big a flake as I am."

Clea laughed. "That I doubt."

Austin tried to look offended. "He is," he insisted. "Next time we go down, I'll get him to demonstrate."

Clea shook her head, still laughing. *Next time.* God, how tempting that thought was. She rarely spent much time in the company of congenial friends. Usually she worked or went out with Ken. Ken was an only child and basically a loner. They saw his family frequently, but that was that. And while Clea saw Rosie socially and Devin socially, naturally she never saw them together. Most of her college friends, too, had dropped out of her life, getting married and moving to Denver or Philadelphia or L.A. or New York, wherever their jobs took them.

She knew she should devote more of her life to developing a circle of friends, but she never seemed to take the time. When she was married to Austin, she had got friends by the dozen by default. Austin knew everyone, liked everyone and welcomed everyone into his world. He was as generous with his friends as he was with his time or his money. She was grateful that he'd shared Miles, Susan and their friends with her. But it also made her a bit wistful.

She had enjoyed the evening enormously, had felt a comradeship with them all, especially Jack Morrisey and Susan, who seemed to understand the Cavanaugh psyche better than anyone else. And, having had a taste of it, she realized now that, like Austin, she'd been missing something in her life.

"Be nice to do that again sometime," Austin ventured now. He lifted the Coke can and sipped it, his eyes meeting hers for a moment.

It would be wonderful, Clea thought. But...

"Shouldn't we get back to work?" she asked.

Austin tipped his head back and poured the last of the Coke down his throat. "Slave driver."

But he already had the second form in place on top of the first and was shoveling in sand by the time Clea had disposed of the cans and sandwich wrappers and had returned to help.

"I'll shovel this time," he told her. "You tamp for a bit."

Doubtful, Clea climbed onto the first two-foot-high layer of sand and stood in the form as he directed her. She took hold of the axle and tamped.

"Huh-uh." Austin shook his head, grinning at her. "Slam it down."

"Slam it?" She gave it an experimental thump.

"Better. Again."

She whacked it down harder, the impact stinging her hands right through the gloves.

"Yeah, like that. Great outlet for your aggressions." He grinned. "We should have had you doing this yesterday when you were mad at me."

Clea flushed, but knew he couldn't tell. "I said I overreacted."

"Hey!" Austin reached up and wrapped an arm around her, bending her down toward him and planting a kiss on her cheek. "You weren't imagining me thinking anything I hadn't thought. Believe me."

Nor anything she hadn't thought herself.

They worked steadily on through the afternoon, fetching more water when they needed it, adding forms as they filled them, trading places periodically until Austin had to do all the shoveling because they were now up to the height of his head. Clea stood in the last form, tamping still, working her way right through her third pair of gloves.

The sun had moved, no longer rising slowly above the California coast, no longer even beating down overhead. When it had been, Austin had made another quick trip into the tent and emerged to toss Clea a hat and to slap a similar one on his head. But by the time they had all four forms filled, the sun had slid considerably down toward the Pacific horizon, and Clea, slamming the tamper down one last time, felt as if she were standing atop a mountain of their own making.

"Now the barrel," Austin said. "I'll bring it up to you. You put it over your head."

"What?" She leaned on the tamper, exhausted, and stared down at him.

"Here." He already had a hold on it and was carefully climbing up each two-foot step. There were four of them now, the last one only three feet square, and it was a bit of a dance getting the two of them and the barrel on top of it at once.

"Stand in the middle," Austin instructed. She did, and he lifted the open-ended barrel, dropping it over her head and settling it down into the top layer of dry sand. Then he poured water on it to seal it to the layer beneath.

"Now what?" Clea was up to the bottom of her breasts in the barrel.

"Tamp," Austin said, handing her up another bucket of water and more sand.

She should have guessed. Clea tamped. And tamped. Austin shoveled. And shoveled.

As the level of the sand rose, so rose Clea, and by the time the sun was beginning to drop into the sea, she was almost twelve feet in the air, with nothing to hang on to but a thirty-pound truck axle and the last dregs of her sanity.

"I'm going to fall."

"You're not."

"Austin, I am. I feel like a bird on a perch."

"We're up to the last bucket."

"There's more?"

"One. Not a big one."

At this point Clea thought bigger would've been better. The last open-ended bucket he handed her was a foot and a half deep and less than a foot in diameter. "I'm not supposed to get in this one, am I?" she joked.

"As a matter of fact, you are."

"What!"

"Set it down in the center and stand in it."

"I can't even see the center anymore, much less stand in it!"

"Hang on."

It was a figurative, not literal command, for there was absolutely nothing to hang on to. Clea heard, rather than saw him scramble back down the forms, then a few minutes later he reappeared with a flashlight.

"So, you scoop sand, I tamp and God holds the flashlight?" she asked sarcastically, glaring at him in its yellowish gleam.

Austin shook his head wordlessly, produced a roll of tape from the back pocket of his trunks and proceeded to tape the flashlight to his head, wrapping it round and round with layers of tape. Clea just stared.

"Now can you see the center?" he asked when he had the light taped to his head and turned on.

"Yes, but—"

"Then put the bucket there and stand in it."

"And then what?"

"Then we fill it with sand."

"You're serious?"

He just stared at her. It was the same look he had given her when they were nine and ten and he had jumped off the bridge into the river and had then expected her to.

Sighing deeply, Clea put the bucket in the center and stood in it. It fit like Cinderella's slipper, not a millimeter to spare.

"Now you know why I asked you along," Austin teased, though Clea heard weariness threading his voice.

"Because your feet were too big." But there was no irritation in her tone now. She had gone beyond that into the realm of amazement at what he was willing to do to build his castle.

"Of course." He hopped carefully back down the forms and shoveled several clumps of sand up to the form two levels below her. Then he climbed back up and passed it up to her one handful at a time. "Almost done," he encouraged when she sighed again. "Just drop this in and tamp it down."

Clea did, but she wobbled as she did so, her legs beginning to tire. And the higher she got, the wobblier she felt. "I— Austin!"

The world tilted suddenly, and she grabbed for his head with both hands at the same instant he latched onto her trembling legs. His face was pressed against her knees, his fingers digging into her thighs, hanging on for dear life. Her dear life, Clea thought, heart thundering.

"You all right? You okay now?" he muttered, not moving.

She took a steadying breath. "Y-yes, but I dropped the axle."

"I'll get it." He started to move.

"No! No," she said more softly the second time. "Not yet. Don't let go." Her teeth were chattering. "Please, don't let me go."

She heard him chuckle, his forehead pressing on her thighs, his breath warm against her legs. "I never thought you'd say that to me again."

"All a matter of circumstances," she said shakily. She loosened her grip on his head fractionally and straightened slightly, taking deep, even breaths in an effort to calm herself.

"How far are you from the top?"

"I'm *on* the top," she reminded him testily.

"I mean from the rim of the bucket."

She explored the bucket cautiously with one foot, sliding it up the side till her toe skated along the edge. "Maybe eight inches."

"So, only half a foot more. That's not bad, is it?"

"Optimist. It's awful," Clea replied promptly.

"But you can do it?" He was leaving her an out. He hadn't let go of her yet. He wouldn't, she knew, if she told him not to. He never had when she'd demanded support. But she'd rarely demanded it, preferring instead to carry her own weight, to be an equal partner.

"Give me the sand," she said.

Carefully he released her. Then at her murmured "Okay," he began to move down again. The light taped on his forehead dipped and arced crazily as he bent for another chunk of sand and handed it up to her. Everything was fine whenever he was standing straight and holding her legs lightly while she tamped the sand down. But when he moved, the play of light disconcerted her.

Two more handfuls tamped and she traced the distance to the rim again. Maybe five inches. She sucked in her breath. He gave her another handful. And another.

At last she said, "There!"

She felt Austin's hand patting around her feet, which were only about two inches below the top of the bucket. "Yes," he said, and with the hiss of breath that went out with the word he sounded like the little engine that thought it could— and just barely did—make it to end of the line.

"Get me down," Clea said.

"Yes." He flicked off the flashlight, then held out his arms to her.

She squatted down and felt his arms come around her, gathering her close. Then she was lifted carefully down so that she stood on the same layer Austin did, crushed against his sandy, damp body, held in his trembling arms.

She thought she should pull free, but she didn't have the strength to do it. She thought she should say she could manage the rest on her own, but the words wouldn't come. It was too warm, too comfortable, too right just where she was with the rough bristle of Austin's jaw against her cheek, the hard strength of his arms cradling her against him, the steady thrum of his heart palpable through the cotton shirt against her chest.

She didn't know how long they stood there unmoving, the only sounds their breathing and the waves against the shore, the only light the half moon that spilled across the water and, to the west, the twinkling red and white of an airplane headed south.

"We did it," Austin murmured into her hair. "You were wonderful."

Clea smiled. "What I am is beat. If I don't get down now, I'll go to sleep right here, standing up like a horse."

"We can't have that, can we?" Austin said softly. He loosened his hold on her slightly, but kept one arm around her as they climbed down form by form. And even when they were on the ground again, he didn't relinquish his hold.

Clea looked back at the tower they had spent the day making and wished she could see the product of their efforts. The moon shed too little light to give her a real sense of what they had done. But she didn't need the moon to tell her they had worked hard. Her muscles—many she'd never met before today—and her hands—which had forgiven her turpentine and stripper and putty and a thousand atrocities, but which might never forgive her this—could attest to that.

But they had built more than a sandcastle tower. They had built the beginning of a new relationship. They had worked together. They had shared, they had laughed, they had talked, and once, briefly, they had kissed.

"Bed," she muttered before she could think about it further, and she started to stagger off in the general direction of the tent.

"How about a swim first?"

"A swim?" Clea croaked. "You still have the energy for a swim? That's obscene."

"Not the energy," Austin said, "the necessity. I'm gritty, grimy, sweaty, and I'm damned if I want to spend the night in a sleeping bag that feels like a rhinoceros skin."

Clea rubbed a hand down his gritty forearm, then down her own. "You have a point."

"C'mon." He was tugging her down toward the water with one hand, tugging the flashlight tape off his head with the other, muttering swear words every time it pulled on his hair.

"Hold still," Clea commanded, and lifted her hands to work it off carefully for him. He winced and pulled away. She tweaked his nose in the dark. "I said, hold still. You're no better now than you were when you were a kid."

"At some things I am," Austin said, and she could hear the smile in his voice.

"Yeah?" Her doubt was apparent.

He laughed, a low weary laugh, and as she freed his head from the tape at last, he dropped his head to rest against her shoulder. "Yeah. And I'd show you, but I moved eleven tons of sand today. I don't think I can move heaven and earth tonight even if I want to."

"Just as well," Clea said and reached for his hand this time. "Come on."

The water made her hands sting, but she kept them in it anyway, resolutely washing her raw palms until she felt no more grit. Then she sank down and knelt on the bottom, letting the incoming waves wash over her and soothe her.

Austin was right beside her doing the same thing. She dipped her head back and let the surf wash through her hair, then felt his hands threading through it, washing it as well.

And then while her head was still back, he rose slightly and loomed over her, his face obscuring the moonlight as it descended, and he planted a gentle kiss on her forehead. "Come on."

He took her hand, and they stood up together, walking back toward the tent, their fingers laced. "D'you want me to get the flashlight?"

Clea shook her head, mussily happy, almost in a trance so tired was she and so content. "No. Just a towel."

He found two in the dark and handed her one. They dried off quickly, then crawled into the tent and slipped inside their sleeping bags, wordless and exhausted.

Then, just as she was drifting off, she heard, "Clea?" Austin's voice was low, barely audible over the sound of the waves.

"What?"

His hand reached out, seeking hers, and, finding it, wrapped it in his roughly callused one. "You were super today."

"Thanks." She gave his hand a quick squeeze. "You weren't so bad yourself."

"If we can do this, we can do anything, Clea," he said softly.

She knew what "anything" was. "Go to sleep, Austin. We're not going to settle our future tonight."

But when they fell asleep their fingers were still entwined.

Chapter Ten

Gentle fingers touched his cheek. Austin's eyes snapped open. The fingers moved, brushing through the hair just above his ear, then stroked his face.

"Clea?" he whispered.

She was snuggled against him, she in her sleeping bag, he in his. But her head rested on his arm, and her hand continued to play havoc with his hormones. He raised his head slightly to see if she looked as if she meant what it felt like she meant.

She was asleep.

His head fell back and he stared at the roof of the tent, despair mingling with consternation in his mind. Talk about torment! He sighed and shifted away slightly, trying to think cool, indifferent thoughts.

Clea muttered indistinctly and edged next to him again, her hand curving now to fit the contour of his jaw. He turned his head, unable to stop himself, and pressed a kiss into the palm of her hand.

She smiled. Her lips puckered slightly and she sighed softly.

Austin ached.

Not surprising, he told himself. He always ached the day after a pound-up. What could you expect after moving eleven tons of sand? But it wasn't muscle aches that bothered him, and no amount of pretending could convince him that it was.

It was Clea.

He wanted her. Desperately.

He wasn't supposed to. He'd convinced himself as well as her that after all he had done yesterday, he would be far too tired to even contemplate making love. He was wrong.

He might have been too tired to do it, but he certainly hadn't been too tired to contemplate it. He had dreamt about it all night long. He was fantasizing about it now. Wanted it more than ever. Wanted Clea.

And if he woke her?

Yesterday had gone well. They had done exactly what he had hoped they would do—fallen back into the routine of teamwork and intuitive understanding that had made them inseparable for so long. Clea, who had started out apprehensive, had relaxed. She had laughed, she had joked, she hadn't pulled away when he'd held her in his arms. So did he dare risk his progress by taking a giant step forward now?

Yes, his hormones shouted.

No, whispered his common sense.

Clea's hand slid down his neck, traced his collarbone and curled in a fist against his chest. He licked his lips. Then, when she turned her head and he felt her breath teasing the hair under his arm, he bit down hard on the lower one.

Every muscle in his body tensed, resisting. And finally the urge lessened, Clea shifted slightly, and with exquisite care he eased his arm out from beneath her head and sat up. She rolled away from him, curling into a ball and facing the tent, presenting him with her naked back.

The urge came back, he shoved it away. He wanted more than a morning's loving, more than the satisfaction of a physical urge. He wanted Clea back in his life. So he had to walk cautiously, make haste slowly. Watch his step every inch of the way.

He got to his feet and pulled on a pair of trunks and a T-shirt. Then with one last hungry look at Clea, he slipped out of the tent. All his life he had sublimated his desires by throwing himself into his work. One more time wouldn't hurt.

"I STOOD on top of *that*?"

In the morning light it looked like Everest, or at the very least, Pike's Peak. A homemade Pike's Peak jutting upward proudly in the sandy cove. And now that Austin had removed the top two cylindrical forms, last night's perch seemed more precarious than ever. But no more precarious than her relationship with Austin.

She had awakened to find him gone again. And in a way she was glad. She didn't know what she would have done if she had found him still there beside her. What worried her was what she would have liked to have done. She had done it in her dreams last night. And even now, knowing that it hadn't really happened, her foundations were shaken.

Austin was standing atop the fourth form, busy squaring off the cylindrical area that would become the top tower, and when he heard her, he turned and grinned down at her. "Finally decided to get up, huh, Sunshine?" Then without waiting for an answer, he went on, "You did a great job last night. Amazing what you can do if you put your mind to it, isn't it?"

"Amazing what you can do in the dark if you don't know any better," Clea corrected dryly as she tugged a hairbrush through the tumbleweed her hair had become.

He slanted a roguish grin at her. "You always did do well in the dark."

Clea blushed, his remark coming too close to the substance of her dreams. "That's not what I meant."

But he was openly laughing now, and Clea, shaking her head at his incorrigibility, feigned throwing the brush at him. He looked horrified.

"Don't you dare! If you knock my tower off, I'll have to rebuild."

"And God knows we don't want you to have to do that," Clea said fervently. "One day of building is quite enough."

"Amen." Austin concentrated on the rectangle he was carving. "Help yourself to whatever you want for breakfast. I've eaten."

"In a minute."

Right now she was simply intrigued with watching him work.

The sun was relatively low still and hidden behind an early-morning overcast, so Austin had tossed his shirt aside. He wore another pair of faded, disreputable-looking bathing trunks that looked as if they were left over from the several summers he'd spent working as a lifeguard while in college. Clea suspected they probably were. They fit him well. His body had filled out a bit more, his back broader, his muscles more clearly defined. He looked a bit like an aging surfer with his straw-blond hair and dark tan. He probably still drew the girls like flies.

He still drew her.

It struck her forcibly how differently she reacted to Austin than she did to Ken. She couldn't remember ever being overwhelmed by Ken's physical presence. He was like a hearth fire, his warm steadiness beckoning her. Austin was like a lightning bolt, sizzling her where she stood. Shaken, she deliberately looked away now, walking back to the tent and rummaging through the ice box for a carton of juice which she drank as she cut a bagel in two. Physical attraction wasn't enough, she reminded herself. Love was far more than that.

But as the day wore on she found that, like yesterday, far more than simply awareness existed between them. As soon as she had finished breakfast, Austin called her over.

"I didn't just want you along for the donkey work," he told her. "You can sculpt as well."

"I don't know how," she protested.

"So figure it out." He was unrelenting, challenging, and just as obstinately demanding as he had been when they were children. When he thought she should be able to do something, he didn't take no for an answer. "I've got complete faith in you," he told her. "Here." He passed her down a copy of a picture he was using as a guide. "You'll know what to make of this."

Clea recognized it in an instant. "That's not a castle. That's the old Barnett house on Pierce Street." It was a notable San Francisco Victorian. A real beauty whose straight verticals and delicately traced stained-glass windows she had always loved.

"Home of our dreams—that's the subject of the contest," Austin said, his eyes meeting hers. "It's mine."

Mine, too, Clea would have said, except he already knew that.

Together they'd spent plenty of time dreaming about it. Many a weekend in college they'd walked through San Francisco, collecting old houses and talking about how they would fix them up if they owned them. The Barnett house had been Clea's favorite. She had gone on and on about what she would do with it if it were hers, and Austin had always listened indulgently, chipping in now and then with ideas that enhanced her own.

It was their least expensive, most inspiring pastime—besides making love, Clea remembered.

The look on Austin's face told her he was remembering, too.

Waves slapped against the shore and overhead a jet droned. But louder than any of it Clea heard the thrum of the blood in her veins and the surging longing of her heart. Suddenly this house was more than just any old sand castle; it was their shared past that they were remaking together. And, out of it, did Austin hope they might bring a future?

Clea grabbed the tool he was offering and set to work.

Austin had given her the back of the house, which didn't need to be as perfect since the detail wasn't as fine and chances were the judges would be more concerned with the front elevation. But even so he was an exacting taskmaster. He wanted everything done just so—all corners squared, all lines determined with a level.

"How's this?" Clea asked him when she'd finished a particularly tricky bit of panel molding.

He stopped work and came around to see. You'd have thought he was constructing a Gothic cathedral that would endure for centuries, Clea thought watching him with an exasperated fondness while he checked her sculpting with a level before he would let her go on.

"It'll be washed away tomorrow or the next day," she reminded him as he frowned and shaved off a bit more that she hadn't got quite level.

"I know. It's the doing that I like. It's like dancing, really. Or singing. A performing art. The results are secondary." A slash of white grin appeared in his tanned face. "Unless I win the prize, of course."

She peered at him around the conical tower he was finishing up. "What is the prize, by the way?"

"Two weeks in Hawaii for two, and all the sand you can eat. Want to go to Hawaii with me?" He gave her a hopeful look.

Clea just looked back at him, not trusting herself to answer.

Austin continued carving. "Imagine what we could build in Hawaii given two weeks."

Clea rubbed her back. "No, thank you."

"I should've warned you. Was it rougher than you expected?"

"A tad more strenuous," she admitted. "Like creating marble before you sculpt it."

"Yeah." He was concentrating on an intricate bit of carving on the pediment. Then, having got it right, he looked up and grinned at her. "But after that, it's a hell of a lot of fun."

It was. As the day went on and the upper stories of the Barnett house were gradually revealed as Austin carved them out of the sand, Clea was enchanted. The backbreaking bit was over. Now it was time for Austin the artist to come to the fore.

In his way, she realized, Austin was every bit the artist that Miles was. His medium was different, his subject was different, but otherwise they were remarkably alike.

She said so, and Austin raised his head in astonishment.

"Me? Like Miles? You must be kidding."

"No." Clea shook her head. "You're both artists. You both have a vision. And you're both terribly talented."

Austin was still staring, shaking his head in disbelief. "You really think so?"

"Yes," she said, meeting his eyes honestly. "I think so."

Austin looked thoughtful. He went back to sculpting again, frowning in concentration. Then, "He has a good marriage," he said off-handedly.

Clea hadn't had Miles's marriage in mind. "It seems so," she agreed cautiously.

"He did it right."

Clea didn't reply, waiting, holding her breath.

Austin moved on, chewing on his lip as he contemplated first the picture, then the sand before him. "Fell in love, courted—took his own sweet time, of course—then married her. Jack Morrisey married them. Church wedding. All very proper. Formal. No loose ends. No backing out." He rubbed a hand around behind his head, scratching the nape of his neck. "Should we have had a church wedding, Clea?"

"How could we?" she asked him sharply. "You wanted a loose end."

He sighed. "I know." He slapped the sculpting spatula he was using against his hand. "Damn it, Clea, I was just a kid. What did I know?"

"What did either of us know?" Clea murmured, keeping her eyes fixed on the sand.

She heard footsteps, and the next thing she knew he was standing behind her.

"Are you sorry we did it, Clea?" His voice was soft, barely carrying over the sound of the waves.

She pressed her lips together and bowed her head. "No."

Suddenly she felt his lips on her neck. There followed a gentle nip and a quick kiss. "Good," he said. "Keep that in mind."

SHE DID. As the day went on, it was hard not to. She'd never felt so comfortable with anyone else. Austin could make her laugh, could tease her, could finish a sentence that she began, and she could do the same for him. It was eerie how much they thought alike.

But there seemed to be no helping it. They were on the same wavelength.

She felt it when they broke for a midmorning snack and he started talking about her house. No one else would talk about her house, much less rhapsodize about it. Even her parents, who generally supported her every move, had expressed their doubts about her purchase, wondering aloud if she hadn't bitten off more than she could chew. And Ken—well, Ken had been even more vocal.

She'd gone ahead and bought it anyway, of course. She could see the potential, sense the possibilities inherent in the rundown, abandoned wreck. But she'd had a hard time convincing anyone else that she knew what she was doing.

Except, it seemed, Austin. He said quite frankly that he envied her.

"You could buy one and work on it," she told him.

He shook his head. "It wouldn't be the same. Not without you."

It was on the tip of her tongue to offer to let him help her. But she stopped herself. She wasn't sure of him. And the thought of sharing her house with Austin, of working on it with him was almost too tempting for her own good.

"Come on," she said. "Let's go for a swim."

But even the swim didn't break the spell. They were living a Garden of Eden experience, inhabiting a world that belonged just to the two of them in which all cares seemed foreign and all worries vague. They were like children, playing by an enchanted sea, creating their own fairy-tale castle. It was like dreaming, and it was tempting not to wake up.

By dusk they had finished sculpting the towers and the top square forms that day. Then they took another swim and shared a cold supper. The breeze picked up and Austin made a fire, then pulled a bag of marshmallows out of one of his packs.

"Marshmallows? Prepared for all eventualities, aren't you?" Clea teased.

"A regular Boy Scout," Austin agreed, squatting down by the fire and poking a marshmallow on the end of a stick. He handed it to her, then fixed another for himself, settling himself down cross-legged on a blanket and smiling at Clea over the flames.

Enchanted, Clea smiled back.

"Remember the first time we did this?" Austin asked, rotating his marshmallow.

"How could I forget? You and Miles were staying with us while your parents were gone somewhere..."

"...and we begged your parents to let us spend the night in the backyard in the tent."

"...and they did. And then Miles got an asthma attack and had to go inside..."

"...which left you and me in the tent. All alone." Austin's grin was a bright wolfish slash of white in the darkness.

"...and you thought the Muellers' dog barking was a werewolf and almost wet your pants," Clea finished, laughing.

Austin looked offended. "You weren't supposed to remember that."

"I remember everything."

"Do you?" His voice dropped. His eyes met hers, all laughter gone now. He got to his feet and came around to her side of the fire, then dropped down again next to her, looping an arm over her shoulders and pulling her close.

For a moment Clea stiffened, but nothing in her wanted to pull away. Her heart, her emotions, her body all cried out, *Yes*.

"I remember," she sighed and turned her marshmallow above the flames.

"It could be like that again, Clea." His arm tightened around hers.

"Could it?" she whispered hollowly.

"We can make it like that."

She shook her head slowly, confused, scared to hope. "I don't know, Austin," she said softly. "I just don't know."

It was harder to sleep that night. They were less exhausted, more aware of each other, more attuned than ever. When one rolled over, so did the other. When Austin cleared his throat, Clea felt hers tickle. When she sighed, he shifted uneasily.

She wanted his touch and feared it at the same time. She wanted a lifetime love, a real and lasting love. What Austin wanted—what Austin was capable of—she wasn't sure.

HE WAS SURVIVING, but it was getting harder all the time.

And there was a pun for you, Austin thought with an inward groan as he rolled over for the third morning in a row and stared into Clea's sleeping face.

She seemed to sense his gaze for she blinked slowly and opened her eyes. Then her lips parted in a sleepy smile. "Hello there."

"Hello," he croaked. He rolled onto his side and eased himself up on one elbow, wincing at the tightness in his muscles as he did so.

"What's wrong?"

"Occupational hazard." He reached around with the other hand and massaged the stiffness.

"Sore?"

He nodded, then gaped with astonishment as she sat up in one fluid motion and crawled out of her sleeping bag to come around and push him over on his stomach.

"Allow me." And the next thing he knew she was straddling his hips, sitting back against his buttocks, while her fingers began a slow, methodical kneading of his back.

He shivered, groaned, squirmed against the delightful pressure of her hands.

"Is that pain I hear?" she asked him, bending down.

"No," he muttered, his voice muffled by the sleeping bag but even more by desire. "It's ecstasy."

"Ah." It was a knowing sound, an acknowledgement. But she didn't pull away.

Her fingers browsed through the hair at the nape of his neck while her thumbs eased the knots of tension below.

Then her hands slid in unison down the length of his spine, and worked their way slowly back up the muscles along either side. Wherever her fingers touched, his body tingled in response, his nerve endings applauded, tiny hairs stood at attention and begged for more.

His hands clenched into tight fists around the sleeping bag, his chest heaved, and he ached deep within. Now her hands skimmed down his sides, pausing at his waist, and he raised his hips slightly, willing her to slide her hands around to the front to touch him where he needed it the most.

But they stopped there, didn't move. And then her weight shifted. He held his breath, felt hers hot against his back, and then he shivered as she pressed her lips lightly to the nape of his neck.

He groaned, turning beneath her, catching her in his arms and pulling her down full against him, molding her soft curves to the hardness of his. His mouth captured hers, his tongue seeking, finding, asking and, blessedly, answered at last.

It was better than he remembered. Warmer and more wonderful. Or maybe he was simply older and wiser, able finally to appreciate what could have been his years ago if he'd but had the sense to accept it.

Well, God knew, he was accepting it now. Reveling in it. Loving every minute of it. Loving every inch of her. His hands slid down her back, pressing her tightly against him. Their legs tangled, their breath mingled, their hearts thrummed as one.

"Yes," Austin murmured against her lips. "God, yes." Clea pulled back from him just slightly, enough so that when he looked up he could meet her eyes. They were glazed with desire, with longing, and tinged with something else. Anxiety, perhaps?

"Clea?"

Her smile was wistful, weary, worried. One of her hands came up and stroked his cheek softly. Then she lay her head down against his shoulder so that his lips brushed against her hair.

"Clea?" he asked again.

She lifted her head slightly, enough so that she could lay a light kiss on his jaw. "Don't push, Austin."

His hands stilled on her back, felt the gradual slowing of her breathing, acknowledged that the passion he had sensed in her moments before was slipping away, vanishing as quickly as it had surged. But in its place he felt acceptance. Surrender.

Austin smiled and kissed her hair. It was enough.

CLEA COOKED BREAKFAST over a small campfire while Austin started work on the two lower levels of the sand castle. She hummed while she cooked, stopping frequently to watch him work—as often as he stopped work to watch her cook.

Their gazes would lock, they would smile, hearts would somersault. Then Clea would flip a pancake and Austin would sculpt another row of shingles. No words passed between them. No words seemed necessary. There was quiet acceptance in Clea's face, triumphant joy in Austin's.

She cleaned up, then came over to watch him work, offering to help if he could give her some boring bits to work on.

"Sure you wouldn't like to try your hand at something a little more challenging?"

"Certain," Clea responded. "After all, you want to win, don't you?"

"There's winning and there's winning." His look told her that if he lost the contest and regained his wife, he would consider that he'd won indeed.

"Anyway, I don't build, I restore," she told him.

He grinned. "You mean if I muck it up, you'll fix it for me?"

"I'll try." She nodded gamely.

But he didn't muck anything up. He was too good at what he was doing to make mistakes. So Clea had the pleasure of simply watching him until a flock of birds let their curiosity get the better of them, and he enlisted her aid, requesting that she flap her arms at approaching sea gulls.

Clea flapped, feeling silly, but not caring in the least. She could be as outrageous as she wanted to with Austin. It went with the territory. One particularly bold brown sea gull with a white belly reminded her of him. Inquisitive and aggressive, he wouldn't leave the tower alone. "What will happen if he sits on your tower?" Clea wanted to know.

"He won't."

She shooed the bird again, but he fluttered back the moment she stopped. "He might," she said darkly. "And if he does . . . ?"

"Don't ask." Austin scowled, remembering. "One did last month in British Columbia."

"And?"

"And he fell off . . ."

"Good."

". . . And so did the tower."

Clea grimaced. "What'd you do?"

"Cast a new one and took the old one down. It was a bit tricky."

"I'll bet."

"Repairing damage is always tricky," Austin said. "You know that. It's the same in houses."

And in marriages, Clea thought. But she was beginning to hope. Things were getting better.

HE WOULDN'T LET HIMSELF HOPE. Not completely. Not yet. He'd hoped too many times in his life. Raised his expectations. Seen them dashed. He wouldn't do it this time, he told himself. *Couldn't.*

Ha.

He couldn't help it. It felt too good, too right. She was smiling at him. She was humming. She was looking at him with eyes of love.

He shook himself, telling himself to get to the business at hand, to concentrate on the house, to finish it. And then...only then...

In fact he was almost done. Clea was working on the back now, close to the bottom, and all he had left was some delicate porch railing and a particularly tricky window. But he looked forward to them—the railing for its discipline, the window for its challenge. When the sun was lower, if he did it right, the carving should look like the lead outlines on a stained glass window.

"Are you sure you can manage that?" Clea stopped her work and came round to watch him begin on the porch. "I mean, I can see it being done in wood. Devin would have a great time with it. But sand? Won't it defy gravity?"

"Might." Austin spoke through clenched teeth, all his concentration centering now on the delicate carving.

The whole sculpture had ceased being simply sand long ago. It was his dream now. His house with Clea. His future with her. If he could create it here, he could create it in life. He wiped the sweat off his forehead with his shirttail and bent again to his work.

It was close to five when he finished, straightened up and stepped back at last. His dream house existed. Whole. Complete. Perfect.

He was exhausted, but pleased.

Pleased? No. Ecstatic.

"Clea?" He turned to look for her.

She popped out from beyond the tent where she had gone to put together some supper. "What?"

He just grinned at her, sandy, disheveled and high on his sense of accomplishment.

"You finished it?"

Clea hadn't looked at the work he'd been doing on the windows once he'd started, saying she was afraid she'd jinx him. She hadn't. She'd given him the inspiration he'd needed.

She came across the sand now, stopping beside him, looking first at the house, then at him. Her eyes were like dinner plates, and her smile—well, she was smiling at him just the way he'd remembered her smiling on their wedding day. His heart lodged in his throat.

"It's beautiful, Austin."

"Not half as beautiful as you are," he whispered, reaching for her, wrapping her in his arms.

Clea hugged him back, her arms locking behind him, lifting his hopes, luring his heart. He buried his face in her hair, inhaling the sweet and salty scent of her. "Fantastic," he muttered.

"It is," Clea agreed, smiling up at him, eyes shining. "It's wonderful."

Austin took a step backward, still holding her loosely in the circle of his arms. Then he leaned forward and kissed her full on the lips. "Yes," he said, and he didn't mean just the house.

For a brief moment Clea was kissing him back, then she pulled back slightly and gave a small half laugh. "Hey, let's don't get carried away now. You've still got to photograph it."

He looked at her ruefully, then nodded. There would be time after for what he'd rather be doing. All the time in the world. "Let me get my camera," he said.

By the time he had, and had set up his tripod, the soft early-evening light cast exactly the shadows he'd been counting on, highlighting the careful sculpting, outlining the delicate tracery and the sharp vertical lines. He took two rolls, moving about as he did so. A step this way, a step that. From the right side, from the left. And while he did it, Clea flapped her arms and waved away the gulls again.

"Shoo," she shouted, charging at two who seemed about to land on the top of the finial. "Go on! Get!"

Unable to resist, Austin put in a new roll and photographed her arm-flapping charge on the birds.

"You didn't!" Clea turned on him, laughing. "Give me that!"

"Uh-uh." Austin shook his head, backing away from her, grinning.

"Austin." She advanced on him slowly, her hand outstretched.

"Nope. If I could convince the judges that you were my sand sculpture, we'd win hands down."

"Those photos aren't even going to see the light of day, let alone be judged." She started running then, and Austin took off scant feet ahead of her. A flying tackle brought him down inches from the surf line. A warm, soft body flattened him face first onto the sand. Austin didn't mind a bit.

"Got you," Clea panted, sitting up and straddling the backs of his thighs.

Austin rolled over beneath her and reached for her, pulling her down against him. "Likewise," he muttered and kissed her with every ounce of need in him.

"Austin!" She pulled back, wiping the sand off her mouth.

He grimaced, then grinned at the face she was making. "Sorry."

"The film, Austin," she demanded.

"They're great pictures, Clea," he protested.

"The film."

Oh, what the hell? He didn't need the film. He had the woman. "Here." He handed her the camera.

She gave him a beatific smile, getting to her feet. "Thank you very much."

He scrambled up and caught up with her, looping an arm over her shoulder and hugging her close as they walked back. "How about a swim before supper?"

Clea glanced at her watch. "A swim? I don't think we even have time for supper, do we?"

Was she that eager then? Austin grinned in anticipation. "I'd be cleaner." He cast a disparaging glance down at his gritty, sweat-stained shirt and shorts.

"Well, make it a quick one," Clea told him.

He grinned all over his face. "You bet."

"I'll get packed."

The earth seemed to have shifted under his feet. "Packed?"

She shrugged. "There are heaps of stuff that need to be stowed away if we're going to get going anytime tonight."

"We aren't, though."

She looked perplexed. "We aren't what?"

"Going tonight." A pause. "Are we?"

"Of course we are. I'm meeting Ken in the morning. You know that."

"Meeting Ken?" He was flabbergasted.

"You knew I had to be back."

"But I—" She couldn't be. What the hell did she think they'd just spent the last four days proving but that they had a future together? "But you—" He couldn't believe it.

Clea turned suddenly brisk. "Don't change the rules on me now, Austin. You knew damned well. Now, how about taking a quick swim to clean off and then helping me load the raft? That way we can make it back by dark."

He still couldn't believe it, but she turned and marched back to the tent and ducked inside and he could hear her clunking around and rattling things, making very obvious packing sounds. He strode over to the tent and stood outside, glaring at the dark green cover that hid her from his view. "You're not kidding, are you?"

She poked her head out. "No, I'm not."

"You don't give a damn about me? Is that what you're saying?"

"No, Austin," she said patiently, "that's not what I'm saying. I'm saying I made a promise to Ken." She was all clear-minded reasonableness in the face of his woolly-minded fury. He glared at her. She looked impassively and unblinkingly back.

Finally he turned on his heel and strode toward the water, plowing right in and hitting the surface with a resounding smack. He didn't take a quick swim. He took a damned long one. He'd have stayed out there all night if he didn't think he might have shriveled right away—and if Clea hadn't yelled at him to stop being so childish.

It wasn't childishness so much as frustration, and he would have pointed that out, but he didn't think that Clea was in the mood to distinguish between the two.

She was packed when he finally dripped out of the water and dried off. He looked at her glumly. She tapped her foot.

He scowled.

"I have to, Austin," she said.

He didn't believe that for a minute. She wanted to. She wanted *Ken*, for God's sake!

A gull lit on top of the finial.

"Shoo," Clea said and waved her arms at it.

Austin sighed. "Let him alone. It's only sand. It'll crumble sooner or later anyway." He turned, slung the towel around his neck and set about loading the raft. "What the hell difference does it make?"

Chapter Eleven

He should, by God, have run out of gas.

He should have stranded them on that miserable lousy island until little Miss Sunshine came to her senses and realized that it hadn't been just a fun-and-games interlude they were dealing with, but their future.

He didn't.

It didn't even occur to him.

He was too stunned, too absolutely shell-shocked to do more than load the damned boat like some preprogrammed mechanical robot, start the engine and head right straight back to Ventura.

He couldn't think, he couldn't talk, he could hardly even breathe. It was as if all the emotions that had been building between them for the past four days—no, scratch that—for the past two weeks, had formed into solid granite and come tumbling down to flatten him.

And he was flattened.

For a time.

Then the anger began to build. And build. And build.

It caught fire slowly as they drove south from Ventura. It flamed steadily as, tight-lipped and rigid, he took her to the airport, and the conflagration nearly burned him alive when Clea turned at the opening of the tunnel to the plane to offer him a tentative smile and the gentle pressure of her hand

on his arm. Then she hooked her thumb around his the way
she'd always done when they were kids. It was like a secret
handshake. Kid stuff.

"Thank you, Austin. It was wonderful. Truly."

The top of his head was coming off. Wonderful? *Wonderful?* When, in effect, she was saying that all they had
between them was what they'd had as kids? It was the most
god-awful day of his life.

IT HADN'T BEEN A PICNIC for Clea either. It had been two-
thirty in the morning by the time he got her to the airport.
Clea had thought he might have suggested going to Miles's
for the remainder of the night, but he drove directly to the
terminal he had picked her up at, parked the truck and,
hauling her duffel bag out of the back, escorted her in.

"I hope you'll get there in plenty of time," he'd said sarcastically.

Clea had just looked at him, hurt. Trust me, she'd wanted
to tell him. But she had no right. Not when she wasn't sure
yet that she trusted him.

"I'm sure I will," she'd said with as much equanimity as
she could muster.

He'd growled something unintelligible, then walked her
to her boarding gate without another word.

She'd longed to say something to take the edge off his
anger. But there'd been nothing to say that wouldn't perhaps cause more pain in the end. So finally just before she'd
boarded the plane, she'd given him a hopeful smile, a gentle
squeeze on the arm, and then hooked her thumb around his
the way they'd done as kids. Solidarity, it had meant. You
and me. Together.

If things were going to come right between them, she told
herself, that would be enough.

"That your boyfriend?" Clea's tiny blue-haired seatmate asked her when she dropped into her seat on the plane.

"My...?"

"Had to be," the woman went on confidently. "Or fiancé," she added with a wink. "You never see a husband looking that distraught when he lets his better half go."

Was Austin distraught? Angry more like, Clea thought. Well, she wasn't overly pleased herself.

Nine-tenths of her—maybe more—wanted nothing better than to forget that the world outside of their tiny island existed, wanted to forget that any man other than Austin existed.

It would have been sheer heaven to chuck commitments, responsibilities and demands to the winds and wrap herself around him and never let him go.

God knew her hormones were all for it. So was most of the rest of her.

But she couldn't.

"I remember my Harold used to look at me that way when we were engaged." The little lady sighed. "My goodness! I'll bet he comes after you on the next flight."

Clea hoped not. She had to talk to Ken first.

She had taken a long hard look over the past four days at herself, at Austin, and at what she thought she wanted out of a marriage to Ken. And she had faced some hard truths.

She couldn't marry Ken.

He was a warm, sensitive man and, in his way, he loved her. But she knew now that a marriage between them wouldn't work. She couldn't give him what he wanted.

She didn't relish telling him so. But she had to. And she had to do it personally, had to do it when he expected to see her. She couldn't stand him up and then explain afterward with an "Oh, by the way..." She owed him more than that.

Of course she couldn't spend the weekend with him now, not under what amounted to false pretenses. But she had to go to see him just the same. Anything else wouldn't be right.

"He's lovely, your man," Clea's seatmate went on. "So strong. Demanding, I'd say."

Amen to that, Clea thought. She'd been tempted, in the face of his fury, to tell him she wasn't going to marry Ken. But she hadn't for a variety of reasons.

First, because Ken had a right to be the first to know that their engagement was off. He was the one involved, after all. Second, and even more crucial from Clea's own standpoint, saying no to marrying Ken did not automatically imply that she was consenting to stay married to Austin.

It was a possibility, of course. But she was still a bit unsure.

If life were nothing more than building castles in the sand, she'd stay married to him in a minute. Short terms with Austin were always top notch. They were fun, exciting, exhausting, demanding.

But how would things be over the long run?

She thought it quite possible now that Austin might've changed. Once she was free of her engagement to Ken, she was determined to get to know him better, to find out.

SHE COULD HAVE CALLED KEN to get her at the airport. But that would have meant explaining herself on the freeway going home, and she didn't think either of them were up to that. So she caught the airport transport into the city and then took a cab home.

It was almost six by the time she got there, and while she would have happily taken a shower and fallen into bed for a full day's sleep, she only did the first before leaving again.

Ken had planned their departure for eight-thirty. He would have to leave his place at eight to pick her up. She didn't want him to get that far. She had enough to feel guilty about without making him drive across town only to learn she wasn't coming with him.

Ken lived on the second floor of a contemporary concrete and glass building that Clea privately thought was soul destroying. Ken simply thought it was easy to maintain. If she'd been thinking straight early on in their relationship, she might have recognized that a disagreement as fundamental as that meant something.

She hadn't because she genuinely liked him. And because she'd decided at last that she wasn't getting any younger, that she really needed to get on with things if she was going to marry again and have a family. So she'd concentrated on what they had in common: a desire to settle down, a desire for a family. The wheres and hows hadn't seemed of especial consequence at the time. They were, she could see now.

She rang the bell and waited nervously on the porch for him to press the buzzer and let her in. Minutes passed and no buzzer sounded. Had she missed him? Oh, Lord. What if she'd come here just while he was going there?

But she'd barely had the thought when the front door opened and Ken stood there in person, staring at her. "You? I didn't press the buzzer because I wasn't expecting anyone. I thought it was a mistake." He looked baffled. "I thought I was picking *you* up."

"Er...well, that's what I want to talk to you about." Clea gave him a hopeful smile. He met it with a cautious one of his own. "Could I...come in?"

"Oh. Sure. Sorry. I'm just surprised, that's all." He bent forward and brushed his lips against hers, then stepped back, letting her walk past him, frowning slightly as he walked alongside her to the elevator.

It was waiting with the door open. Thank heavens, Clea thought. She hadn't relished the notion of standing there mute waiting for an elevator while Ken wondered what was going on.

"Did you have a nice time?"

"Nice time?" she echoed vaguely. Busy rehearsing what she was going to say, and knowing she was going to say it badly, she hadn't the vaguest idea what he was talking about.

"With the sand castle," he prompted.

"Oh." She recovered quickly. "Oh, yes. It was...interesting."

Ken looked doubtful. They reached his floor and got off. He unlocked his front door and held it open for her. Clea darted past him, headed directly for the couch and tucked herself in one corner. Then she swallowed hard and prepared to begin.

Before she could, though, Ken regarded her solemnly for a long moment, then said, "You look like you could use some tea."

Clea nodded, briefly grateful for the reprieve. "Yes, please."

Ken started to back out of the room, but suddenly she couldn't let him go, couldn't put it off a moment longer. "Forget the tea, Ken. How about some brandy instead."

He halted in the doorway, blinking in astonishment.

Clea shrugged. "False courage?"

Ken frowned, but when she didn't change her mind, but just stared at him implacably, he walked over to his small liquor cabinet and pulled out a bottle. He sloshed some into a glass and looked over at her. "Me, too?" he asked her, lifting one eyebrow.

"You might want one," she admitted.

He grimaced, poured a generous dollop into a second one, then carried them across the room and handed one to Clea. Holding his own, he sat down beside her and met her gaze squarely. "So. What's going on?"

It wasn't fair, Clea thought, what she was about to do. But it would be no fairer to continue things the way she felt. "I owe you an apology," she said quietly.

"For getting the instructions wrong?" He smiled slightly. "For not waiting at your place?"

Clea shook her head miserably. "No."

Ken swirled his brandy in his glass, watching the movement of the liquid, then lifting his eyes and meeting hers. "What, then?"

She took a sip of the brandy, looking for courage, and found fire instead. She coughed, her eyes watered.

Ken slapped her on the back. "Are you all right?"

"I...I'm fine," she gasped. "I...I... No. I'm miserable," she admitted. "I shouldn't be doing this, saying this...but..."

Ken sat back, his knuckles whitening against the amber glass. "Clea?"

"I...can't...marry you."

"Cavanaugh." It wasn't a question.

Clea sighed and raked a hand through her hair. She bent her head. "Cavanaugh," she admitted softly.

"You going back to him?"

"I...I don't know."

"He got to you." It was matter-of-fact. Ken nodded his head slowly, resigned.

"Not entirely," Clea said quickly. "I admit he had a lot to do with it. But it was more than that. Seeing him again, being with him again," she added softly, "got me to thinking about marriage—about what I wanted in a marriage, about what you wanted, about what I could give you. And—" she met his gaze, seeing hurt there and hating herself for having caused it "—I don't think I can give you what you want."

"Love."

"I do love you, Ken. In my way. But, it's not...not..." She floundered, at sea with an explanation she didn't fully comprehend herself. "Not what you have a right to expect. It's not blinding passion. It's not flash-bang—"

"We're not talking fireworks, you know."

"No." She smiled sadly and reached out to touch his hand momentarily. "But maybe we should be."

"Cavanaugh made you feel that way?"

"He...I..." There was a long pause. "Once upon a time, yes, he did." She ducked her head, studying the weave of the upholstery, unable to meet his eyes.

"And you're going back for more?"

"I said, I don't know yet. There's more to life than fireworks."

"But you just said—"

"I said I think they're important, Ken. But alone they're not enough."

"Then what we had—"

"No." She shook her head, then put out her hand, squeezing his again briefly. "That's not enough, either. Or it wouldn't be after a while."

He didn't answer. For a moment his fingers clenched beneath hers, then gradually they relaxed and he turned his hand over, wrapping it around hers and holding it gently, his thumb softly stroking the finger that wore his ring.

Clea shut her eyes tightly, squeezing back the tears that threatened. Then she reached down and eased the diamond solitaire off her finger. Laying it in his palm, she folded his fingers around it, then leaned forward and brushed a kiss across his cheek. "I'm sorry. I wish—"

But she couldn't have said what she wished. Her life was too confused, her thoughts and emotions too tangled.

"Nobody wishes more than I do," Ken said quietly.

Clea set the glass on the table and got to her feet. "I know," she said softly. "I'd better go now."

He gave her a rueful look. "You're quite sure?"

"Yes."

"You're not just saying all this because you're exhausted, out of sorts, miserable, and feeling like hell?" A hint of a smile flickered across his face.

It got an answering one from Clea. Trust Ken to let her out gracefully. "I don't think so."

"Well, if you wake up tomorrow and find you're wrong, come back."

"Don't say that."

He shrugged. "Why not?" He gave her a crooked grin. "So maybe we didn't have a grand passion, I still thought we were pretty great."

"I think you're pretty great."

He smiled wryly. "Nicest rejection I've ever got."

"You should hate me," Clea said, despairing.

Ken's hand came out and lifted her chin so that her eyes collided with his. "No. You'll be hard enough on yourself for both of us."

"You know me well," she admitted.

"Not well enough, apparently. I wish I had. Is there a moral here, do you suppose?"

Clea sighed. "Life isn't always what you'd have it be."

"Sounds about right to me. So what do you guess that makes us? Friends?"

"Are you serious?"

Ken shrugged. "Why not? Maybe it's the hand of fate, steering us toward a greater destiny. You know the old saying about God never closing a door without opening another one..."

Clea smiled wryly, wondering if Austin was hers, and if so, what sort. A trap door, perhaps? "Right." Impulsively she stood on tiptoe and brushed her lips lightly across his cheek. "For you I hope so, friend. You were more than I ever deserved."

He winked as he walked her out the door. "Hold that thought."

THE TROUBLE WITH CLEA, Austin thought as he stared at the sloping ceiling of Aunt Grace's story-and-a-half bungalow in Pasadena, was that she didn't know her own mind. No, not her own mind, her own heart.

If she did, she would realize that Ken Hollister was all wrong for her and that she couldn't possibly love him the way she loved Austin—even if her mind told her she should.

But Clea's mind, apparently, was locked. At any rate, he hadn't been able to reach her. Damn. His fist smacked down on the feather mattress. How could she be spending the weekend with Ken Hollister? It boggled the mind, sent the blood pressure soaring, and kicked the imagination into overdrive as he tried to figure out what to do next.

He wasn't giving up, that was certain.

There was no way he was going to let her make a mess of her life by marrying such an unsuitable man. No. He had to do something. But what?

"Are you home yet?" Aunt Grace tapped on the door and poked her head round for the tenth time that morning.

"Not if it's Miles," Austin said promptly. He purposely hadn't gone back to Miles's after he'd left Clea at the airport. He could do without his brother's solicitous questions and his sister-in-law's well-meaning but painful sympathy at this point. He might have lost the battle, but the war was far from over, and Austin Cavanaugh had no intention of discussing momentary defeats.

"It's not Miles," Aunt Grace said. "It's an Englishman."

Baxter, Austin thought glumly, debating whether to answer it or not.

"He's called before. Several times," Aunt Grace said. "I know you're tired, Austin. But as long as you're awake, it's only polite..." She gave him a reproving frown, one of the sort that she gave him frequently as a youngster when she'd despaired of civilizing him.

He heaved himself to a sitting position. "All right. I'll be right down."

Aunt Grace only had one phone. It was in the kitchen, and so was Aunt Grace. She was slicing apples, which she could do with both ears free, and that she was going to listen avidly Austin had no doubt.

"He's not English, you know," he said conversationally as he reached for the phone, knowing that Baxter could overhear him. "He's a fake."

Aunt Grace sniffed. "He's got manners, at least, which is more than I can say for some," she added darkly and split an apple with a thwack.

Austin grinned. "What's up?" he said into the phone.

"Your father's offer."

"What?"

"He offered Dennis Houston half a million."

"What?" This time it was a yelp of outrage.

"Half a million," Baxter repeated calmly. "His lawyer called me this morning while you were sulking."

"Sul—?" Austin frowned in Aunt Grace's direction. "I was sleeping," he corrected not altogether honestly. "I had a hard four days."

Baxter made a noncommittal noise. There was something about sand castle building that he seemed to feel was licentious or, at the very least, not quite respectable. That someone could actually claim exhaustion after having done it didn't even merit comment. "Nevertheless," he said starchily, "we need to respond."

"So respond."

"With?"

"No."

"But—"

"No. Tell the old man no. Tell him he's not going to get whatever he wants all the time. Tell him Dennis Houston's furniture business is out of his reach now and forever. Tell him that this time we don't have a price.''

"But Dennis might want to take the offer," Baxter said. "It's a lot of money. He could—"

"No. No, he couldn't. He couldn't go on making his furniture the way he has been with my old man controlling the show. He'd be doing patterns, making prototypes. And a bunch of robots would be putting them together!''

"But if he had the—"

"Just tell him, Baxter. Tell him no." And Austin slammed the phone down on his lawyer's ear. "You heard?'' he said to Aunt Grace as he stalked from one end of the room like an angry cat.

She turned and nodded. "Yes.''

Austin slammed his fist against the counter. "What's the matter with him? Why does he do this? What makes him think he can run everyone's life?''

Aunt Grace sighed and shook her head.

CLEA SPENT THE WEEKEND at the Carrutherses' house making up for lost time. She felt dithery and at a loose ends, and she desperately wished that Austin would show up so that they could continue getting to know each other again. But she knew he wouldn't.

He thought she was with Ken.

She wondered if he was still angry. Probably. Austin didn't mellow quickly. When he came back on Monday she had planned to tell him that she'd rethought things and had broken off with Ken. Now she thought it might be wisest to tell him over the phone.

So she called Miles's, but he wasn't there.

"Haven't seen him," Susan told her Saturday night when she tried the first time. "Anything wrong?''

"No," Clea said softly.

"I'll tell him you called if he shows up," Susan promised.

But when Clea called back on Sunday morning and twice on Sunday afternoon, Austin still hadn't shown up.

"I don't know where he is," Miles told her the last time. "Susan thought he might've gone to Aunt Grace's, but she says he isn't there."

"Well, thanks for trying anyway," Clea said in a small voice. She went back to work on an upstairs bedroom, telling herself to forget about Austin and concentrate instead on patching the plaster in the walls.

It looked as if Devin had made some progress on repairing the built-in cabinet while she was away. But he didn't seem to have got as far as she thought he would. Maybe he'd come over and work today if she called him. A little company wouldn't hurt, Clea decided. And Devin was a good bet since he was forever complaining that his social life was zilch.

"Work? This afternoon?" he said when she finally got him on the twelfth ring of his phone. He sounded as if he'd just got up. "I . . . I don't think I can, really. I . . . I'm sorry, Clea. It's just . . ." There was a muffled noise in the background. Another person, Clea thought. His social life had obviously picked up.

"That's all right, Dev," she said quickly. "I was just working myself, and—" She couldn't think of how to phrase it so that she didn't make herself sound pitiful.

She needn't have worried. "Good for you," Dev said cheerfully. "Get a lot done." And he rang off.

Clea, distracted, didn't get nearly as much done as she'd have liked.

A MAN OF ACTION, Austin ordinarily got his best ideas while climbing on rooftops or swinging from rafters. He rarely had them sitting still. And he'd never yet had one lying on his back reading the Bible. But he did this time.

He was lying on his back because Aunt Grace's roof was in fine shape, her bungalow lacked rafters, and he'd already mowed her lawn to U.S. Marine regulation-haircut length and scalped her hedge without figuring out what to do about Clea and Ken. Aunt Grace had finally banished him upstairs because, she said, he was driving her insane crashing around her knickknack-strewn living room like a bull in heat. Austin had said he didn't think bulls were in heat ever, that they were continually that way. Just so, Aunt Grace had replied and pointed up the stairs. He'd left.

He was reading the Bible because he'd already counted the number of roses in each climbing vine of wallpaper (two hundred and thirty-two), the number of small rectangular openings in the heat register (eighty-four), and the number of pine planks in the highly polished floor (fifty-five), and because, like in a hotel, it was all Aunt Grace provided to read.

It was enough.

There in the first chapter of the Book of Ruth, he discovered what to do about Ken.

"'Wither thou goest, I will go,'" he muttered. Would Clea follow Ken wherever he went?

Austin was willing to bet his future that the answer was no.

ROSIE DIDN'T COME IN to work on Monday.

"Are you sick?" Clea asked when she phoned. "I hear there's a lot of flu going around."

"Maybe," Rosie said vaguely. "I'm...tired."

"Flu," Clea said. "Drink lots of water, get lots of rest. Stay in bed."

"Yes," Rosie agreed readily. "I will. See you tomorrow."

"Right." Clea hung up the phone slowly and sank down onto the settee to think. She shouldn't take the time. She should be getting over to the Carruthers' place right this minute. She'd got a lot done over the weekend, but she still had plenty to accomplish.

Her heart wasn't in it, though. Her heart was wandering aimlessly about, wondering where Austin was. She'd thought for sure she'd have heard something from him by now. She hadn't. Her phone hadn't rung until Rosie called just now.

She reached over and twitched the cover off Thurber's cage. "What do you think, Thurb?" she said to him.

Thurber thought it was breakfast time. Clea filled his food dish and hung it back on the inside of his cage. He pecked her fingers as she withdrew them. Then he tucked his head inside the feeder. His answer was obvious: life must go on.

Life did, and so did Clea. She put a message on her answering machine, giving the number at the Carruthers'. Then, having done that, she went to work.

All day long she expected Austin would drop in. All day long she listened for the phone to ring. But all day long she waited in vain until at last, at almost five-thirty, just as she was getting ready to quit, she heard the shrill of the telephone.

"Hello?"

"Hi." It was Ken.

Her spirits sank. His sounded better than ever. "How are you?" she asked perfunctorily.

"Fine. Super. Couldn't be better. How about a drink?"

Clea frowned. "Are you sure you haven't been drinking already?"

"Positive." She could hear the smile in his voice. "I've got news."

"Oh?"

"Have a drink with me," he coaxed.

"I'm really bushed, Ken. I—"

"I'll bring the champagne to your place."

"Champagne?"

"What time will you be home?"

"I...er..." She felt as if she had long ago lost the thread of the conversation.

"Half an hour?"

"How about forty-five minutes?"

"See you there."

He hung up before she had time to say another word. Champagne? Fine? Super? Couldn't be better? She shook her head bemusedly. She didn't know whether to be offended or not. He'd certainly got over her fast enough.

Just as well, she told herself firmly. And she knew it was true. But it didn't help her make sense of it all the way home.

It didn't help either to discover Austin on her doorstep. For the first time in two full days she'd forgotten him for half an hour, and—bang—he popped out of the woodwork. He was wearing a burgundy polo shirt and a pair of jeans, huaraches and no socks. He'd shaved, but his eyes still looked a bit bloodshot, as if he hadn't had a lot more sleep over the weekend than she had.

But he was smiling. Clea breathed a little easier. Climbing out of her truck, she smiled back.

Austin stood as she came up the stairs, lifting the tool case out of her hands. "Hi." He leaned across the tool case and kissed her lightly on the lips.

His restraint surprised her. Over his anger, not fighting mad, not possessive beyond good sense. Hmm. Things were definitely looking up. Her smile broadened. "Hi," she said and kissed him back.

He took her key, unlocked her door and opened it wide. "After you," he said, sweeping as much of a bow as he could with the heavy tool case in one hand.

Clea swept in ahead of him, then turned in the parlor. "I think I should tell you, Austin," she said, "that in a few minutes Ken is coming over. He—"

Austin shrugged complacently. "No problem."

Clea blinked. This was the man who threw a tantrum three days ago when he'd discovered she was going to keep her date with Ken?

But before she could comment, a navy-blue Volvo pulled up to the curb and Ken bounded out, a magnum of champagne in his hand. He came up the steps smiling as brightly as Clea had ever seen him.

"I've been transferred," he said. "To Madagascar."

Chapter Twelve

"Mada..." Clea's voice trailed off.

"...gascar," Ken finished for her, brandishing the champagne bottle. "See? I told you. It's true about the door and window bit."

Clea was still staring at him, dumbstruck. But Austin was shaking his hand. "Madagascar?" he said heartily. "Hey, that's terrific. A promotion, is it?"

Ken beamed. "Gets me on the international track. And that's promotion enough in itself, but yes, I'm moving up a bit."

Austin clapped him on the back. "Fantastic." He looked over at Clea, a grin on his face. "Isn't it fantastic, Clea?"

For a long moment Clea didn't say a word.

Her mind was busy adding, subtracting, and otherwise divining the meaning of the news she'd just heard. It seemed, to her, extraordinarily suspicious. First Austin had a fit about her going back to meet Ken, wanting Ken out of the picture. Then Ken called with great news. Then Austin arrived, calm and self-possessed. Then Ken revealed his new job overseas and, upon hearing about it, Austin gave an award-winning portrayal of the Cheshire Cat.

Clea's eyes narrowed, her jaw tightened, her teeth came together with a snap. That snake.

"Clea?" Ken looked at her with real worry in his eyes. "Is something wrong? Aren't you pleased? I mean, I told you..."

"I remember what you told me, Ken," she said slowly and deliberately, her fingers tightening into fists. "I'm very...pleased...for you." She managed a brittle smile for him. She didn't even look at Austin.

He didn't seem to notice. He had bounded off to the dining room and was rooting through the boxes of glasses and dinnerware that she still hadn't unpacked.

"Where're the champagne glasses, Clea? I know you got custody of them."

She didn't know, and he was lucky she didn't, because if she had, she'd have thrown them at his head. Stalking past him, she went into the kitchen and let the door swing closed behind her. Once there she clenched the countertop with such force that her knuckles went white. A moment's respite was all she got, though, for she had scarcely got a grip on herself when the door swung open again.

"Got any glasses in here?" Ken poked his head in after her. "We can't find any in the dining room."

Clea sucked in her breath, counted to ten and turned around. "I've got some wineglasses. I'll get them."

"Thanks." Ken grinned at her, more boyish enthusiasm on his face than she'd ever seen. "Isn't it something, Clea? The way this worked out. You're the first person I've told. I still can't believe it, can you?"

"No," Clea said flatly and with complete honesty. "I can't." She didn't think she'd have believed Austin could stoop this low in a million years. "I'll get the glasses," she said.

She took her time getting them, telling herself that now was not the time to make a fuss, that there was always the remotest chance she was mistaken. But she doubted it.

Ken had the champagne uncorked by the time she got back. And when he had poured them each a glassful, Austin proposed the first toast. "To Ken. To a bright and unencumbered future."

Her worst suspicions were confirmed.

Austin raised his glass, clinking it against Ken's, then against Clea's, frowning suddenly at the expression on her face. "What's this? You surely don't begrudge him the opportunity to..."

"I don't begrudge *him* anything," Clea said tightly.

"Cheers," Ken broke in, tapping his glass against hers, then taking a long swallow.

Obediently, feeling as if she were drinking hemlock rather than Dom Perignon, Clea lifted her glass and sipped.

Ken filled his and Austin's empty glasses again and lifted his once more. His grin faded, settling into a warm smile and his eyes sought Clea's. "To Clea, the most lovely woman I've ever known."

There was an enduring pause. A cable car clanged, a ship whistled, Mrs. Gianetti's dog barked across the street. Then Austin said a touch too huskily, a touch too heartily, "Hear, hear."

The champagne tasted like bile in Clea's throat.

"So, tell us more," Austin encouraged Ken. "When do you leave?" He dropped onto the settee, crossed one ankle over the other knee and looked up at the other man with an expression of eager enthusiasm on his face.

"Soon, they say," Ken replied. "I've got a passport. I'll need a visa. But since it's an American bank, they say it won't be a problem. A matter of weeks really. And here I thought I'd be stuck playing golf forever just to get ahead. They must've noticed, don't you think?" He went on enthusiastically, and Austin sat back, nodding happily, commenting appropriately and smiling all the while.

Clea stood and seethed. She'd never been assailed by such a maelstrom of conflicting emotions in her life. She was genuinely pleased for Ken. She knew he liked his work and wanted to succeed. She knew he counted even a place as remote as Madagascar as a step on the road to success. And he was quite right—for him it couldn't have come at a better time. After Clea, he'd want a new start.

But not a start instigated the way she was willing to bet his had been.

Not that she was going to say anything, of course. Not yet. Not to Ken. But she prayed he would leave soon. She didn't know how far she could get her control to stretch.

"Are you sure you won't have another glass?" Ken asked her once.

Clea shook her head. "No, thanks. You go ahead."

She needn't have bothered to suggest it. They went ahead quite readily, laughing, talking. Between them, he and Austin killed the bottle of champagne. It looked, she thought sourly, as if by the time Ken left, they would be fast friends. Suitable, inasmuch as she'd have been willing to bet that Ken owed the reason for his celebration to the man pretending ignorance while he quaffed champagne with him.

She sat down in the armchair next to Thurber's cage and watched both men stonily. They didn't seem to notice. Ken discovered that Austin had been to Africa once, and plied him with a thousand questions, all of which Austin was quite ready to answer.

Good old Austin.

Pity, Clea thought, that she didn't have eyes like those women in sci-fi movies who turned people to stone right where they sat.

It was an hour before Ken decided he'd really ought to be going. "I'll call my folks tonight," he said. "Give them the good news."

"I'm sure they'll be pleased," Clea said, though she wasn't, entirely. Ken's mother was all for him advancing in his career, but even she might think Madagascar was a bit of an extreme to go to just for that. But maybe not. Clea was discovering she was not a very good judge of character, after all. If she had been, she'd have slammed the door on Austin the first night he'd come back into her life.

"They'll be horrified at first," Ken said. "But then they'll adjust. Hollisters are good at that." He gave her a knowing look.

Clea nodded and put her hand on his arm. He wrapped his over it and held it there while he reached out and shook Austin's hand again. "You're not a bad guy, Cavanaugh," he said as Clea walked him to the door.

Austin had the grace to turn a faint red.

"That's what you think," Clea muttered under her breath.

Ken didn't hear. He opened the door, then turned and smiled down at her. "I hope I wasn't out of line in calling you, in coming over to tell you."

Clea shook her head. "No. No, I'm glad you did." *For more reasons than you can imagine.*

He touched her cheek. "I'm glad you were here to share it with. See? I told you we could be friends. Even Cavanaugh was pleasant tonight."

Why shouldn't he be? Clea thought bitterly. *He got his own way again.* She brushed a lock of hair away from her face. "Yes, I guess we can."

"And since he seems like he's in a good mood, he can't begrudge me this," Ken said and, bending his head, he planted a kiss on her lips. "For old-time's sake."

And he was gone.

Clea stood on the porch watching him go, gathering strength, like a hurricane heading for the coast. She heard

Austin get up off the settee and come out into the entry hall so that he stood just a few feet behind her.

"Well," he said cheerfully to her back. "Madagascar. Imagine that."

Clea turned slowly, hooking her fingers in her belt loops, rocking back and forth on the balls of her feet. "Yes," she said, sarcasm dripping. "Madagascar. Imagine that."

Austin's jovial grin faded. His face went momentarily blank. Then he mustered up another smile and pasted it in place. "I didn't even know they had U.S. banks in Madagascar," he ventured.

Clea arched an eyebrow. "Really? You mean you weren't that specific in your request?"

The blank look came back. "Huh?"

"Don't 'huh' me, Austin Patrick Cavanaugh! You know damned well what I'm talking about!"

"Clea?"

"You snake. You rotter. You swine. How dare you just jump in and run somebody's life that way!"

Austin's eyes widened. "Are you saying that you think I—"

Clea's eyes rolled heavenward. "Oh, spare me that look of wide-eyed innocence. I know you, Austin. Ken didn't get that overseas position by accident. He got it because you set it up!"

"Me? How the hell could I set it up? I don't own the damned bank!"

"You wouldn't have to own the bank, Austin, and you know it." She paused, looking him squarely in the eyes, her voice low and level when she spoke. "You never used to lie to me, Austin."

He licked his lips, tucked his hands into the back pockets of his jeans, then ducked his head and cleared his throat. "I didn't get him sent to Madagascar," he said in a low tone at last.

"The Madagascar bit wasn't your idea, you mean?"

Austin rubbed a hand round the back of his neck and kneaded taut muscles there. Cornered, he flared back at her. "Yes, damn it, all right. That's what I mean."

"You did want to get him sent somewhere." She took a step forward.

Austin took a step back. He scratched his head. "Well, what the hell was I supposed to do?" he demanded angrily. "We'd had a fantastic four days together. We had the start of a marriage again. You can't deny that, Clea," he said when she opened her mouth. "And then, pert as you please, you said you were going back to him!"

"He was expecting me. He'd made a weekend's worth of plans. We had a date."

"You could've broken it."

"No. No, I could not have," she contradicted. "Not like that. Not and had any respect for myself. I don't do things that way, Austin. I play fair. I consider other people's feelings. I—"

"You damned sure didn't consider mine!"

She stared. "I spent the better part of my life considering your feelings! How can you even stand there and say that? Who married you in the first place to help you out of a jam? Who divorced you when you said it was time to get out?"

He scowled at her. "You wanted out, too."

"Did I?"

"Didn't you?" He was staring at her now, nonplussed.

"No, actually, then I didn't. Then I thought I'd die of missing you, of wanting you back!"

He stared at her, incredulous. "Then why the hell didn't you say—"

"But now I wouldn't have you on a plate!"

She stalked past him and strode into the living room, staring out the window, trying to ignore him when he followed her.

"That's absurd," he countered, reaching for her arm, hauling her around to face him. "You love me and you know it."

"I *loved* you. I probably still do at this moment," she said bitterly. "I haven't had time to break myself of the habit yet. But believe this, buddy, I will!"

"Why?"

"Why?" She was shouting now, jerking her arm away from him, glaring up into his furious face. "You have the audacity to stand there and pretend you don't know why?"

"I don't know why." His voice was flat.

"Then you're a bigger jerk than I thought."

A muscle ticked in his cheek. "What the hell is that supposed to mean?"

"It means that if you don't know why I'm angry, you're worse off than I ever thought you were. You're blinder, stupider, and more selfish than even I ever thought!"

"Selfish? Blind? Oh, come on, Clea. I was doing it for you. And you're the blind one if you think—if you ever thought for a minute—that some bland banker could make you happy for the rest of your life!"

"Ken is not bland!"

"He gives a good imitation of it then. You wouldn't last a year with him."

"Longer than I lasted with you at least!"

Austin strode over to the fireplace and slammed his hand against the marble mantelpiece. "I don't believe you," he said, shaking his head. "You actually think you could've made it work?"

"That's not the point!"

Austin's brows lifted. "Oh? Then what is the point?"

"The point is, the choice was mine to make. Not yours, Austin. *I* was the one who should have had the chance to say I wanted him or didn't want him. I didn't need you coming along and deciding what was right for me. I didn't need you deciding that just because you wanted to stay married to me that it was all right to eliminate him from my life."

"It needed to be done. For God's sake, Clea, you might've married the guy!"

She gritted her teeth. "You know who you remind me of?"

Austin blinked, as if she'd switched tracks and he hadn't followed. "What?"

"What you did, do you know who it reminds me of?"

He looked blank.

"Your father."

The color drained from his face. "Oh, get off it, Clea. It's not a bit like—"

"It is every bit like the sort of thing he'd do. It's exactly the sort of thing he always did. Think about it, Austin. When old Crafty Eddie wanted something, what'd he do?"

Austin glared at her.

"He went after it. And he didn't take no for an answer, either, did he?" She smiled tightly.

"Damn it, Clea—"

"Just like you."

"Now wait a sec—"

"And if he ever got a no, what'd he do?"

Austin scowled, his jaw working.

"I'll tell you what he did," Clea said bluntly. "He tried to buy out whoever was standing in his way. He eliminated the competition. Exactly the same way you eliminated Ken!"

"I didn't buy him out, for God's sake," Austin raged.

"In a manner of speaking, I'd be willing to bet that that's exactly what you did. You went to the bank, didn't you, Austin?"

He dug at the edge of the throw rug with his toe. "So?"

"So what did you do there?"

He looked furious, stomping around the room, flinging himself into the armchair, then immediately popping back out of it again to pace another circle of the room.

"Austin?"

He stopped and drew a long slow, reluctant breath. "I talked to some guy."

"Some 'guy'?" she prodded.

The toe of his huarache dug into the hardwood floor. "A vice president." He looked up and gave her a quick, fierce glare. "I don't remember his name."

"His name is Gleason," Clea said. "What'd you say to him?"

Austin sighed and ran his fingers through his hair. "For God's sake, Clea, you already know more or less what I said. What difference does it make?"

"I just want to know, for the record, Austin, how low you stooped."

"I love you, damn it! I stooped pretty low." A dark red flush stained his cheeks.

Clea waited, tapping her foot.

"I raved about him," Austin said finally in a low voice. "Said what a good administrator I'd heard he was. Talked about his customer relations ability." He paused, chewed on his upper lip, took a deep breath, then exhaled slowly. "I told 'em I'd move my millions there."

The last sentence was so soft that Clea scarcely caught the words. And wished with all her heart that what she heard wasn't true.

She sighed raggedly. "Just like your father," she confirmed.

Austin shook his head, glowering at her. "He never did it for love, Clea."

"Maybe not," she agreed wearily. "But does love make it right, Austin? Do you even know what love is, I wonder? Do you really care how I feel at all? Or is the only thing that concerns you simply getting me back? The way you moved heaven and earth to get your Roberto Clemente baseball card back after you'd traded it to Miles?

"Did you really want a marriage this time, Austin? You know, once upon a time, not so very long ago, I really thought it was possible that you might have changed, that marriage might have begun to mean more than simply a convenience to you, that *I* might have had some significance to you as a person instead of simply as an object you wanted the way your father wanted whatever he didn't have."

Clea's gaze fixed on him and she shook her head slowly and sadly, shutting the door on her dreams. "Well, I was wrong. You used to want to be your father's son, Austin. Well, congratulations. I'd say you've really made it big."

Chapter Thirteen

"I thought you were in San Francisco." Baxter looked up, startled, when the door to his office was flung open and Austin stalked in.

"I'm not."

"No. I can see that."

Austin was practically caroming off the walls, pacing hurried circles around Baxter's elegant office. He hadn't been able to stay in San Francisco a moment. He had to put as many miles between himself and Clea as possible. If he hadn't he might've wrung her neck. How dare she suggest he was like his father!

Austin prowled the room, changing the angle of the blinds, picking up the crystal walrus paperweight, tossing it in the air, catching it again, to Baxter's great relief, and setting it back on the desk. Then he raised the blinds all the way to the top and snapped them down again with a crash.

"Er...do you want something?" Baxter asked finally. "I haven't got a response from your father yet. I told you I'd call you when I did."

"My father," Austin muttered. "Damn my father." The blinds went up and down once more.

Baxter winced.

Austin swiveled around and scowled at him. "Do you think I'm like my father, Baxter?"

The lawyer adjusted his tie. "Well, you're taller certainly. But I believe he was blond when he was younger and—"

"Not do I look like him, Baxter. Am I *like* him? Do I *act* like him?"

"Er... well, sir..." Baxter tugged at his tie again, reddening enough that Austin wondered if it was strangling him. "You have the same sort of...assertiveness, sir," he offered tentatively.

"You mean I'm pushy."

"Well," Baxter hedged, but Austin nailed him with a steely stare. "In the vernacular, I suppose you could say that, sir."

Austin grimaced. "Am I overbearing, Baxter?"

"You, uh...lean a little hard sometimes, sir."

"On you?"

"On...me. On...everyone, sir. But you do it with the best of motives," Baxter assured him quickly.

Austin groaned. "Why didn't you say something?"

Baxter looked surprised. "Like what, sir?"

"Like 'lay off,' I suppose." Austin raked his fingers through his hair. "Like, 'get off my case.' Or just 'stop bossing everyone around.'"

"Well, I did...er, try, sir."

Austin looked blank.

"Just the other day. About the Houston Furniture Company. I tried to say you should at least let Mr. Houston consider your father's offer, but you said—"

"I remember what I said," Austin said heavily. He sucked in a deep breath, wandered from the window to the Gainsborough painting on the wall and then to the desk again. "It's not the same," he muttered to himself. He reached for the paperweight again, rubbing the smooth glass against his fingers, worrying it the way he had been worrying every word Clea had said to him three days before.

It had taken him until this morning to do more than simply deny it. He had stalked out of Clea's house, incensed, feeling wronged, misunderstood, maligned and a whole host of other things detrimental to his emotional health. He'd told her flatly she didn't know what the hell she was talking about, and he'd taken off for L.A. so fast that Mrs. Gianetti stood spinning in his wake.

Tuesday he had seethed, then he had drunk himself into a stupor, slept hours, achieved a humdinger of a hangover and not much else. He certainly hadn't convinced her that she was wrong.

Wednesday he'd gone to Aunt Grace's and scalped her lawn and bushes again, letting the unrelenting Pasadena sun beat down on his head and bake the alcohol out of him. After he was finished he flung himself down on the bed and glowered at the Bible that still sat on the nightstand.

So much for scriptural inspiration. It probably worked great for saints like Miles. But he should've known it would backfire for a sinner like him.

Thursday morning he'd got up and stared at the red-eyed, scruffy face that wavered in the mirror in front of him and actually let himself consider seriously for the first time that Clea might be right. Her words, which he'd tried to deny, had rung in his head so long that he felt as if they were indelibly imprinted on each and every cell of his brain.

"You're just like your father!" she'd accused. "You want to run everything. You make the decisions. What you want counts and to hell with everyone else!"

All morning he'd lain on the feather bed in Aunt Grace's upstairs bedroom and probed the notion carefully, skirting around it, poking it, testing it.

He was beginning not to like what he saw.

But he wouldn't accept what he saw, either. Not without unbiased confirmation. So he'd come to Baxter.

And now?

Now he was gritting his teeth, clenching his fist around the crystal walrus, and breathing shallow, surprisingly labored breaths. He felt as if he'd run a marathon. In fact he'd climbed half a dozen stairs. Twenty minutes ago.

He sighed now and sagged against Baxter's mahogany desk, then he ran his hand through his hair and sighed again.

"Don't concern yourself overly much with Houston's business, sir. It will all work out to your advantage. It always does."

"That, Baxter," Austin said heavily, "I sincerely doubt." He hauled himself to his feet and rubbed a hand round the back of his neck, trying and failing to massage the tension out.

"Is something the matter, sir?" Baxter's face creased into a worried frown.

Austin made a wry face.

The lawyer's frown deepened. "Is there any way I can help?"

Austin balanced the walrus momentarily on its nose, then set him down and patted him on the head. "No, thanks, Bax. You told me everything I needed to know." He gave his attorney a wan smile, a weak wave, and walked out the door as wearily as he'd come in."

If he'd wanted confirmation, he'd got it.

He was every bit as big a bastard as his old man.

"Damn it!" He slapped both his hands down hard on the hood of his Ferrari. His throat tightened, his vision blurred. He was reminded of when he was a child and Miles, a great Pogo comics fan, used to go around quoting the possum, "We've met the enemy, and he's us."

He opened the door to the car and sank down into the luxurious upholstery, lay his head back, closed his eyes and hurt.

He'd done it for her, exactly as he'd told her he had. He didn't want her flying off half-cocked, marrying the wrong man. Exactly the same way he'd wanted Dennis Houston to have the chance to work at his own business, undisturbed by his overbearing, abrasive father.

And in arranging both, Austin had become just like him.

"Shit," he muttered. "Oh shit."

Undoing his actions with regard to Houston was easy. He could simply pick up a phone and tell Dennis about his father's offer. He still didn't think Dennis should take it. He thought Dennis would detest working under Crafty Eddie's thumb. He thought that it would be the death knell of Dennis's creativity.

But Clea was probably right: the choice should be Dennis's.

Dennis was an adult. Dennis had every right to make his own decisions, to make his own mistakes. And Austin would just have to grit his teeth and give it to him.

Resolving the disaster with Clea was not so easy.

There was no way on earth he was going to be able to go back to the bank, look up the vice president, and say, "I changed my mind. I don't think Ken Hollister is overseas material, after all."

There was no way he was going to be able to undo what he had done to Ken's career by waving a magic checkbook and saying a few dozen persuasive words. Ken was going to Madagascar and that was that.

And Clea? What about Clea?

What did she want?

Him?

No, he conceded. Not after what he'd done.

Ken?

The thought made him physically ill. Thinking about Clea with another man twisted his guts.

But if she really wanted him...

He sighed. There was no escaping it. No matter how much he didn't want to, Austin knew precisely and painfully exactly what he had to do.

ROSIE WAS SINGING in the kitchen when Clea dragged herself to the Carrutherses' house on Tuesday morning.

"Well, you made a quick recovery."

Rosie turned around, beaming. "I wasn't sick."

Clea raised her brows. "No?"

"No." Rosie gave her a beatific smile. "I was following your example."

Clea looked baffled. She hadn't slept all night, tossing and turning, aching over the mess her life had become, aching over Austin again just as she'd feared she would. She couldn't imagine what example Rosie was talking about.

"I gave him a second chance," Rosie enlightened her.

"Who?"

"Devin."

Clea felt the floor shift under her feet. "Say what?"

"He's Nicky's father."

Clea just stared, her mind whirled, patterns of reality shifting, clashing, spinning in her head. "Devin Flynn is...Nicky's father."

Rosie nodded. "Years ago we were...lovers. We shared an apartment for almost two years. It was a sort of 'no commitments' type relationship. You do your thing, and I'll do mine. At least that was what we thought it was. Then I got pregnant and I wanted all the traditional things—marriage, a house, a name for my child. And Devin wanted out. He left me flat."

"Ah." And Clea thought she'd been led down the primrose path by Austin. It wasn't hard to understand Rosie's animosity now. But had she just said something about a second chance?

Before Clea could ask, however, Rosie went on. "He came back about three years ago. Reformed. Or so he said. He said he'd got all his 'wanderlust' out of his system. He said he loved me, wanted to love Nicky, to share our lives. I told him to go take a flying leap." She grimaced. "And I kept telling him until you gave your fella a second chance."

Oh, God. Clea blanched.

Rosie didn't even notice. Consumed by her own cheerful news, she didn't even seen Clea's pallor, her sunken eyes and listless expression. "Then I thought," she went blithely on, "that maybe I ought to take the risk. I mean, your fella was coming back after seven years and you were willing to give him a shot when you had hardly even seen him. I'd seen Devin for three whole years, and though I didn't much want to admit it, I could see he'd changed. So while you were gone, I took the leap myself." She beamed. "We're getting married."

Clea swallowed. "How...nice."

"It is," Rosie agreed. "And Nicky's thrilled. Sometimes Devin would come over and take him to a game or something when I couldn't, and he really liked Dev even when I didn't. But he never thought he'd have him for a father." She threw her arms around Clea and hugged her tightly. "And we owe it all to you!"

Clea winced.

IF THERE WAS ANY CONSOLATION to having a love life as disastrous as hers, it had to be how appealing it made working, by comparison. The Carrutherses' house had never seen such devotion in all its ninety-odd years. Clea got there early in the morning, she worked until past ten at night.

"You're making marvelous progress," Mrs. Carruthers told her on the following weekend. "I'm beginning to think you were right about how to do the house after all."

Clea supposed it was nice to be right about something. She nodded, shoved her hair out of her eyes and went back to work.

"You're killing yourself here," Rosie said to her when she and Devin stopped because they'd driven by at ten and had seen a light still on. "My word, this isn't a Guinness Book of World Records house restoration contest, you know."

But Clea didn't answer her, either. Work was therapy, solace, balm to a wounded soul. And other than having long, unreciprocated talks with Thurber about what a fool she'd been, she had nothing else.

"I should never have interfered," her mother said. "Will always says I should keep my big mouth shut."

Clea did answer that. "It's not your fault," she said.

It was her own and no one else's. She was the one who'd given in. She was the one who'd dared to hope. She was the one who'd been the fool. Still was, for that matter, unable even now to stop loving a man who'd never change.

In time, of course, she would get over it. On the surface at least. She'd got over him before. She could do it again.

It was harder this time, though, if possible. She'd had the resilience of youth on her side earlier. She'd had plans, hopes, dreams to hang on to, certain in the knowledge that if she couldn't share them with Austin, she would someday be able to share them with someone else.

Now she was certain she would not.

She would have her work. She would have her friends. She would have her house. She would have her bird. But she would not have a husband.

Maybe she would get a cat.

It was the thought of possibly getting a cat that she was using to keep everything else at bay on Monday evening two weeks from when her life had crumbled around her. She had come home at seven because Rosie, Devin and Nicky had come by and insisted that she looked like a wreck and that she needed some rest.

Needing and getting, Clea could have told them, were two different things. Insomnia went with the territory these days. But because she didn't have the strength it would take to argue with them, she had let Devin chivvy her out the door and tuck her into her truck. She might've gone back in once they'd left. But Devin seemed to sense that, for he said, "I'll follow you home," and damned if he didn't.

Then Rosie went to the Chinese carry-out down the hill and brought her beef and asparagus tips and a bottle of Tsingtao beer, set it on the table in front of her and said, "Eat."

"I suppose you're going to stand over me until I do," Clea grumbled.

"We could," Devin offered equably.

"It won't be necessary," Clea said with bad grace.

He tapped her on the nose. "Good. Eat hearty, then go to bed and get a good night's sleep. It'll help what ails you, believe me." He winked at her and hugged Nicky against his side. "There're five more beers in the fridge if one doesn't do the trick."

Clea gave all of them a wan smile. "Thanks, you guys. You really don't need to bother about me. I'll be fine."

"Of course you will," Rosie said briskly and she hustled her men out the door.

In the silence that followed their departure, Clea started thinking about the cat. It would be more company than Thurber. It might do more than look bored when she talked to it. It might even allow her to scratch it under the chin and stroke its silky fur while it sat on her lap.

Not much, Clea conceded. But she wasn't asking for much these days. Her hopes-and-dreams threshold had lowered quite a bit.

The sound of the doorbell startled her. She wasn't expecting anyone.

Rosie would've just walked in. And unless she was checking up on Clea, she wouldn't be coming back so soon. Her parents never came without calling first. Ken was already in Madagascar. Whatever influence Austin had exerted, it worked fast. Barely a week and a half after Ken had announced where he was going, he'd gone.

Pushing her chair back, Clea went to answer the door, peeking warily out the peephole she'd installed last week, and breathing a sigh of relief when all she saw was a mail-man.

"Ms. Clea Maxine Bannister?" he asked when she opened the door.

"Yes?"

He handed her a thick manila envelope. "Special delivery, miss. Sign here."

Clea signed, then weighed the envelope in her hands. The address was typed, the return a post office box in Los Angeles. No clues at all. She smiled a vague thanks to the mailman, shut the door and carried the envelope to the parlor where she sat down.

It looked ponderous, weighty and official, the sort of letter you got when they foreclosed on your house or you inherited a million dollars. She slit it open.

In this case it was neither.

On top was a letter signed by someone with the unlikely name of Thaddeus Baxter Thatcher, Jr. It said merely, "I am sending you these at the request of my employer, Austin P. Cavanaugh. He hopes you will find them satisfactory." A note in Austin's own spiky scrawl was stuck to the bottom.

I can't undo what I did. It may not be what you want, but this is the only choice I can give you now.

Paper-clipped to the letter were newly filed divorce papers, a visa and an open-dated airline ticket to Madagascar.

DENNIS HOUSTON took Edward Cavanaugh's offer.

And Clea was probably on her way to Madagascar this very minute, Austin thought glumly as he lay flat on his back in the lonely king-sized bed in the Tiburon house he rarely used.

"Half a million bucks compensates for a hell of a lot of artistic integrity," Dennis had told Austin. "I'm sure you understand."

Austin had tried to. He'd smiled tightly, saying not a word. At least Dennis had taken the trouble to tell him. Clea hadn't acknowledged his letter at all.

Such was the price of nobility, Austin told himself. But it was cold comfort.

In fact, he didn't find comfort these days in much of anything at all. Not even having won second place in the sand sculpture contest for the house of his dreams. The stuffing seemed to have been knocked right out of his dreams lately. And the prize of a weekend in Acapulco would only be tempting if he had Clea to share it with. For the first time he lacked the initiative even to get out of bed.

He stayed at Aunt Grace's for a week, worrying her sick. She fluttered around, waving her arms at him, saying things like, "The grass is nearly two inches tall. Why don't you cut the grass, Austin?" Or, "Perhaps you could paint the fence."

He hadn't wanted to cut the grass for once. Or paint the fence. Keeping busy didn't seem enough. It didn't distract. It didn't amuse or divert. Even sculpting in sand, which had been his life preserver when he'd been adrift last year, wasn't as satisfactory as it had been.

One day, at Aunt Grace's insistence, he'd got out of the house, wandering aimlessly around until some remote homing instinct sent him to Susan and Miles. They had both been off that day, and the three of them had taken Patrick, a beach umbrella, and a cooler down to the sand. Miles had swum and Susan had dug tunnels, but Austin had just lain silent and unmoving on a towel until finally Susan had coerced him into helping her build a castle.

He had agreed to please her, but his heart wasn't in it. He couldn't enjoy it, for it recalled too strongly the time he and

Clea had spent on the island, the time when paradise had been within his grasp.

He got to his feet abruptly, leaving Susan to stare open-mouthed at him. "I can't do this. I'm going for a swim," he said. He must've swum a mile.

And when he came back, he didn't look at the castle again.

The next day he bade farewell to them and to Aunt Grace and drove up to Tiburon.

"Are you sure?" Miles had asked him, concern written on his face. "I mean, you're welcome to stay. I know how hard it can be to—"

"No." Austin shook his head. "I've got to go."

"Is it this thing with Clea?"

"It's over with Clea."

"But—"

"She wants it that way," Austin said, and laid a restraining hand on his brother's arm when Miles would have protested. "Don't worry. I'm a big boy. I'll get over it. I'll be fine."

Someday, of course, he would be. But someday was a long time coming.

It had been almost five weeks now since he'd last seen Clea, three weeks come Monday that she should have got the letter he sent.

Maybe she'd already flown to Madagascar. Maybe she was already Mrs. Kenneth Hollister. Maybe he should get off his butt and stop feeling sorry for himself.

It was Saturday. He could get dressed, go jogging, maybe answer a bit of the correspondence that Baxter kept forwarding to him with urgent little prodding notes. There was a convention in Jamaica that wanted a sand castle built. "A flight of fancy," the letter had said. "We look to you for a work of art that will inspire creativity in our employees."

Austin felt about as creatively inspiring as a toad.

A soft tapping sound reached him. He scowled, listening harder. Sometimes the paperboy hit the door with an awful thud. But he rarely tapped. Unless he'd inadvertently flung the paper on the roof.

Groaning, Austin hauled himself out of bed, pulled on a pair of jeans and padded to the door. Stifling a yawn, he jerked it open.

Clea stood on the doorstep.

He gaped, swallowing his yawn, his heart suddenly lodging in his throat.

She gave him a wary, tentative smile. "I'm sorry," she said politely. "I must have got you up."

He shook his head, wanting to blink, not daring to, afraid she was a mirage destined to vanish if he even briefly closed his eyes.

"Clea?" he croaked when he found his voice at last. *Oh, God, please let her be real!*

"I came to thank you for the ticket, for the visa," she said.

"Oh." His spiking emotions felt suddenly flat. "You're...welcome."

She looked marvelous. Her hair was shining, freshly washed and curling under at the ends, just brushing her shoulders as she moved. She wore a simple rose-colored, scoop-necked dress, tailored but feminine. It showed off her tan, the tan she'd got on the island. He did shut his eyes then, fighting down the memories before they completely swamped him.

"Could I...uh, come in?" she asked almost diffidently.

Austin backed up quickly. "Oh. Sure. Sorry, I...I didn't think you'd want to."

She came in, looking around curiously, and Austin followed her, curious himself.

"I...I thought you'd have gone by now."

Clea looked blank. "Gone?"

"To Madagascar."

"No."

"No?"

She shook her head. "I chose not to."

"I...see." He didn't. Not really. He hoped, of course. He couldn't help it. But at the same time he told himself he was a fool to do so. Other than Ken, she would have no real reason to want to go to Madagascar. Her business was here. Her house...

It probably meant nothing.

"This is a nice house," Clea remarked, looking around.

"Thanks."

"Your design?"

"Yes."

"You've come a long way."

"Not so far," he said meaningfully.

She met his gaze, and he knew that she understood what he meant. "You've made progress, Austin," she said firmly.

He gave her a rueful smile and stuffed his hands into the pockets of his jeans. "Thanks. I'm trying."

She wandered across his living room and looked out the windows at the view down the hillside, then ran her hand over the smooth oak mantel above the rough stone fireplace. He expected any moment that, having delivered her thanks, she would walk out the door. The thought panicked him.

"How about a cup of coffee?" he suggested quickly.

"I can't." She shook her head. "I have to get back to the City. I just came because...I..." She hesitated a moment, then went on, "I have a business proposition for you."

"Business proposition?" His brows drew together. "For me?"

"I was talking to Jack Morrisey the other day. You remember? The priest friend of Miles's."

"I remember."

"He's interested in having me do some restoration at his church. I went to see it last week. A lot of it I can handle, but some of it is structural. It requires an architect. I thought maybe you..."

"Me?" Did that mean she was willing to work with him? That she was leaving a door open? That he wasn't out in the cold forever?

"Well, I know you're really more interested in just pursuing sand sculpture, but I thought you might like—"

"I'd like," Austin said emphatically. His heart was beginning to work again.

Clea started to smile. "Really? Well, I was wondering...do you think you might want to take a look at it this morning, then?"

"Now?"

"Well, I have to go see him at ten-thirty, and I thought that perhaps, if you were free, you might want to come along."

"I'll come," he said eagerly before she could change her mind. He glanced at his watch. It was almost nine. "Let me get dressed." He looked over her dress again. "You're wearing *that*?"

Clea shrugged. "I've already climbed all over the church. This isn't a climbing day, really. More of a sit-down-and-discuss-possibilities."

Austin considered that. "Can I...that is, I wonder if maybe afterward, you and I could...maybe have brunch and...discuss...possibilities?" he ventured, hardly daring to hope. Did her mouth lift slightly? Did he spot a tentative smile?

"Perhaps," she said quietly.

Cool it, Austin warned himself. *Don't push her. Don't be overbearing. Just take it as it comes.* But it was like holding back a runaway stallion. Everything in him wanted to grab her and make her his.

"Go ahead and get dressed," Clea told him. "I'll wait out here."

He went. But despite reminding himself again and again that she'd said "business" and nothing else, he dressed for brunch, not for church climbing, putting on a pair of gray slacks and an open-necked blue-and-white-striped shirt. And all the time he was in the bedroom, getting ready, he kept her talking, asking questions about the Carrutherses' house, about her parents, Thurber, anything at all, fearing that silence would mean she'd changed her mind and gone away.

But when he came out at last, she was still there waiting for him, and she even gave him a smile that made his heart kick over in his chest.

At her suggestion, they took her truck. He didn't mind. In fact, he was delighted. It meant she would have to bring him home. It meant she couldn't just dump him once they'd seen the church. At least he hoped she wouldn't.

He seemed to have exhausted all safe avenues of conversation while he was dressing, and once they were underway Clea didn't have much to say. She seemed distracted. They wound down the hill and onto the highway with scarcely a word between them. When they talked at all, they talked about the church. Joists and plastering, dry rot, termites, side altars, and mildew. There were a thousand things Austin wanted to say, but he was afraid to mention anything else, afraid to bring up what had happened between them the last time they were together. He practically sat on his hands the whole way, and bit his tongue as well.

He almost made it. But when they were turning into the side street where St. Adelbert's was located and Clea, finally having found her voice, was going on nonstop about removing the communion railing and using it in the choir loft to keep people from falling through, he knew he couldn't pretend any longer.

"Clea, I'd give anything to go back, to do things over! I'm sorry. I really am—"

Clea pulled the truck to a stop in front of the church and turned to him, touching his lips with her hand to silence him. "I know that, Austin. I know that now."

"Then you've got to try to understand! It's just—"

She gave his hand a squeeze. "Don't worry about it. Come on."

"But—"

But Clea was getting out of the truck, and there was nothing he could do but follow her. She went up the steps and quickly disappeared into the vestibule of the church.

Austin caught up with her, expecting to find her already talking to Jack Morrisey. But Clea was alone.

"We're supposed to meet Jack here?"

"Inside." Clea nodded toward the closed doors that led into the nave of the church.

"Sounds like they're having some sort of service now," Austin said. Soft murmurings from behind the doors indicated that the church was clearly occupied.

"Yes."

"Well, maybe it'll be over soon. We could go have brunch first," he said hopefully.

"No." Clea was adamant. "He's expecting us." She smiled at him slightly.

"But if he's busy with a wedding or a funeral or a baptism or something, we could—"

She shook her head. "No. Just poke your head in so he'll know we're here."

Austin looked doubtful. "Are you sure?"

"Go ahead," Clea urged him.

"But if we had brunch—"

"Later, Austin." She touched his arm. "I promise."

It was the promise that convinced him. It was the most positive thing he'd got out of her so far, the biggest commitment. He crossed the vestibule and eased the door open slightly, sticking his head in.

The organ burst to life, the first bars of The Wedding March reverberating from the rafters. And all the people clustered at the front of the nave turned around.

Austin stared. He saw Miles, Susan and Patrick, Susan's brother, Brian, Aunt Grace, Clea's parents, all the Craigs, Griff, Lainie and what must be the brand-new little Tucker wrapped in a blue blanket, Chase Whitelaw, Dennis Houston, Clea's friend Rosie with a little boy and a tall lean hawk-nosed man, an obviously bemused Baxter, and, standing directly in front of the altar, Jack Morrisey, smiling at him.

"God in heaven!" Austin jerked his head back, letting the door bang shut as he whirled around to stare at Clea in the sudden silence. She was looking back at him, a tremulous, tentative smile on her face, a promise of love in her eyes.

He swallowed painfully, his eyes stinging. "Clea?"

"I love you, Austin." And she opened her arms to him.

"Oh, God." Three strides closed the gap between them. He wrapped her in his arms, felt hers lock around him, holding him tightly against her pounding heart. He buried his head against her hair, shuddering, and surrendering at last to the emotions that swamped him.

Clea's hands stroked his back, then hugged him hard, and his hands tightened against her, wanting to never let her go.

Then he pulled back to stare down into her eyes. They brimmed with tears just like his own. "Clea, do you mean it? Are you sure?"

She touched his cheek. "Oh, yes. I'm sure. All I needed was the chance to make the choice."

He dropped his forehead against her shoulder. "I love you so much," he said unevenly. "I know I don't show you the right way. I know I'm not always—"

"You showed me," Clea assured him, kissing his cheek. "I had to show you. A church wedding seemed the best way to do it. It's for real this time, Austin. Forever. You and me. All right?"

He raised his head and looked at her long and hard. "Absolutely."

Clea dug into her purse. "I thought perhaps we could honeymoon in Madagascar..." she went on tentatively, extending the unused ticket.

Austin shook his head, his once boundless enthusiasm returning, the creative force surging within him anew. "I have a better idea. How about Jamaica?" he suggested. "Building a 'flight of fancy' out of sand. Or Acapulco?" The prize was worth winning now.

"I don't care, as long as we can build a future at the same time," Clea told him with shining eyes. "I'll follow you wherever you go."

Austin grinned. So there was something to this business of scriptural inspiration after all! "You'd better believe it."

He took her hand and drew her to the doors that opened onto the nave. Sticking his head in, he grinned at the assembled congregation, then hollered up at the organist, "One more time. Take it from the top!"

Then he turned to Clea and winked. "Come on, Sunshine. Let's get married."

The laughter and action never stop with
ANNE McALLISTER

You've just seen how Austin Cavanaugh "fell" back into his wife Clea's life—literally—and with his inimitable style recaptured her love in #234 *Marry Sunshine*.

So don't miss their friends' stories . . . as respectable Cassandra Hart, M.D., is upset by the scourge of her childhood, Brendan Craig, who makes a nothing-short-of-spectacular reentry into her life in #108 *Quicksilver Season* . . . as Griffin and Lainie Tucker beat the odds—with a little help from their friends, of course—in #132 *A Chance of Rainbows* . . . as Susan Rivers turns her third "disaster"—the bedeviled Miles Cavanaugh—into her one true love in #186 *Body and Soul*.

Catch all the action. Don't miss the books that started it all!
